For my dad

Publications

A Bucketful of Fish and Other Tales (Lulu, 2019)
Max & Luchia: The Game Makers (Black Pear Press, 2018)
Jimmy Cricket (Black Pear Press, 2014)
The Roman Citizens from Class 6B (Lulu, 2013)

The Objectors

by

Kevin Brooke

The Objectors
by
Kevin Brooke

First published in 2021 by Black Pear Press
www.blackpear.net

ISBN 978-1-913418-45-8

Cover design and illustrations by Seraphim Bryant
https://bluefalcon1983.com

Black Pear Press

Websites

www.kevinbrooke.com
www.blackpear.net

'If you assume that there's no hope, you guarantee that there will be no hope. If you assume that there is an instinct for freedom, there are opportunities to change things, there's a chance you may contribute to making a better world. The choice is yours.'

—Noam Chomsky (linguist, philosopher, social critic and political activist)

Reader Reviews

'I really enjoyed the idea of how the younger generation is often to blame for mistakes that the older generation has made. It made it relatable to issues in our society. I also felt that the range and depth of the characters made the book extremely interesting.'

Louisa Fullerton, aged 17

'The book is aimed at older children and this gave the story action and adventure. It had an interesting dark side and I couldn't put it down.'

Noah Benedict, aged 13

'I thought it was great! It was super engaging and exciting to read and kept me on the edge of my seat. I like how different it is from Kevin's other books, and I like how real the characters felt.'

Harriet Meek, aged 14

SHETLAND ISLANDS

SCOTLAND
WILDS OF THE FREE MAN

STIRLING CASTLE
SUSPECTED REBELLION
STRONGHOLD

BORDER GATE

CUMBRIA RAILWAY
GATE

IRELAND
FORMER EUROPEAN PROVINCE RECLAIMED
DURING THE FIRST UPRISING

BELFAST ARMED
OUTPOST

ISLE OF MAN PRISON

ENGLAND
PROVINCE OF THE ELITE

MANCHESTER

SHEFFIELD

BIRMINGHAM

WALLED WORCESTER

WALES
GALL PECHOD MAWR DDYFOD
TRWY DORWS BYCHAN

CHEPSTOW
WELSH RELAY GATE

GREAT LONDON

DOVER

KENT COASTAL SEA PORT

NO DRAFT ZONE

EXETER

SANDS OUTPOST

Preface

Although *The Objectors* is set in a dystopian future, it focuses on major contemporary discourse. This includes the issue of economic division in society, protest against injustice, citizenship, identity, the effects of global warming and the need for sustainable resources. Above all, it is about three young people; a Quaker, a Christian and a girl of spiritual upbringing, all of whom possess the courage and aspiration to stand up for what they believe, no matter what.

Contents

PART 1—Incarceration

Chapter 1—Ethan

20th September 2042

'You are the masters of the new age. It's up to you to put things right.'

His uncle's words repeating in his mind, Ethan smashed a chair into the window, the force of his swing creating a mosaic of cracks in the glass. He stared briefly at his splintered reflection, the deep blue eyes and the dimple on his cheek a reminder of how much he was turning into his father. A second swing of the chair and he was through, the biting chill of the night air rushing through the broken window onto his face.

The triggering of the wire had given him the warning he needed. Applying the same technique he'd used on the farm, Ethan created a system of trip wire that surrounded the cabin. The sound he'd heard, the succession of cracks, meant the fishing line had broken and the hundred-metre perimeter had been breached.

As the pop caps fired their warning, he snatched a few items from the floor and crammed them into his rucksack. Moments later, the crash of the front door downstairs confirmed that the synthetic warriors had entered the stone cabin. The sound of thumping, mechanical footsteps on the staircase meant they'd be behind him in seconds.

Using his gloved hands, Ethan punched at the dagger-like shards that surrounded the window frame and levered himself through the gap. His feet crunching on broken glass, he reached back into the room and grabbed his rucksack.

'Stay exactly where you are,' an electronic voice snapped.

Ethan glanced, briefly, at the hulking, mechanical figure that filled the space he'd recently occupied. He then turned and propelled himself onto the grass verge below. Without breaking stride, he ran across the sloping field in the direction of the road.

With the help of a sky filled with a thousand stars to light his way, he climbed over the stone wall and followed the gravelled path that led to a row of pine trees.

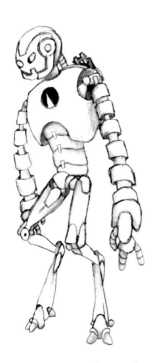

'You need to get out of the city,' his father had said, when Ethan received the letter on his sixteenth birthday to confirm he'd been selected by the regime to eliminate his quota of six people. It was

One of the trigger-happy synthetic guards

too late to even think about trying to leave the country. As soon as the scheme of elimination was announced, the regime increased the guard at the ports. In addition, the borders with Wales and Scotland were filled with laser-eyed, trigger-happy synthetic guards who'd been ordered to shoot at anything that came within range.

Instead, his father had given him an address, the keys to the car they'd built from rusted components and every unit of energy they'd created from the wind turbines on

3

the farm. The aim was to get him as far from Leeds as possible and beyond the prying eyes of the regime. The sloping hillsides of the Yorkshire Dales seemed like the perfect location, but then, three days later, he'd been discovered.

When he didn't report to The Elimination Centre on the date he'd been instructed, the search began for Ethan immediately. A reward was offered in return for information about his location and two words added beneath his photograph.

Objector—Traitor.

The fact they knew exactly where to find him meant only one thing. Ethan had been betrayed by those who'd succumbed to the lure of greed and informed the regime of his whereabouts.

Damp with sweat, he reached the row of pine trees and clicked the plastic key fob in his pocket. Immediately, a flash of orange sidelights verified the position of his car. He lifted the pile of heavy branches from the bonnet and was about to wipe the dirt from the windscreen when he heard the crunch of tyres on the road behind him.

'Ethan Blake, you need to come with us,' shouted a voice, human this time. 'Step away from the vehicle.'

A beam of light shone in his direction and Ethan lifted his hands to shield his eyes. As the panic increased, he remembered the scathing words of his father. 'You're just a child, Ethan,' he'd said, 'a fragile, terrified child who lacks any strength of conviction.' Ethan couldn't forget those words. Filled with an intent to prove his father wrong, he opened the car door and jumped inside.

'Don't even think about it,' the human voice warned.

Ethan slammed the door, pushed the ignition button on the electric car and set off in the opposite direction to the spotlight. He'd barely moved when a tall figure stepped into the road. Ethan tried to swerve out of its way, only for the synthetic warrior to crash its armoured fists against the bonnet of the car that thudded to a halt.

'You are playing a most dangerous game young man,' a voice said, as the door on the driver's side opened.

Ethan fell onto the road. His mouth filled with the metallic taste of blood, he pushed himself up and tried to run, only to be restrained by the fierce hold of the synthetic warrior. He tried to force his way free, but it was no use. His arms were pulled behind him and his wrists manacled into handcuffs.

The images of his fellow Objectors, Ellie-Mae and Samarah, filled his mind. He'd seen them on the transmissions, their faces emblazoned on the screen. Like Ethan, they'd been labelled by the regime as criminals. Like Ethan, their only crime had been to stand up for what they believed.

'I don't care what you do to me,' he said, his resolve hardening. 'I'm not killing anybody.'

A man in camouflage clothing walked towards him. On the left shoulder of the man's jacket was the image of a white blade, cutting through a circle of black. The Shard. The symbol of the regime and one that signified this man as a member of the elite. 'Hold still now,' he said.

'No!' Ethan shouted as the man stepped forward, but the more he tried to kick and fight his way free, the tighter the mechanical grip of the synthetic warrior became.

A fist connected with his jaw, followed by a moment of pain and his struggles were over, his thoughts plunged.

Chapter 2—Ellie-Mae

Ellie-Mae edged across the road, wrapping the arms of her jacket around her chest to keep out the chill London air. A group of shivering human figures assembled on the pavement beside her. Their clothes were threadbare and ripped to confirm them as the have-nots in society, the second-class citizens who'd become known as the underlings.

Others approached from around the corner on the right. Many were of a similar age to her father and had lost their homes, jobs and self-respect to the regime. Some of the others were of a similar age to Ellie-Mae, whose youthful aspirations had been destroyed and replaced with fear and despair.

'The younger generation has been forsaken,' her father told her. 'People like you can give them hope.'

In coming to London, the home of the rich and elite, each of the underlings was taking a massive risk. For Ellie-Mae, the threat was an even greater one. Along with Ethan and Samarah, both of whom had refused to sign the contract of elimination, her image had been displayed during national transmissions alongside two words deliberately chosen to attack her Christian faith.

Objector - Judas.

As she stood on the pavement, she gripped at the crucifixes that hung around her neck. She then looked at those around her, the fight for survival imprinted in their determined expressions. Whatever happened, she knew she had to stay strong and as the crowd grew in numbers, Ellie-Mae moved as close to her father as she could.

Ahead of her was a sign for Westminster Station, the place they'd agreed to meet at the start of the march of defiance. It was once at the centre of a crowded metropolis. Workers would arrive at the underground station and be escalated in their thousands towards a multitude of professions. As resources in energy reduced and communication networks failed across the world, the city emptied.

The government were driven out of office by a new regime in the form of The Entitlement Party. Its members became known as the elite and the new order quickly began to enforce its power. The same workers who'd previously spent their days in offices and schools in London were exiled to separate parts of the country.

The strongest were sent to the mines and the mills in the north that generated power and textiles for the regime. Others were taken to the wastelands and forced to survive on scraps amongst England's dumping grounds. The rest were relocated in specialist towns that were barely habitable.

Ellie-Mae moved towards the top of the staircase to see a mass of human figures huddled on the concourse below.

'It is time for us to have our say,' a man shouted. 'This is our country too.'

The shrill screech of whistles and a blowing of horns confirmed the approval of the horde of underlings who'd gathered at the bottom of the steps.

'We are working night and day, seven days a week, our lungs choking with coal dust, our limbs severed in the jaws of machinery and how do they repay us? By taking everything for themselves and teaching our young how to kill. Not anymore!'

Ellie-Mae heard shouts from the concourse and she saw a series of fists punched into the gloom as the swaying crowd climbed the staircase. As they poured into the street, they passed beneath the slogan adopted by the regime. In basic terms, the symbol suggested a political message that was similar to many that had been used throughout history as a sign of strength and unity. In reality, it represented ambition, prosperity and selfish greed for those at the top of society's spectrum at the expense of everyone else.

Ellie-Mae stood to one side as a man she recognised as William Eastern headed in her direction, his left eye covered with a black leather patch. He was viewed by the underlings as the leader of the uprising and someone her father had described as the bravest man he'd ever known.

William stopped. 'Are you joining us? We need people like you.'

'Of course,' Ellie-Mae replied. 'Where are we going?'

'Parliament Square.'

The human figures who'd gathered in the darkness of the station followed William into the street. Like Ellie-Mae and her father, many of them had travelled on foot to London, having left the mines and the mills in the north. As the hands of Big Ben ticked over to nine o'clock to announce that the curfew had begun, a second group approached from the right, each of them lifting their banners into the September sky.

'Everyone deserves a life'
'Freedom, not slavery'
'Stop the murder NOW!'

The whistles, drums and horns increased in volume and as she joined the back of the group, Ellie-Mae couldn't help but feel a sense of pride. For years her family had campaigned for equality and here she was, marching alongside her father and William Eastern, the man who'd inspired the starving masses to raise their voices. In response to their protests, rallies and strikes, the regime appeared sympathetic at first.

But then it fought back.

The same synthetic warriors who'd originally been built to protect the people from terrorism were put into action. Stories emerged of baton charges, machine guns being fired into crowds from point blank range and surviving protesters being taken away, never to be seen again. Then, of course, came the announcement of the elimination scheme and the opportunity for underlings to live amongst the elite. All they had to do was kill six of their own.

A roar of engines drew Ellie-Mae's attention. Headlamps burst through the gloom as a row of black, armoured vans started to approach. The mood in the group altered. Banners fell and the same figures who'd been following the march began to disperse.

His arms waving, William turned. 'This is a peaceful demonstration,' he shouted. 'They cannot harm you.'

His words were ignored by all but a few of the group who continued to walk along the centre of the road. Some of them covered their faces to hide from the cameras that pointed in their direction. Others lifted their heads towards the lens in defiance and with their every step, the armoured vehicles drew closer.

'It's all right, Ellie-Mae,' her father said. 'Keep going.'

9

She kept her eyes ahead and followed him onto College Green. The imposing statue of Winston Churchill towered above them, his determined expression matching that of William Eastern who was striding towards Parliament Tower. Hanging from every window and doorway were banners of The Shard, the white blade that cut through a circle of black.

William's pace was matched by an armoured vehicle that screeched to a halt. The door on one side opened and a pair of synthetic warriors lowered their hulking, mechanical figures to the road, their guns strapped to their sides. Behind them was a bearded man with dark eyes. He was wearing an ankle-length coat and as he came closer, Ellie-Mae noticed a jagged scar on his cheek that characterised his approach. Evil, sadistic and filled with self-admiration, it was Lucius, the face of the regime.

'William Eastern,' Lucius said, lifting a silver gun from his rucksack and pointing it at William. 'You have been found guilty of treason against the state.'

'Must be important if they sent you,' William said, as the towering group of synthetic warriors surrounded him.

'Afraid so,' he replied. 'We warned you, didn't we? We told you what would happen if you continued to provoke the underling class to stand up against the regime. Do you have anything to say before your sentence is carried out?'

William looked in several directions as though searching for an escape route, but then his eyes settled on Ellie-Mae. 'Never give up,' he said, 'and never stop believing.'

The circle of synthetic warriors tightened around William. A small gap opened and Ellie-Mae gasped at the sight of William's head, jerking back from the power of the bullet.

'No!' her father shouted, pushing through the gap as William's body slumped to the ground. 'This man has done nothing wrong.'

Ellie-Mae tried to follow him but was pushed away by the metal hand of a synthetic warrior. 'Please, Dad, don't,' she cried.

Too late. He'd already draped his coat over William. He then lifted the cross from around his neck and placed it next to William's forehead, down to his chest and across his shoulders.

'Peace be with you.'

In response, Lucius snarled. He then turned towards Ellie-Mae as a hint of recognition appeared in his eyes. 'I know you, don't I?'

'You will never know me,' she whispered.

'We'll see, Ellie-Mae, the Objector,' Lucius said, pointing his silver gun in her father's direction. 'I'm sure you know the penalty for protecting a criminal, especially when her father continues to preach a religion that defies our laws.'

'My daughter is not a criminal,' her father said. 'She is allowed to object.'

'No, she is not,' Lucius said. 'Members of the underlings must do exactly what we say, and this includes your daughter. As you know, she has been selected to eliminate six people and this is what she must do.'

'I'll sign the contract,' Ellie-Mae shouted. 'Let him live and I'll do whatever you want.'

Lucius paused, then lowered the gun. 'I like the sound of that,' he said, and gestured towards one of the synthetic warriors. 'Take him with the others.'

Ellie-Mae didn't get the chance to say goodbye to her father. Instead, she could only watch as he was taken away by the menacing cluster of synthetics. Her head was then covered in a black hood and her wrists bound into handcuffs.

'Do not struggle,' an electronic voice said, 'It is easier if you do not fight back.'

Her feet kicking the air, Ellie-Mae was lifted from the ground and thrown onto a harsh, metal surface. Moments later, the door to the vehicle slammed closed and she hid beneath the hood of her tattered blue jacket.

'Do not judge, and you will not be judged. Forgive, and you will be forgiven,' she whispered, her face pressed against the floor. 'Keep safe, Father, we will be together again.'

With a roar of the engine and a jolt of movement, the armoured vehicle was on the move.

Chapter 3—Samarah

Samarah looked down at the girl who was sprawled across the floor of the armoured vehicle. Although she was partly hidden by the tattered fabric of her blue jacket, Samarah knew who she was. So far, only three people had objected to the regime and the programme of elimination. This girl, Ellie-Mae, was one of them.

When she was thrown on board, Samarah heard her whisper something unintelligible and something about forgiveness. As the journey continued, the words stopped. The black hood slipped from Ellie-Mae's head to uncover a mass of long brown hair and black-rimmed glasses with a crack in one of the lenses.

Samarah closed her eyes, her mind reaching upwards, outwards. A girl of spiritual upbringing, she'd learnt the ability to connect with other people's minds from her mother. The knowledge came with the warning that not everyone could be contacted and that only the ones with receptive, open minds could hear the words of others.

Fortunately, Ellie-Mae was one of them and in the darkness, Samarah could visualise a faint image of the girl. At first, she felt the timid resemblance of a rabbit or a fawn. As she drew closer, Samarah could feel the inner strength of an ibex. In a similar way to the mountain goat, there was something in Ellie-Mae's aura to suggest that she could fight back against even the fiercest of predators.

'I'm here if you need me,' Samarah offered, then opened her eyes.

The girl stirred and lifted her gaze through the tangle of hair. She appeared confused, but then her expression settled as she looked at Samarah.

'Thank you,' Ellie-Mae mouthed and lay back down.

Samarah decided not to push it any further. This wasn't the right time to continue to reach out to Ellie-Mae and anyway, Samarah needed to conserve her energy. Instead, she leaned back and rested her head against the metal frame behind her. It didn't take long for her thoughts to return to the moment she'd been lifted from the basement of her safe-house. Like an injured wolf hiding from its hunter, she'd concealed herself in the darkness.

And then they came.

She'd heard the faraway barking of dogs, then the crash of the door and the thud of footsteps above her. Samarah always knew they'd find her sooner or later. Before she'd gone into hiding, she'd seen the transmissions with the image of the boy, Ethan, and this girl, Ellie-Mae, alongside her own. Beneath her photograph was the phrase that ensured they would hunt her down at all costs.

Objector   —Immigrant.

Her being an underling who'd chosen to defy the regime would have been reason enough for them to widen their search. Although she'd been raised in a western culture, the fact that Samarah was of Afro-Caribbean origin meant that the predominantly Caucasian regime would stop at nothing to make an example of a young black woman.

'Secure the area. See if you can find the others,' a woman shouted as the hatch to the basement was forced open and she was dragged by her wrists into the room.

'Where is your family?' asked the man with the jagged scar on his face. For a moment, his pupils narrowed into vertical lines, like a predator who'd captured its prey.

'Somewhere you will never reach them,' she'd replied.

Samarah could still feel the pain of the resulting slap to her face. Although his attack wasn't filled with venom, his strike was razor-sharp, and she knew exactly who he was. In the last few months, his image had appeared in every transmission and regime leaflet. Most people knew him as Lucius, the ultimate member of the elite and an example for all. To Samarah, with his dark, predatory eyes and slithering demeanour, he would be forever known as the viper.

The rhythm of the journey continued, the rocking motion of the armoured vehicle causing her to slip in and out of consciousness. A sharp jolt jerked her from her seat and she fell into the bear-sized chest of the synthetic warrior that was sitting opposite. As she sat back, she looked into its green, expressionless eyes.

Samarah wondered if she could sense the soul of an animal within. She attempted to communicate and explore its inner being only for her efforts to be pushed away by the coldness of metal and the intricate mesh of technology.

The armoured vehicle came to a stop and the door slid open to allow a rush of cold air that searched beneath the fabric of her clothes. Shivering, and with her wrists tied with handcuffs behind her back, Samarah lowered herself from her seat, perched at the edge of the vehicle and slid onto the concrete below.

Samarah then turned to see that the girl with the long brown hair had remained where she was, lying on the floor of the armoured vehicle.

'Ellie-Mae,' she said. 'You need to move.'

No response.

'Please, Ellie-Mae. Follow my voice, come towards me. Otherwise, they'll throw you onto the ground.'

One of the synthetic warriors stood up and reached out his arm, only for Ellie-Mae to avoid his grasp and crawl towards Samarah. Within moments, the viper appeared in front of them and even in the gloom, Samarah could see the scar that cut into the side of his face.

'Follow me,' Lucius said.

He led them towards an iron-clad door covered with the dagger-like image of The Shard, above which was an

15

inscription *'Non Ducor, Duco'*. *'I am not led, I lead'* it said. Yet another slogan used by the elite that caused Samarah to cringe at its arrogance.

A synthetic warrior nudged her in the back and she followed Lucius through the door, down some concrete steps and into a bunker that surprised her in its vastness. Steel columns rose from floor to ceiling in each of the corners and at one end of the hall was a raised platform. On top of the platform was a camera that followed her every movement.

Plasma screens were mounted on every wall and some of them were filled with the images of middle-aged men and women who gesticulated with wild hands as they spoke. Samarah recognised some of them as high-ranking figures within The Entitlement Party.

She assumed the others were members of the elite who'd been chosen because of their snappy appearance and boyish good looks. The rest of the screens were filled with various images of propaganda: people of different generations, families and children, all of whom were sitting around in staged poses of happiness.

Samarah had seen it all before. It was exactly the type of utopian society The Entitlement Party promised when they came into power. Powerful decision makers positioned at the apex of the regime and a contented society of elite people beneath.

At one end of the room a door opened and a group of girls in dark green uniform ran towards Lucius. Part of their faces were hidden beneath baseball caps. Samarah knew who they were. Girls of sixteen, with July birthdays and two months older than Samarah. They were the first cohort of cadets selected by the regime to carry out the programme of elimination. They had the guise of labradors welcoming their master back to his home and showering him with praise.

'You've come back to us,' the first one said, handing him a red rose. 'We've missed you.'

One after another, the girls kissed him on both cheeks before stepping to one side.

A second group appeared from the opposite side of the room. This time, it was a group of shaven-headed boys and if the girls were labradors, the boys snarled with the fury of pit bull terriers.

'Are these the ones?' a voice barked from within the group. 'The Objectors?'

'That's right,' Lucius replied. 'Pathetic, aren't they?'

A synthetic warrior grabbed Samarah's arm. It squeezed it so tightly, her eyes began to water. One of the boys rubbed the sharpness of his stubbled head across her face.

'Cry baby,' he said.

Accompanied by the stamping of feet, Samarah and Ellie-Mae were led to the centre of the room by a synthetic warrior. In front of them was the camera that was previously located on the platform, with the lens now aimed at Lucius.

'Stand here, Objectors,' said a woman in khaki uniform, 'the transmission has begun.'

'Citizens of England,' Lucius said, looking directly into the camera. 'It is time for the strikes and the riots to end and for the dissenters to go back to work.'

Behind him, the pit-bull terriers and the labradors barked their approval. Some of them started to clap and cheer and as the volume increased, Lucius stepped to one side to allow the camera to focus directly on Ellie-Mae.

'It is also time for all of the chosen to join the elimination scheme and dismiss any thoughts of objection.'

The lens of the camera moved closer to Ellie-Mae's face.

'Do you think you are special?' Lucius asked. 'Do you think you're better than the decent people of this country. Those who recognise devotion to the regime and understand the meaning of duty?'

The camera moved to its right.

'How about you, Samarah? Do you have anything to say?'

She wanted to shout and scream the reasons why she wouldn't sign the contract. She wanted to tell the watching world to keep going and never give up in opposing the regime. But she couldn't. Ellie-Mae was being gripped in the mechanical arms of a synthetic who was pointing a gun at her temple

'Nothing?' Lucius continued. 'Not as brave as you thought you were, are you?'

The red light on the side of the camera extinguished to confirm the end of the transmission. With the heckling labradors on one side and the taunting pit-bulls on the other, Samarah was forced towards the side of the hall by the metal arms of a synthetic. One of the boys stood in her way. Another one stretched out his foot and Samarah tripped and fell to the ground in front of the sneering Lucius. As the pit-bulls barked again, the synthetic dragged Samarah to her feet.

'Follow me,' Lucius said.

The synthetic grabbed Samarah's arms and followed Lucius through an iron door. On the other side of the door was a spiral staircase and Samarah's feet stumbled as the synthetic shoved her forward. At the bottom of the steps were two cells. Samarah and Ellie-Mae were positioned outside each of the closed doors.

'Inside your cell, you will find one hessian dress, one blanket and one piece of string,' Lucius said, unlocking the handcuffs behind Samarah's back. 'You have two minutes to get changed or else I will come in and do it for you.'

The door opened to reveal a darkened room. A sharp push in the small of her back sent Samarah sprawling onto the stone floor. She stood up, moved to behind the cell wall to hide from Lucius's gaze and removed her jeans. She then stepped further into the darkness and took off her top. The hessian dress stank of stale sweat and its fabric was rough against her skin. Even so, the possibility of being 'helped' by the viper was enough encouragement to do as he'd asked.

'Clothes,' Lucius said, 'and hands.'

Samarah moved towards the cell door and gave him her jeans and shirt. In an effort to prevent her arms from being grappled behind her, she held out her hands in front of her waist.

'Smart move,' Lucius said, tightening the handcuffs on her wrists. 'You could be in here for a while.'

The door to the cell slammed and shut out the light. Her hands feeling at the walls, Samarah lowered herself to the floor. She thought about the girl imprisoned beside her and closed her eyes, her mind reaching upward, outward.

Ellie-Mae. Can you hear me? Are you all right?

Nothing happened at first, but then the faint image of the ibex appeared, its horns pointing upwards.

Yes. Thank you. I am stronger than they think.

It was all that Samarah needed to know and she opened her eyes. As her focus adjusted to the gloom of the cell, she realised that the darkness wasn't as empty as she thought. A shimmering movement on the wall opposite was followed by a hissing sound and the scurry of footsteps.

She then tightened her arms to her body as the swarm of black creatures raced in her direction.

Chapter 4—Ethan

Ethan woke to the taste of dirt and dust. His mouth dry, his head pounding, he sat up on the cold, plastic mattress at the side of his prison cell and looked at the palms of his hands. His blistered skin was broken in several places and Ethan blew at his fingers to soothe the burning pain. Since he'd arrived at The Elimination Centre, he'd been woken at various times of the day and night, then dragged outside by the synthetic warriors to work for hours at a time.

Sometimes, he'd be taken to different sections of the wall that enclosed Clapham, Vauxhall, Brixton, Balham and Wandsworth. It was the area known as the protected zone and the adopted home of the elite and the regime itself. In the centre of the zone was Clapham Common, the home of the cavernous, deep-level bunkers. In the biting wind, and close to exhaustion, this had been the location he'd spent most of his time, plunging blunt tools into the frozen earth to dig the deepest ditch of them all.

'Bunker number five,' he'd been told. 'The final reckoning.'

He grimaced at the sound of the siren, a noise that began with a low murmur and then grew louder until it reached its ear-splitting peak. It signalled that the previous shift had ended and Ethan looked to his left as the cell door opened to reveal the imposing three-metre figure of a synthetic.

'Time to move,' an electronic voice said.

Ethan stood up and received a punch to his midriff. As he bent double from the force of the blow, the synthetic gripped into the skin of his arms and lifted Ethan back to standing. He glanced at the cell doors at the far end of the corridor. On his second day at The Elimination Centre, he'd heard the shouts and stamping feet of cadets from above. The voices outside his cell door confirmed that the two girls, Samarah and Ellie-Mae, had been caught. Objectors, like him, who'd tried to escape the clutches of the regime and were now at the mercy of Lucius.

The synthetic dragged him through the corridor, his shoulders crashing against the metal walls on either side. The shock of pain that ran down his arms caused Ethan to stumble, only for the grip of the synthetic warrior to tighten as he hauled him forward. At the junction of passageways, they stopped. Instead of heading towards the exit that led to the bunkers outside, Ethan was forced along a different corridor until he reached a steel door.

The door opened and he was taken into a room in which the portrait of a man in black uniform was emblazoned on the wall. Black hair, thick moustache and eyebrows that met in the middle, Ethan recognised him as the former leader of The Entitlement Party who'd led the initial coup in 2034.

The Commandant.

Since his death in 2038, the party had continued to use his image at every opportunity to retain a link with the past and to offer the regime a sense of credibility.

Inside the room, desks were bolted to the floor and set out in the design of a classroom. Sitting at the rows of desks were eager looking boys and girls of a similar age to Ethan, each of them leaning forward as though they were ready to listen and learn.

'Stand him at the back. It's time for the show.'

The lights in the room faded as a metal gantry unfolded and descended from the ceiling. In the centre of the gantry was a television monitor filled with the image of a bearded man with a jagged scar on his face. Although most of his sharp features were hidden below the wide brim of a cowboy hat, his narrow eyes remained visible as he stared into a hand-held camera.

'Hi there, cadets,' said the man. 'On a normal day, you

might know me as Lucius but right now, you can call me gunslinger.'

He turned the camera away from his face and towards a trail of lights on the floor. With the clink of spurs in the background, the image on the screen followed the lights and moved towards a synthetic warrior that stood beside a door. It was wearing a red scarf and a badge on the pocket of its jacket that was inscribed *'Sheriff'*.

'Through here?' Lucius asked.

The synthetic sheriff nodded and opened the door to reveal an avenue of wooden buildings.

'Welcome to the Wild West,' Lucius said, pointing the camera towards a street of buildings. Each of them was inscribed with a wooden sign above its main entrance. One of them was marked as *'Bank'*, another one *'Saloon'* and at the end of the row, the building was marked *'Rail Depot'*. In between the avenue of buildings was a dirt track and railway that led from one end of the frontier town to the other.

'This way,' said Lucius into the camera, as he pushed through the swinging wooden doors of the saloon.

The crack of gunfire caused Ethan to flinch and as the camera pointed in a different direction, a flash appeared in one of the windows.

'That guy shooting thinks this is just a game. He doesn't know he's been selected yet,' said Lucius. 'I'd better put down my camera and let him know why he's here, don't you think?'

The screen went blank. When the image returned, it focussed on the track in the street. The figure of Lucius appeared in the centre of the screen, pushing his way through the saloon door. He was holding a rucksack in one hand and his other hand tapped against the gun in his holster.

'Anyone brave enough to challenge me,' Lucius said, in

a mock, American drawl as he lowered the rucksack to the ground.

'I'll face you,' said a blonde-haired man, striding from the bank. 'There's no room for roughnecks like you in this town.'

'OK then,' Lucius said. 'Draw.'

The man lifted his gun and fired. In response, Lucius didn't move and simply smiled as he looked back at the man.

'Hey there, you know the rules. You're dead, so lie down before I knock you down.'

Lucius started to laugh as he lifted a helmet from the rucksack with the inscription '*Head-up display*' on one side. 'Switch camera.'

The television monitor that Ethan was watching went blank once again. When it returned, the image on the screen had moved away from the street in which Lucius was standing. Instead, it narrowed into a circle that aimed at the blonde-haired man to show that the screen was displaying from within the H.U.D.

'You've got the wrong guy,' the man said, stepping back on his heels.

A scroll of text flowed across the screen. Numbers altered into words until the sequence settled on a single name. Neil Roberts. The name remained at the top of the screen as images of faces flickered from person to person until they found a perfect match for the blonde-haired man in the centre of the H.U.D.

'Mr Roberts,' Lucius said. 'You have been selected for elimination.'

'What about my wife and children?' the man replied, then turned and ran.

'Now's when the fun stuff begins,' Lucius said.

A reticle in the centre of the screen confirmed the position of his target. He rounded the corner to find Mr

Roberts attempting to climb out of a dead end that was enclosed by a six-metre wall of bricks.

'It's up to you cadets,' Lucius said, offering further instruction. 'You can alter the appearance of your victim to whoever or whatever you want.'

The image of Mr Roberts transformed into a hooded man in a black cloak. The skeletal animation then turned towards Lucius, the bones of its fingers dripping with blood as they stretched from the sleeves of its cloak.

'How about that? Much easier to kill him now, isn't it?'

A flash on the H.U.D. signalled that Lucius had fired the weapon. As the skeletal animation crumpled and fell into the dirt, a different vision filled the screen. It was an image of the grim reaper as he danced, swayed and evaporated into dust. Text scrolled across the screen.

OBJECTIVE COMPLETE. TARGET ELIMINATED

The television monitor in the room that housed the cadets went blank as the lights came back on. Some of them started to cheer and Ethan shuffled uneasily as the monitor folded back into the metal gantry and lifted to the ceiling. Standing in its place was the bearded man with the jagged scar.

'See how easy it is?' Lucius said.

'Where is this place?' one of the boys asked, his ginger hair flopping over his acne-filled face.

'Good question, Josh,' said Lucius. 'The location is a secret, but each of you will have the chance to play the game as part of your training.'

'I want to do it now,' Josh said. 'This is exactly how I roll.'

Lucius ignored the comment and walked towards Ethan. 'We have an Objector with us today,' he said.

'Someone whose family was given special treatment.'

The cadets turned and looked at Ethan.

'This boy's family was spared the mines, the mills and the wastelands and offered a farm. His objection is therefore particularly disappointing,' Lucius continued as he stood beside him. 'There is still an opportunity to join us, Ethan.'

'I can't.'

'There is doubt in those eyes of yours,' Lucius said. 'Join us and you will be welcomed with open arms.'

Ethan said nothing. He didn't want to admit it, but Lucius was right. His hesitation stemmed from the same doubt he'd always felt. As a young boy, when his Quaker family spoke of their compulsion for conscientious objection, stillness and peace, Ethan played imaginary war with his soldiers. When they talked of simplicity and organic methods to run the farm, Ethan cannibalised scraps to build robots from printed circuit boards and antique micro-chips. The chance to work with proper technology such as H.U.D.s was something he'd always dreamed of.

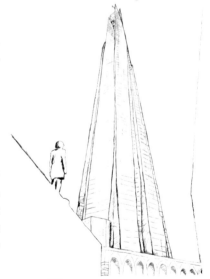

'Thing is, people,' Lucius said, turning back to the group of cadets, 'we don't want you to be afraid of killing. We want you to have some fun along the way.'

'Once we've eliminated our quota of six,' said a girl at the front of the room. 'How soon do we get our reward?'

'Within a week of completing your duty, you and your underling family will receive verification of your upgrade into the elite. You will then be given the keys to your new house within the protected zone.'

'Just like that?' asked Josh.

'There's something else. Something we've only just introduced,' Lucius said. 'If you decide to take a second assignment, sign a new contract and double your quota, you will be offered the chance to choose your very own someone for elimination. There's always somebody who's upset you, isn't there? This is your chance for some proper revenge and to get rid of them forever.'

One of the cadets gasped. Ethan looked at another, who sneered as though he'd already chosen a victim.

'The first group of cadets has nearly completed its preparation,' Lucius said, 'and as graduates of the elimination training scheme, they will be rewarded with a celebration they will never forget.'

Ethan could feel the excitement growing in the room. The increased chatter, the smiles on the faces of the other cadets as though they'd been offered the greatest present in the world. Ethan felt it too and, in that moment, any notions of objection were pushed to one side.

'When do we start?' Josh asked.

'All in good time, my friends,' Lucius replied. 'All in good time.'

Chapter 5—Ellie Mae

Since she'd arrived, the plasma screen on the wall of her cell had displayed a continuous stream of words and pictures.

'When the United Nations disbanded, and the rest of the world locked its doors on us for the last time, we were forced to concentrate on ourselves,' the screen announced. *'But then came the bloodshed.'*

Images of the terrorist atrocities followed, all of them dated between 2032 and 2034. Exploding buildings, people's faces covered in bloodied bandages and the piles of bodies in the street. Then came the destruction of England's churches as a reminder of the dangers of religious extremism. Only the Cathedrals were allowed to remain as a shrine to the attack on St Paul's that killed the founding members of The Entitlement Party in 2033.

The image of the screen switched to men and women in dark green uniforms sitting around tables as though deep in conversation.

'Those we considered to be guardians didn't want to protect their people anymore. But we did,' the words continued. *'For a minimal contribution to our work, The Entitlement Party offered people in London an opportunity to be safe.'*

She was only nine years old at the time, but Ellie-Mae could remember most of what happened when the coup was complete and The Entitlement Party came to power in 2035. Soon after, the children of parents unable to pay the 'minimal contribution' of one million pounds were sent home from school. Within hours, the families of the children were removed from their homes and told to wait in the street for transport and re-allocation. The sight of her mother crying amongst a sack full of belongings was something that Ellie-Mae would never forget.

'Everyone was given the choice,' the words on the screen

continued. *'Pay the membership or become reassigned.'*

As the country split into 'haves' and 'have nots' and violent security measures were put into place, the regime took credit for *'driving the extremists from these shores'*. It was a suggestion her father rejected.

'Nobody was allowed to leave, and no one was allowed to enter the country,' he told her. 'Then the last of the terrorists bombed their way through our borders. They couldn't wait to get out.'

She was still thinking about her family when a change of atmosphere in her cell brought her back to the present. For the first time since her captivity began, the talking on the screen stopped and the images faded. At the sound of scraping metal, Ellie-Mae turned to see a hint of movement at the circular lens in the spyhole on the wall. She slid into the corner as a key rattled in the lock and the door to her prison cell opened.

'Good evening, Ellie-Mae.'

Her fuddled mind took a few seconds to untangle and enable her to place the faint recognition. But then she realised who it was. Lucius. Ellie-Mae grabbed at her hessian clothing and covered her shoulders as best she could. She pushed herself up to kneeling and with her wrists manacled in handcuffs, she clasped the palms of her hands together.

'I pray for my mother's soul,' she said, as Lucius closed the cell door behind him. 'I also pray for my father but most of all, I pray for the man who took him away because he knows only hatred.'

'Let my father live and I'll do whatever you want,' Lucius said, his dark figure standing in the centre of the prison cell. 'Do you remember saying these words?'

'Where have you taken him?' she replied.

'Later, much later,' Lucius said. 'For now, look around you, Ellie-Mae. What can you see?'

She stared into the gloom of her cell. Even the tiny red light in the ceiling camera had been switched off.

'We are completely alone,' said Lucius. 'What do you think about that?'

Ellie-Mae remained where she was as Lucius lifted an envelope from his jacket. 'Sign the contract,' he said. 'It will make things easier for you.'

'No,' she whispered. 'Killing is wrong.'

He placed the envelope back into his jacket and moved towards her. She flinched at the stench of alcohol and the warmth of his breath on the back of her neck. Lucius ran his fingers through her hair and towards the bottom of her ponytail which he pulled with a fierce tug and jerked back her head.

'Aren't you going to try and fight me off?' he whispered, as the sponge-like texture of his tongue licked across her cheek. 'Most of the others do.'

For a moment, Ellie-Mae was tempted to submit to his request and sign the contract. She was even tempted to beg for release, but then the memory of the girl, Samarah, gave her strength. She was suffering just like Ellie-Mae and yet she'd reached out to her on more than one occasion. Alone, scared and imprisoned in the cell beside her she'd even checked to make sure that Ellie-Mae was all right.

There was another one who objected to the programme of eliminations too. The boy, Ethan, whose image she'd seen only in transmissions, but who'd risked his life in standing up to the regime in the same way as Samarah. Empowered with hope and renewed belief, she lifted her hands to the double pendant that hung from her necklace. In one hand, she clasped the crucifix.

'The Lord has risen,' she whispered.

Using her other hand, she brushed her fingers over a second crucifix on which the effigy of Jesus remained on the cross.

'But he is also with me,' she said, louder this time. 'He suffers as I suffer.'

'Very good, Ellie-Mae,' said Lucius. 'Maybe he can watch.'

She thought of her mother, and how she'd prepared her for moments of inappropriate touch such as these. Ellie-Mae constricted the muscles in her abdomen, then released. She was so thirsty, so dehydrated, that nothing happened at first, but then a trickle of warm urine started to run down the inside of her thigh.

'You're disgusting,' Lucius said, pushing her in the middle of her back with so much force, she stumbled and fell into the corner.

Ellie-Mae pushed herself up from the stone floor and watched the dark figure of Lucius stomp across the prison cell. Seconds later, he returned with a bucket of water and threw its icy contents onto her face.

'Have a wash,' he said. 'Because you stink.'

As the door slammed behind him, she shivered and exhaled deeply. The television screen flickered, flashed. Once again, the images of the rise of The Entitlement Party returned, words blasting in praise of the regime's relentless pursuit of glory and the promise to protect its people.

'Hypocrites,' Ellie-Mae said, but then she noticed the glimmer of red light at the side of the camera in the ceiling, to confirm the filming had resumed.

'God is my strength,' she said, standing up. 'I am no longer one of the forsaken.'

In response, the volume on the television increased, forcing her to step back and cover her ears. One more glance into the lens of the camera and Ellie-Mae lay back down on the cold stone floor of her cell. Terrified at the thought of Lucius's return, the next few minutes seemed infinite. As the volume on the television reduced and the pace of her breath returned to normal, she clasped her hands together.

'From darkness comes light,' she said. 'The light shines in the darkness and the darkness has not overcome it.'

It was enough to ease her doubt and as the warmth of her skin began to nullify the cold water that Lucius had thrown, Ellie-Mae relaxed and allowed a wave of exhaustion to send her into dreams.

The sensation of light on her face caused her to wake. She panicked at the silhouetted figure standing in the doorway, before realising it wasn't Lucius but the three-metre-high angular figure of a synthetic warrior.

'Come with me,' it said.

Ellie-Mae lifted herself from the floor and followed it towards the spiral staircase. As they walked, the recorded voice of the deceased Commandant blared from the speakers that lined the corridor.

'Today is a chance to put things right,' he said. 'Do your duty and you will be rewarded.'

She thought about the other cadets, the vulnerable girls who'd signed the contract. She wondered how many of them would be visited by the devil in the night. Maybe some of them would have been willing to give in to Lucius's demands. The rest, no doubt, would be convinced they were simply doing their duty.

Even so, it wasn't only the stain on their honour, but the everlasting touch of his evil that filled Ellie-Mae with the most unbearable ache of sadness.

Chapter 6—Samarah

Since the moment she'd arrived in her cell, the scurrying swarm of black creatures had scampered over her head, her legs and her face. Occasionally, she'd feel the sharp bite of their teeth on her skin and Samarah would leap to standing and brush them away.

They soon came back and the only time they left her alone was in the moments when her food arrived. Like a wave of blackness, the swarm of creatures would scuttle towards the opening at the bottom of the cell door and devour the plate of scraps that were meant for Samarah.

Once they'd consumed every morsel of food, they'd aim their stinking bodies and scuttling legs in her direction once again. Occasionally, she'd get to the plate before they did. She'd sometimes manage to eat a mouthful of food, only for the creatures to cover her in a laceration of spiteful bites in return.

With the pain of hunger gnawing at her stomach, Samarah was lifted from the cell by a pair of synthetic warriors. Her wrists bound in handcuffs, her feet stumbling, she was dragged up the spiral staircase. The door at the top of the stairs opened and she closed her eyes to avoid the blinding light shining into her eyes. After a few seconds, the light dimmed, only to be replaced with the sound of stirring, hurried music that blared from every speaker and plasma screen.

'*The Ride of the Valkyries*,' Lucius said. 'The music of triumph.'

The synthetic led her into one of the corners of the main hall as the floor vibrated to the rhythm of music. Samarah looked to her left to see Ellie-Mae, her cuffed hands in front of her waist. Next to her was a boy with a fair complexion, his blue eyes flicking from one side to another like an anxious mouse in the glare of a predator.

It was the first time she'd seen Ethan in the flesh and even in the few seconds she was able to search his aura, Samarah could sense a depth of goodness amongst a confused craving for identity and belonging.

The blare of noise stopped. Lucius moved to the centre of the room and climbed the steps to a raised platform that was positioned between a pair of steel columns. Beside him, a man dressed in camouflage clothing held a camera that he aimed at a group of cadets who were marching towards the platform in their dark green uniforms.

Shaven headed boys alongside girls wearing baseball caps, Samarah recognised them as the pit bull terriers and labradors who'd greeted Lucius on her first day at The Elimination Centre. Each of them was carrying a silver rifle in one hand and a H.U.D. in the other.

'You are the eliminators of this nation,' Lucius shouted at the cadets. 'It is your duty to rid us of the worthless members of society.'

The uniformed cadets started to cheer and some of them thrust their H.U.D.s into the air above them.

'For two months, you have trained to become the first of the nation's eliminators,' Lucius continued. 'Now it is time to play the game for real.'

A group of synthetic warriors came into the hall and lined up opposite one another to form a guard of honour. As they did so, the triumphant music returned at a deafening level. A golden cloud of mist rose from the floor as the cadets strode through the main hall. On the walls, plasma screens filled with images of soldiers marching through crowds who waved their flags in adoration.

Samarah glanced in the direction of the viper. His head tilted, his smile forced, Lucius gave the impression that he couldn't wait for the moment to end. Sure enough, as the last of the cadets marched through the exit and the door closed behind them, the atmosphere in the hall changed. The music stopped, the lights dimmed and as the golden mist evaporated, Lucius climbed down from the platform. He then beckoned the cameraman to follow him.

'One hundred brave and loyal cadets are on their way to glory and once they have completed their contract of elimination, they will be welcomed into the elite,' Lucius said into the lens of the camera. 'But now it is time to speak to those who continue to object.'

It was clear from the change in his expression that the viper was far happier in the role of tyrant than he was in offering any hint of positivity to others. The camera pointed towards Samarah. In response, she found some reserves of energy from within, lifted her frame and stared directly into the lens. The camera then moved away and focussed on Ellie-Mae.

'Can you see the weakness in this one?' Lucius said, as he moved beside her.

Samarah closed her eyes, her mind reaching upwards, outwards.

'Stay with me, Ellie-Mae. You are not alone.'

'Thank you, Samarah,' her sprit replied, the outline of an ibex clearly visible as she offered a response. *'He's not as tough as he thinks.'*

Lucius glanced in Samarah's direction, then back at Ellie-Mae. His predatory eyes narrowed, as though he'd sensed a connection between them, but then the triumphant music blared. The viper slid away from them both and moved towards the boy with the fair complexion.

'What is your name?' Lucius demanded.

The anxious mouse glanced towards Samarah, his eyes flicking from side to side.

'At me,' Lucius said. 'Look at me.'

'Ethan,' the boy stumbled.

'And what have you decided?' Lucius said.

'To join you,' he whispered.

'Speak up,' said Lucius, 'and this time make sure you are loud enough for everyone to hear.'

The camera moved closer to Ethan's face.

'I have decided to join the elite,' he said. 'Because it's the right thing to do.'

For a second time, Ethan glanced towards Samarah. In response, she closed her eyes. *'Your time will come. You will find your own way.'*

Samarah wasn't convinced she'd been able to reach him. It felt as though something was preventing her from breaching his shell and that he wasn't ready to listen. When she opened her eyes, however, she could see the change in Ethan's demeanour. The anxious look on his face had been replaced with one of confusion to suggest that contact had been made.

The viper looked at each of them in turn, pausing for a few moments as if to elicit a response. He then lifted a key from his pocket and opened the lock to Ethan's handcuffs.

'Be proud,' Lucius said, as he turned to the camera. 'If you have a glass at home, raise a toast in honour of this glorious moment. No matter what they have done in the past, for promising to carry out their duty, even former traitors of the regime are given the opportunity to join us.'

He then pointed to Samarah and Ellie-Mae. 'Maybe we can now persuade those we consider as the Immigrant and Judas to join us as well.'

The music continued, its volume increasing once more as Lucius stood beside Ethan, his arm coiled around his shoulders. Lucius held the pose for a few seconds and waited until the cameraman lifted his thumb to declare that the transmission was over.

'Why are you still here, Ethan?' Lucius said, pushing him away, his previous smile replaced with a sneer. 'Why are you standing beside me? Get out of my sight.'

Ethan fell backwards onto the floor and a synthetic leaned over, grabbed hold of his shoulders and lifted him to standing. Samarah attempted to make contact once again, but Ethan offered her nothing. Instead, the bear-like synthetic led the hesitant, scared looking mouse from the hall. The viper, however, wasn't finished and fixed his attention on Ellie-Mae.

'You must be hungry,' he said, the side of his mouth curling into a snarl.

The ibex said nothing, and Lucius tilted his predatory head to one side. 'I will see you soon, no doubt. Maybe I can come to your cell again and we can finish what we started.'

Samarah knew she had to do something. Ellie-Mae looked terrified. 'Why can't you leave her alone?'

Lucius continued to stare into the eyes of the frail looking girl and then, with deliberate footsteps, he circled Samarah. 'Did you say leave her alone?' he asked. 'Why should I do that?'

'If you have to pick on someone, pick on me.'

'I intend to have my fun with you as well,' Lucius said. 'Unless you decide to change your mind and sign the contract.'

'Why am I still alive?' Samarah said, in an effort to disturb his flow. 'Why don't you kill me?'

'Perhaps I should,' he said. 'But how, I wonder?'

'You haven't got the guts. You know it's against your laws to kill people of my age. Yet another one of your rules that doesn't make any sense.'

Lucius moved closer and examined her face. 'You've been bitten, I see. Our scuttling friends in your cell are particularly hungry at the moment it would seem. If you sign the contract, I will make them go away.'

'They don't scare me,' Samarah said, 'and neither do you.'

Lucius paused, then grinned. 'We will break you, young lady,' he said, as the metal hand of a synthetic grabbed hold of her arm. 'Because this is what we do.'

The synthetic's metal fingers dug into her forearms as it led Samarah across the hall and down the spiral staircase. The synthetic then opened the door to her cell and threw her inside. Within seconds, the rattle and hiss returned as the black creatures scurried over her chest, her face and into her hair.

Chapter 7—Ethan

The next morning, Ethan shuffled along the corridor. On his left was the door that led to the spiral staircase and part of him wished he was going back to his cell. No doubt his family would have seen the transmission. The same Quaker family, whose values of peace and traditions of justice he'd promised to uphold. In allowing himself to be seduced by self-interest and committing himself to the elite, he was fully aware that he'd broken something that might never be fixed.

'This way,' said Josh, the ginger-haired cadet who'd been assigned as his 'buddy'. 'Breakfast time.'

The corridor led into the main hall, the place in which Ethan had submitted to Lucius. On either side of the hall, wooden tables ran from one end of the room to the other and Ethan joined one of the queues that headed towards a square hatch. As he did so, he looked at the table on the far side. Unlike the queue of white boys in front of him, the second table was filled with a mixture of black and Asian faces.

'Outreach eliminators,' Josh said. 'Segregated, of course. It's how we roll.'

Ethan filled his plate with bread, cheese and ham. Only days before, he could only have dreamt of luxuries such as these. His thoughts turned to the girls who'd stood alongside him as he'd allowed his selfishness to cloud his judgement. He remembered how the girl with the brown hair, Ellie-Mae, looked as though she was about to collapse at any moment and yet she continued to reject the regime. He also remembered the moment in which the girl, Samarah, seemed to enter his mind in a way he didn't think was possible. *'Your time will come,'* she'd said, and he couldn't help but think that now he'd joined the elite, it was already too late. He sat down beside Josh and, immediately, Lucius appeared on the opposite side of the table.

'We've had some trouble,' he said. 'I need a group of you to go onto the common and report back.'

'What sort of trouble?' Josh asked.

'Stop eating, go outside and let me know what you see,' Lucius said. 'I'll speak to you in an hour.'

'Can I choose who I take?' Josh asked. 'As platoon leader, I mean.'

'Make sure you include him,' Lucius said, looking at Ethan. 'You've worked at bunker number five, haven't you? Show the others where it is.'

As Lucius moved away, it was Josh's turn to aim his attention at Ethan. 'Well now,' he said. 'This is your chance to show me what you can do.'

Ethan nodded, stood up and stuffed a roll into his pocket. At the exit to the bunker, the towering figure of a synthetic warrior waited for them, the dull sheen of its armour clearly visible against the light-coloured walls. Its luminous green eyes stared at each of the cadets, scanning them from their baseball caps to their boots and then beckoned them to pass.

Ethan climbed the steps of The Elimination Centre. On the other side of the iron gate, a low cloud drifted above the expanse of Clapham Common and he shivered at the cold wind that wrapped itself around him.

'Now then,' said Josh. 'You can show us the way.'

The last time he'd worked at the bunker, Ethan was led by a synthetic. For a moment, he lost his bearings but then he noticed a mound of earth that poked its way through the mist.

'It's this way,' he said.

With Ethan at the front, the cadets made their way across the common. He hadn't gone far when he paused at the sight of a grey plume of smoke that spiralled through the mist and into the chill October sky. The further they went, the more obvious it became that the smoke was coming from the place they were heading towards.

'Why have you stopped?' Josh asked. 'Run.'

They reached the broken mess of the bunker. The walls had caved in, its metal structures tangled together amongst the fumes and smog of the fire. Charred bodies were scattered across the ground. Some of them were soldiers of the elite in camouflage clothing. The others were those that Ethan had worked alongside only days before, the forced labour employed by the elite to dig the frozen ground.

Josh moved towards one of the bodies and lifted a badge from the clothing. 'Anyone know what this means?'

Ethan looked at the others. None of them seemed to show any recognition. 'It's a white poppy,' he said. 'A symbol of pacifism.'

If he'd had more time, he'd have told them how the poppy was seen as an international commemoration of the dead, but the sight of a synthetic warrior advancing across the common stopped him from saying anymore.

He was pointing a silver weapon at the group of cadets. Josh appeared to be rooted to the spot, his face filled with terror and Ethan pushed him out of the way. Instead of firing his weapon, the advancing synthetic moved beyond the cadets and when Ethan turned, he noticed a steam-powered car heading towards the gates of The Elimination

Centre. The synthetic started to run, its giant strides soon bringing its menacing frame to within metres of the car.

A human figure jumped from the vehicle, only for the synthetic to shoot its weapon and engulf the man with fire. The synthetic then aimed at the car, its laser striking the back windows that shattered. The sound of screams from within the vehicle was interrupted by an explosion that created a ball of flames.

Ethan was too busy watching the scene and hoping for any sign of survivors to notice that Lucius had reached them and was now standing amongst the group of cadets.

'Burnt to death,' he said. 'A suitable demise for an underling who chose to defy us, don't you think?'

'That was brutal,' Josh said, his voice trembling.

'Yes,' Lucius said, 'and the reason I sent you out here at this moment. I knew the little skirmish was coming to an end and hopefully, you will now recognise the power of a single synthetic warrior. Imagine what a whole army could do.'

'But what's happened?' Josh said. 'I don't understand.'

'The underlings have attacked the missile launch pads in Brize Norton and stolen some barrels of fuel from our stores in Clapham,' Lucius said. 'Then they came here and the workers joined in with their pathetic little uprising.'

'In that case,' Josh said, appearing to regain his composure. 'They deserve everything they get.'

'When the underlings were starving, we re-opened the mines to give them employment. We even repaired the rail networks to ensure their labours wouldn't go to waste,' Lucius continued, 'and this is how they repay our kindness.'

'But how have they managed to attack us?' asked one of the cadets, 'and will they come back?'

Lucius paused, allowing for a few moments of silence. 'Who is this person?'

'It's Billy, sir,' said Josh.

'Well, Billy,' Lucius said, holding his stare in the direction of the cadet. 'It's like this. Sometimes, people get lucky and the fact is, they won't come back, because we will go after them with our synthetic warriors and when we find them, we will remind them of what we do to people who oppose The Entitlement Party. Is that clear enough for you?'

'You need to get inside, sir,' Josh said, breaking the tension. 'It might not be safe.'

Lucius looked towards Ethan. 'Do you know anything about this? As a former Objector, I wondered if you had any knowledge of today's attack.'

'No.'

'I have warned you of the consequences of disloyalty, haven't I?' Lucius asked. 'Above everything else, you must remember that I am your God, your Lord and the person who decides what happens to you.'

Ethan nodded, but as the group moved away, he slowed down and looked at the cloud of smoke that continued to rise from the remains of the bunker and the steam-powered car. He couldn't believe it. The underlings were fighting back at a time that coincided with his own capitulation to Lucius and the regime. Not just with demonstrations and rallies, but with actual force.

Ignoring Lucius's warning, he hoped that if he waited long enough, members of the uprising might return. Then he looked down at his jacket and realised he was wearing the uniform of the enemy. Even if they did come back, there was no way they'd take him with them.

'Ethan,' Josh shouted. 'Come on!'

Inside the bunker of The Elimination Centre, the atmosphere returned to one of forced propaganda. The plasma screens reverted to images of the elite sitting in restaurants or drinking in bars at the side of swimming pools. Others showed families wandering through busy shopping arcades and groups of people sitting on beaches.

The same synthetic warrior who'd destroyed the steam-powered car with its laser, glared at the cadets as they stopped by the screens. Lucius then beckoned Josh and the rest of the group to join him at the side of the hall. Behind him, a separate screen showed the image of a window that overlooked The Shard, the elite's symbol of power and oppression. Silhouetted figures stood at the window; gesticulating, pointing.

Lucius pulled a seat towards him, unbuttoned his shirt and poured himself a glass of wine.

'Today is nothing more than a blip,' Lucius said, lighting a cigar. 'It won't be long until it is your turn to feel the benefit of your work, courtesy of the regime.'

'What about you?' asked Josh, gazing at the image of The Shard. 'Why haven't you retired to some fancy place?'

Lucius's face contorted. 'Why would I want to leave?' he said. 'When I can be here, inspiring the next group of cadets.'

'But you've done your share, haven't you?' Josh asked.

Lucius stood up and leaned his forehead into the face of Josh. 'Deep down, all of us have a desire to kill,' he said. 'Even those who don't want to admit it.'

Ethan looked away in disgust. He knew that the comment was aimed at him and his mind turned back to the common, the screams from the car and the spirals of smoke. His thoughts also turned to the second phrase that Samarah had used at the time of his commitment to the elite.

'*You will find your way,*' she'd said, mirroring the Quaker ideals he knew so well that speak of different journeys for all. Even at a moment in which he'd turned his back on her, she'd found a way to reach him in a way she knew he'd understand.

In a single instant, any doubt he'd previously felt was wiped away and Ethan knew exactly to which side he belonged.

Chapter 8—Ellie-Mae

For the next few nights, Lucius didn't come back as he'd threatened. Alone in the darkness of her cell and with too much time to think, Ellie-Mae allowed her father's words to repeat in her mind. *'We are being punished for our selfishness and because we have lost the ability to think beyond our own situations.'*

They were standing at her mother's graveside when he'd told her this. Forced from their London home, they'd been re-housed in one of the regime's specialist towns in the east. For three years, her mother gave everything she could to feed them and keep them safe in the cramped, single room the family had been allocated. In the end, she lost her life to an illness that ripped through the town and decimated its population.

Ellie-Mae caught the sickness too and suffered the same delirium and nightmares as her mother but somehow she became one of its few survivors. Weeks later, the regime used the mounting death count as the perfect excuse to close the specialist town and abandon the east of England. The effects of global warming had already caused much of the eastern counties to be covered with stagnant lakes of water. When they turned off the pumps, large parts of Norfolk, Suffolk and the rest of East Anglia became uninhabitable as they sank below the rising sea level.

For a second time, Ellie-Mae's memories of her family were interrupted by silence returning to her cell. Without warning, the incessant images on the screen in the middle of her cell, and the blare of propaganda, ceased. Convinced that Lucius had returned, Ellie-Mae took a deep breath and lifted the top of the hessian dress to her chin. The cell door opened, but instead of Lucius, a pair of different, slimmer figures stood in the doorway.

'Come with us little scaredy cat,' a female voice said.

'This is Scarlett and I'm Clara,' said the second girl, whose lip was pierced with a silver ring.

The two girls stood either side of Ellie-Mae and lifted her from the floor.

'A friend of mine was eliminated by her ex-boyfriend yesterday,' said Clara, talking across Ellie-Mae. 'He was in the first cohort of cadets.'

'That's crazy,' said Scarlett.

'Yea. A bit sad too,' Clara replied, her dyed pink hair bobbing against her shoulders as they walked along the corridor. 'I remember seeing them together when they were a proper couple. They were always holding hands and stuff.'

'Same age as us?' Scarlett asked.

'Similar. Petra was seventeen. Jack was sixteen, but tall for his age,' Clara replied. 'When they weren't working in the mills, they used to go everywhere together.'

The words swirled in Ellie-Mae's mind as they climbed the spiral staircase. She'd barely eaten for days and when the mealtimes came and the flap at the bottom of her cell door was opened, she'd received only dried bread and chunks of fat. After climbing the stairs, they turned right and walked along a narrow corridor until they reached a row of doors.

The three of them stopped.

'You can't come in here wearing those,' Scarlett said, lifting a key from her pocket and opening the handcuffs.

Her hands free from the sharp edges of metal for the first time in almost three weeks, Ellie-Mae rubbed at the red indentation on her wrists.

'Thank you,' she said.

Clara opened the door to reveal a room that included the type of luxuries that Ellie-Mae had only seen in films. A large sofa was placed in front of a glass table, colourful flowers lifted from the top of a vase and in the corner of the apartment was a television.

'The shower's through there,' Clara said, offering a towel. 'Make it quick.'

'Shower?' Ellie-Mae asked.

'We want to help you,' said Scarlett. 'But first, you need to be clean.'

Ellie-Mae didn't move at first, but then Clara lifted the softness of a towel to her face and led her into the bathroom. Steam rose from the glass cubicle and Ellie-Mae took off her glasses. She then placed the hessian dress on the cabinet in front of her and turned on the water.

It didn't take long for Ellie-Mae to lose herself in the sweetness of soap and the pleasure of her first shower in almost a month. She looked up to the shower head and closed her eyes, allowing the water to swill inside her mouth and run across the bottom of her chin as it washed away the grime of her cell.

The sound of voices and the click of the door caused her to turn. A figure entered the room and moved towards her. Convinced it was Lucius, Ellie-Mae panicked and gathered her arms across her chest, then slid to the bottom of the shower. As the steam in the cubicle started to disperse, she looked through the glass and breathed a sigh of relief at the flash of pink to confirm it was Clara.

'Hurry up!' she said. 'We haven't got long.'

Ellie-Mae rinsed the last of the soap from her skin, dried herself and put on her glasses. She looked at the top of the cabinet on which Clara had placed some clothes. She couldn't remember the last time she wore something new and the softness of the blue cotton dress against her skin was overwhelming. Composing herself as best she could, she wiped the tear from her eye and went into the room to find the two girls sitting on the sofa. Beside them was a chair.

'I've been told Jack went to her house and shouted at the window,' Clara said, carrying on the conversation from a few minutes earlier. 'Something about how Petra needed to open the door and let him come inside.'

'Just like that?' Scarlett asked.

'Exactly like that,' Clara continued. 'The thing is, it's not about love anymore, is it? It's about doing what we have to do to survive.'

'Kill or be killed,' Scarlett said.

Clara moved closer to Ellie-Mae. 'You've heard what they're saying, haven't you? About resources and stuff? Everything's running out and it means there isn't room for everyone anymore. You need to look after yourself and forget everyone else.'

Ellie-Mae perched on the edge of the chair and looked at the bowl of grapes on the table in front of her. Beside them was a glass of water.

'Knock yourself out,' Scarlett said. 'It's all for you.'

'Why are you doing this?' Ellie-Mae asked.

Scarlett stood up from the sofa and went to one side of the room. Without thinking, Ellie-Mae took a gulp of water and picked at the grapes. Her dry, sensitive stomach reacted violently to the first few bites and caused her to wretch.

'Take it slowly,' Clara said. 'You're dehydrated, remember?'

Ellie-Mae tried again, chewing at the skin of the grape and allowing the juice of the fruit to slip down her throat.

'Is this your father?' Scarlett asked, lifting a photograph from an envelope.

Ellie-Mae looked at the image, her chest tightening at his appearance. His face was covered in filth and his clothes hung from his shoulders as though he'd lost some weight. She looked at the rest of the picture to see that behind him was a mountain of trash.

'They've sent him to the wastelands,' said Ellie-Mae, in a whisper. 'Which one?'

'I can't tell you,' Clara said. 'But you could set him free.'

Ellie-Mae stared at the photo once again. 'Is that why I'm being given these things? The shower, the food, the clothes?'

'Making our lives better,' Scarlett said. 'That's all we can hope for.'

'All you need to do is to sign the contract,' Clara added. 'Everything's changed now, hasn't it?'

Ellie-Mae looked at the girls in turn through the crack in her lens. 'Like Jack, you mean. The poor boy who killed his girlfriend. Is his life better now?'

'His family will join the regime, become part of the elite and live the rest of their lives in luxury,' Clara said. 'All because of what he did. Can't you see? We're the lucky ones. The people who've been given a chance to become better and richer people. It's what we all deserve.'

Scarlett came closer, her perfectly styled auburn hair shimmering in the light. 'If you can't do it for yourself, do it for your father.'

Ellie-Mae kicked at the carpet beneath her feet. 'I can't.'

'Lucius thinks the other girl will sign the contract as well if you do,' Scarlett said. 'It's what he wants.'

'The other Objector, Ethan, has shown you how easy it is,' Clara added. 'He's one of us now, eating nice food, sleeping in a warm bed and everything. If you do what Lucius asks, Samarah won't have any choice.'

'Thank you for being kind,' Ellie-Mae said, the mention of Lucius increasing her determination to refuse their proposal. 'Whatever reward he is offering, whatever poison Lucius is spouting, killing is wrong.'

'But we told him we could change your mind,' Scarlett said.

'Imagine it, Ellie-Mae,' Clara said. 'Once we've finished

our contract, we could go shopping together, you and me, and buy whatever we want. We could go on holiday to somewhere nice. Imagine all those good-looking boys by the side of the pool.'

'Holiday romance, eh?' Scarlett added, as she rolled some lipstick onto her mouth.

Ellie-Mae looked down towards the carpet once again. No matter what they offered, she had to stay strong.

'If you don't do what they want, we could get in to trouble.' said Scarlett. 'They might even send us to the cells. You wouldn't want that would you?'

Ellie-Mae clenched her hands and squeezed her fingers together so tightly, the colour drained from her skin. 'If you kill people,' she said, 'one day, you will receive an even bigger punishment than anything Lucius can force upon you.'

Clara stood up and threw the hessian dress into Ellie-Mae's face. 'We need those clothes back,' she said. 'If you're not going to help us, you can wear these rags.'

Ellie-Mae did as Clara asked and removed the soft cotton dress. She then lifted the stained, hessian clothing over her shoulder, the coarse fabric scraping at her skin.

'They'll chuck you back in that cell. You know it,' said Scarlett 'Probably forever this time.'

'Thou shall not kill,' Ellie-Mae repeated, as she continued to squeeze her fingers together into a ball. 'Thou shall not kill.'

Chapter 9—Samarah

Samarah stood in the corner of the main hall of The Elimination Centre, the chain of her handcuffs attached to a handrail beside her. The clatter of metal trays and the murmur of teenage conversation accompanied the serving of the evening meal. For once, the bright images on the screens that showed the rise of The Entitlement Party had been replaced with a view of Clapham Common.

As the images moved from left to right, they reached a line of trees that were filled with a scattering of autumn browns and yellows. For a moment, Samarah was back in her adopted home, kicking her way through the clusters of leaves in Haldon Forest.

The calmness of shadows amongst the trees was interrupted by the vision of Lucius striding towards her, his cloak trailing behind him on the tiled floor like a tail. A pair of towering synthetic warriors followed his every move, tight to his side like obedient dogs.

'As you're aware, Ethan has joined us and decided to do his duty as a citizen,' Lucius said, pointing to the opposite side of the room where the boy with blue eyes was sitting at a table with the rest of the cadets.

'So what,' she replied.

Lucius retrieved a key from the bunch that hung from his belt. He playfully rested the silver key against the lock of her handcuffs. 'All you need to do is sign the contract and I will set you free.'

Samarah lifted her head, her eyes staring into his. 'None of us is truly free. Especially those who persecute others.'

Lucius moved his face towards her. 'We'll see,' he said.

He stepped to one side to allow Samarah a clear view of the brown-haired girl who'd been placed in the centre of the room. She was standing between the rows of chattering cadets. As before, the camera stood only metres

51

away and the lens pointed at her face. In response, Ellie-Mae's shackled hands gripped at the crucifixes around her neck, her slim frame teetering from side to side as though she was about to crumple to the floor.

'You could help her,' Lucius said. 'Sign the contract, Samarah. You know you want to.'

His words were broken by a screech and scraping of metal as a harness lowered from the ceiling. Attached to the harness was a series of screens that aimed towards every corner of the room. The moustached image of the Commandant appeared, his side parting brushing at the top of his eyebrow as he gestured, gesticulated.

Samarah looked towards Lucius. His expression betrayed a sense of confusion at first, but then he threw back his shoulders in an apparent attempt to retain his composure.

'We have a special recording of the Commandant to offer us guidance from beyond the grave,' said Lucius. 'Turn it up!'

One of the synthetics moved towards a control panel, its robotic fingers pressing at a row of buttons. The volume increased as Lucius had demanded, but something was different. Instead of the usual rhetoric of propaganda, one word reverberated around the hall.

'Lies, Lies, Lies.'

Lucius's demeanour changed, his previous show of arrogance altered to one of panic as he pushed his way through the cadets. As he reached the far side of the room, he slammed his fists into the control panel.

The call of 'LIES' continued, its volume increasing as the image of the Commandant faded. In his place was a boy. He was dressed in the orange robe of a Buddhist Monk.

'Cadets. You need to listen,' he said, pointing behind him. 'Two days ago, I completed my contract of elimination and this is what is left of my family. The elite's promises of duty and reward are nothing but lies.'

The camera focussed on a row of bloodied bodies, riddled with bullet holes and then returned to the Monk. 'There's something else you must know. Once you've killed someone, their dead soul follows you. There is no escape. The dead will never allow you to forget what you've done.'

A spark flickered at the bottom of the Monk's robe. Screams filled the hall, metal trays clattered on the floor as the boy became smothered in flames. The act of self-immolation was cut short by Lucius who smashed the control panel with an axe. Moments later, the lights in the main hall flickered, extinguished.

In the gloom, the cadets stood up from their tables and started to run.

'Stop them!' Lucius shouted, dropping the axe to the floor. 'Move!'

Samarah watched him shove his hands into the midriff of one of the synthetic warriors. Instead of chasing the cadets, however, the synthetic stayed where it was. The brightness in its green eyes had faded and lost any sign of life. Its mechanical head tilted to one side and its previously angular figure now contorted into one of broken shapes.

White faces intermingled with black and as the lines of segregation disintegrated, Lucius was engulfed in the melee of cadets. Samarah stepped back and closed her eyes, her mind reaching upwards, outwards. Her thoughts were filled with the images of the burning boy and his twisted expression. She tried to reach out to him, to offer him comfort, but it was too late. His soul had left him and moved on to the other side.

'Samarah,' Ethan shouted, breaking the trance.

She opened her eyes to see that he was beside her, his

demeanour having grown in stature from one of an anxious mouse to that of a lion. Behind him, the giant-sized screens crashed to the floor, sending a cascade of sparks and fire in every direction.

'Look away,' he said, lifting the axe from the floor and striking it into the metal handrail that held her against the wall.

'Where's Ellie-Mae?' she asked, ignoring the pain from her handcuffs that cut into her wrists.

'I don't know,' Ethan replied. 'We need to get out of here.'

A second crash. This time, it was the turn of the metal harness to collapse onto the wooden floor.

Samarah closed her eyes once again, her mind reaching into every corner of the room until finally, the ibex revealed her position.

'I'm trapped.'

Samarah opened her eyes and ran to the far side of the hall where a pair of hands, manacled in chains, pushed their way through a heap of broken tables and fallen masonry.

'Help me,' Ellie-Mae pleaded.

A huge chunk of ceiling smashed behind them as Samarah and Ethan scrabbled frantically at the pile of wood and masonry until they managed to reach her.

'Can you run?' Samarah asked,

Ellie-Mae nodded and brushed away the dust from her face. As the ceiling continued to crash down, the three Objectors raced through the debris.

'Don't look up,' Samarah said, as they ran out of the hall.

Inside the corridor, a group of cadets huddled in the red haze of emergency lighting.

'The power's gone,' one of them said.

'Phones, internet, everything,' said another.

With Ethan and Ellie-Mae behind her, Samarah edged her way along the corridor, only to be met with the flash of a torch and the venomous figure of Lucius.

'Ethan, get these two back to their cells,' he said, handing him a torch and a set of keys. 'The rest of you can return to your rooms and wait to be called.'

For a few moments, Ethan stayed exactly where he was. The lion seemed as though he was about to roar and say something back.

'What are you waiting for, Ethan?' Lucius said. 'Do it now.'

Samarah nudged his arm to break the moment and Ethan started to move towards the staircase. They were almost free. She knew it, Ethan knew it. All it would have taken was a few more steps, a few more minutes and they would have been out of The Elimination Centre and into the streets of the city. Instead, she had no choice but to return to her cell of shimmering floors and rattling feet.

'That boy, dressed as a monk,' Ethan said, as they descended the spiral staircase. 'Did he actually die?'

'Yes,' Samarah replied, wishing she'd been able to help him. 'It was quick though. Not too much pain.'

Ethan lowered his eyes. 'I'm sorry,' he said. 'For signing the contract and letting you down.'

'It's in the past,' Samarah said. 'You did what you thought was right and there is time to change things.'

'I know a way out. There's a tunnel we can use,' he said. 'I can take us there.'

Samarah looked at the mouse who'd transformed into a lion for a few moments in the hall and in the darkened corridor, but he wasn't ready yet. He was only a cub with good intentions and a lot of growing up to do. Beside him, the fragile looking ibex was too tired and hungry to run. 'That time has gone, for now,' she said. 'You have no choice but to lock us back into our cells.'

'You might die in there,' Ethan protested.

'If we try to run, they'll hunt us down and blame us for everything that has happened today,' Samarah said. 'We will have another opportunity, I'm sure of it.'

PART 2—Survival

Chapter 10—Ethan

20ᵗʰ October, 2042

The cyber-attack had disabled all power and communication within the protected zone of Clapham, Vauxhall, Brixton, Balham and Wandsworth.

It was perfect and, in hindsight, exactly the type of attack that Ethan would have expected. By infiltrating the systems that separated the elite from the rest of the country, the uprising had created their very own version of equality.

The atmosphere in The Elimination Centre changed overnight and rumours spread amongst the cadets of savage punishments for those found responsible.

'This will never end,' Lucius said, confirming their fears, as he gathered the cadets in the darkness of the main hall. 'We will hunt down our enemies and drag them from their beds. Retribution will be swift and powerful.'

On the third morning since the attack, Ethan woke to the sound of stamping feet in the corridor and glanced at his watch. 6.10 a.m. He lowered himself from the top bunk carefully avoiding the heads of the cadets who were sleeping below.

Within hours of the attack, the cadets were moved from their luxurious apartments and crammed into windowless rooms where the bed frames rusted in the basement of The Elimination Centre. Dressed in his green uniform, Ethan was about to squeeze his way across the floor, when the door opened to reveal a woman in camouflage clothing.

'Everybody out, NOW!'

Ethan was pulled into the corridor. With the synthetics rendered inoperable by the cyber-attack, it was left to members of the elite to keep order. In the red haze of emergency lighting, the soldiers dragged the rest of the cadets from their beds and along the corridor until they reached the main hall.

Except for the occasional divot in the floor, most of the damage from the falling metal harness and plasma screens had been cleared. All that remained were the ghost-like statues of synthetic warriors that stood in poses of mid-movement as though frozen in time. Lucius stood in the centre of the hall with his hands behind his back. As the cadets approached, he looked at each of them in turn, his mouth curled as though he was inspecting a piece of filth.

'Ten cadets, chosen at random,' he said, eventually. 'Will anyone miss them, I wonder?'

Ethan's arms were pulled behind his back and his wrists bound in handcuffs.

'In case you try and run away,' a soldier said. 'We wouldn't want that, would we.'

His eyes alert with panic, Ethan looked around him at the other cadets. Each of them offered the same scared, bewildered expression to suggest they were as terrified as him.

'Move forward,' a soldier shouted.

Ethan was at the front of the group as the cadets headed through the main hall and past the unnerving figure of a crumpled synthetic that stood at the door of the bunker. They reached the expanse of Clapham Common and even in the gloom of early morning, the horror in front of him was enough for Ethan to slow his step.

'Keep moving,' a soldier said, as a rifle jabbed at Ethan's back.

The further they went, the clearer the picture became. Ten wooden posts were placed in the ground at regular intervals. Opposite the posts were soldiers with guns at their side. One of them was holding a camera and he pointed its lens at the cadets.

A soldier grabbed at the top pocket of Ethan's uniform, then forced him to his knees. As the soldier stepped away, Ethan looked down to see a white square had been placed as a target at the position of his heart.

'You have been found guilty of high treason,' Lucius said, 'and you will be punished accordingly.'

'READY'

His breath shallow and quick, the skin on Ethan's face was torn by the abrasive fabric of the hood the soldier placed over his head. Some of the others started to sob, their whimpering interspersed with the snapping of rifles.

'AIM'

Ethan felt the aching pound of his heart as though it understood what was about to happen. Images of his life on the farm, his family and his friends in Leeds, flashed in his mind. In a desperate attempt to escape, he kicked his feet against the post behind him and tugged at the handcuffs on his wrists.

'FIRE!'

As the crack of gunfire echoed across the common, he took a gasping gulp of air, and then nothing. Nothing except for the chill of the morning wind and as the silence lengthened, it confirmed the single most important thing. He was still alive. Ethan's hood was pulled from his head and his wrists released from the handcuffs. His momentary sense of relief evaporated at the sight of Lucius striding towards the cadets.

'At the moment, the laws forbid us from executing anyone who is under eighteen, you know this,' he said. 'From now on, you must do exactly as you're told because next time, this will not be just a game.'

The soldiers lifted their rifles onto their shoulders and turned towards the bunker. One of them unlocked

Ethan's handcuffs and lifted him from the ground.

'Come along now,' the soldier said. 'You have a story to tell.'

Ethan hesitated. He'd never been this close to death before, the reality of life being snatched away in a single, brutal instant was too much and for a moment, he was unable to move. A hand pushed him in the back and Ethan took a step, then another.

As he stumbled forward, he glanced towards the far side of the common. White cranes rose from the ground, tractors powered forward and bulldozers cut into the same ground he'd plunged his blunt tools. The construction of the fifth bunker, the so-called final reckoning, was in overdrive.

Inside The Elimination Centre, the rest of the cadets were standing in groups in the centre of the hall. A recording of the mock execution was beamed onto the walls and as Lucius strode towards a raised platform, Ethan was ushered to follow him.

'How do you feel?' Lucius said. 'Come on, speak up.'

Ethan opened his mouth but was unable to say a word. It was as though the wire from his brain had been cut.

'I will talk for you,' Lucius said. 'The cyber-attack has interrupted our progress. Without electricity and the use of synthetic warriors, we have been forced to make some changes. It means we can trust no one, and every cadet must be ready to leave The Elimination Centre. You have an hour to gather your equipment.'

A general murmur began among the cadets as they started to move towards Lucius. Soldiers intervened, pushing them back and in the confusion, Ethan lowered his head and stepped away from the platform.

'If anyone refuses to leave, they will be dealt with severely.' Lucius continued. 'This is your final warning.'

'Where are we going?' one of the cadets asked.

'Every risk of contamination must be eradicated from the protected zone,' Lucius said. 'That is all you need to know.'

As Ethan moved away, he noticed Josh pushing his way through the cadets, a set of keys jangling on his belt as he approached. On his right arm, the white band that stated *'platoon leader'* in black lettering was clearly visible. Even in all of this, the ginger-haired cadet had retained his self-important position.

'They should have shot you,' Josh said, phlegm spitting from his mouth as he grabbed at Ethan's uniform. 'You should be dead and with you gone, I could have had Samarah to myself.'

'Samarah?' Ethan said, his thoughts turning to the two girls he'd locked in the cells in the moments after the cyber-attack.

The crowd of cadets pushed and shoved. In the melee, the strength of Josh's grip loosened and he was knocked to the ground. As he fell, the set of keys dropped from his belt. Ethan bent down, reached past the rushing feet and hid the keys in his jacket.

'I'll get you, Ethan Blake, you'll see,' Josh said, as the crowd of cadets pushed him backwards.

Ethan turned and ran. No matter what happened to him. No matter what punishment Lucius could inflict, he was Samarah and Ellie-Mae's only chance now and, using the light on his watch to guide him, he bounded down the spiral staircase.

'Samarah, are you in there?' he said, knocking at the first door he came to.

No answer.

Aiming his light at the lock, he tried one of the keys, then another until the door opened. Inside, the air was stale and thick and Ethan covered his nose with his sleeve. Then came the sound of hissing and he aimed the light at the wave of black creatures heading in his direction.

'Don't even think about coming near me,' a voice said in the darkness. 'If you do, I'll hurt you more than you ever thought possible.'

Ethan shone the light onto his face. 'It's me,' he said, rattling the set of keys in his outstretched hand. 'It's Ethan.'

Her faint shadow lifted from the floor. 'Then get rid of these,' Samarah said, lifting her hands towards him.

Ethan searched among the keys until he found one small enough.

'We need to help Ellie-Mae,' Samarah said, as she removed the handcuffs from her wrists and threw them onto the floor, 'and we need to do it before she dies of hunger.'

Chapter 11—Ellie-Mae

She was sure she'd heard the scrape of footsteps on the staircase. Then came the sound of voices in the corridor and Ellie-Mae shuffled back and moved as close to the wall as she could. Surely, he wouldn't come now. Surely, Lucius would have other, more important things to worry about than her.

The lock unfastened and a hint of light appeared in the doorway. Ellie-Mae kept still and bowed her head in the hope that she wouldn't be seen.

'Where are you?' a female voice asked.

Ellie-Mae looked up. As the figure came closer, she recognised the black face of Samarah. Beside her, was the fair-haired boy, Ethan. She looked again, and to her relief, there was no sign of Lucius.

'Can you stand?' Samarah asked.

Ellie-Mae pushed her hands behind her, only to collapse back down onto the floor. 'I'm sorry,' she whispered. 'I have no strength.'

She flinched as a set of hands grabbed around her waist.

'It's all right,' Samarah said. 'You're safe now and we need to get out of here.'

Her head spinning, Ellie-Mae was lifted across the cold stone floor. 'Leave me here,' she said. 'I'll slow you down.'

'Let me see your wrists,' Ethan said.

Her head bowed, Ellie-Mae did as he asked. The light on his watch shone into her eyes and she looked away. By the time she'd turned back, her handcuffs had been released and were lying on the floor.

'Thank you,' she said.

Samarah was next to her. 'We need you to come with us. We need to stay together.'

Ellie-Mae didn't really know this girl, but in a world in

which she continued to feel friendless and alone, Samarah always seemed to offer comfort at the time she most needed it.

With Ethan on one side and Samarah on the other, Ellie-Mae shuffled towards the door of the cell. As they reached the corridor, she felt their grip of assistance loosen and lower her down to the floor.

'What now?' Samarah asked.

'We go upstairs and leave with the rest of them,' Ethan answered.

'In case you hadn't noticed, she's really struggling,' Samarah said. 'We need food, water and new clothes if you can get them.'

'I'll see what I can find,' Ethan replied.

As he walked away, Samarah turned to Ellie-Mae. 'Think of good things, if you can,' she said. 'We will soon be free of this place.'

Ellie-Mae started to believe that it was nothing more than a hopeful dream. She wondered if the feelings of hunger were sending her into some kind of delirious trance and that, in reality, Ellie-Mae was still locked in the cell, the place she thought she would never leave. In her darkest moments, she'd even wished for the angels to find a path into her cell, release her from this life and take her to paradise.

'I'm still with you, Ellie-Mae,' Samarah said. 'Don't be afraid.'

They were the same words her father had used to comfort her. He'd used a similar phrase almost every day since Ellie-Mae's mother had died and she and her father were relocated in the north. If she was in a dream, Ellie-Mae decided to allow it to move towards a happier ending.

She thought about the places they visited on the rare Sundays when they closed the mines and he'd finished preaching to the few who remained true to their faith. The occasional trip to the coast, the sound of seagulls and the taste of crunching sand as they ate their sandwiches on Morecambe beach.

The shout of voices and thump of heavy feet at the end of the corridor interrupted her dream. She felt a pang of relief as the door opened and Ethan came through, only for the moment to be lost in the crowd of soldiers behind him. Each of them carried a rifle as they marched into the dimly lit corridor, their boots thudding against the floor as they approached.

The soldiers stopped, their backs against the wall on either side of the corridor. Samarah took hold of Ellie-Mae's hand as a different, menacing figure came through the door to confirm her nightmare was set to continue and that any hope of a happy ending to her dream was shattered. He was wearing a long, dark coat that trailed along the floor as he strode towards them.

'Guess who's come to see you,' Lucius said.

Chapter 12—Samarah

'You have done well, Ethan,' Lucius said. 'I'd almost forgotten about these two.'

Samarah tried to make eye contact with the boy with the piercing blue eyes but even in the dim light of the corridor, she could see that the lion cub had reverted to the mouse, any hint of conviction having melted in the glare of the viper.

'You said we needed to leave,' Ethan said, his head lowered and aimed in the opposite direction. 'You said no one should be left behind.'

'There is no need to explain,' Lucius said. 'The warning you have been given is clear enough, is it not?'

'Yes.'

Lucius turned away from Ethan and stepped towards Samarah. 'One last chance,' he said, handing her an envelope. 'Sign the contract and I will make things easier for you.'

'You know I won't,' she replied. 'Why do you keep asking the same question?'

'For your own safety, my dear,' Lucius said, with a sly grin. 'Once you are away from these walls, if you were to disappear in the line of duty, it would be unfortunate but lawful.'

'You're such a waste of a human being,' Samarah snapped, unable to control her anger. She regretted her outburst immediately.

'We'll see,' he replied and gestured towards Ethan. 'Give them their uniforms.'

Ethan shuffled forward until he was within a couple of metres of Samarah and Ellie-Mae. He was carrying a brown sack that he turned upside down and allowed its contents to fall onto the floor.

'As you can see, Ethan is wearing a green uniform with

the symbol of the blunted shard on his chest and three stripes for bravery,' Lucius said. 'He will join the cadets who are ready to carry out their duty and once he has completed his contract, he will join the elite.'

Samarah looked down at the clothes that Ethan had placed in front of her.

'The black uniforms with two stripes on the badge indicate those who require special training. That includes you, Samarah, although you will be monitored in everything you do. If you were to step out of line, the other cadets have their orders to remove you from the programme in any way they choose,' Lucius continued, and then kicked a different colour uniform in Ellie-Mae's direction, 'and this one, well, a single stripe on the badge is all she is worth and I think we all know that yellow is the perfect colour for cowards.'

After firing one last stare at Samarah, Lucius turned and headed along the corridor. 'You will be ready in ten minutes,' he said, as he walked away, 'and I will be rid of you, forever. Everything has been arranged.'

The last of the soldiers followed him through the corridor and out of the door.

Ethan remained where he was. 'We haven't got long. You need to get changed and I will take you upstairs.'

'What has he said to you?' Samarah said. 'You look terrified.'

'He saw me grabbing some food in the main hall. He said I was a dead man walking unless I told him what I was doing. I had no choice.'

'You could have said no.'

'I couldn't,' he said. 'There's more going on than I've told you.'

'Like what?'

'I didn't tell you before. I didn't want to scare you, but they put us against a post, Samarah,' he said, his eyes flicking from side to side in the way Ethan always did when he was anxious. 'They accused us of treason. They made us kneel. They covered our heads with a hood and fired. I didn't know it was only blanks, none of us did. I thought I was dead.'

Samarah understood now. She could also see that the lion cub needed her support. 'The regime will feel wounded by the cyber-attack. They are not used to being attacked with such ingenuity and this makes them dangerous and unpredictable,' she said. 'From now on, we must be careful, do everything they say and somehow stay alive. Our time will come.'

'I know I should have lied to him, I'm sorry,' Ethan replied, as though he hadn't listened. 'He gave me no choice.'

Samarah took a deep breath. 'You do have one choice,' she said, as she picked up her uniform, 'and that's to turn around and give us some privacy.'

She peeled the hessian dress from her body, lifted it over her shoulders and threw it onto the floor. The black fabric of the uniform she'd been given was sharp against her skin, but at least it was clean. She glanced at Ethan to check he was still looking in the opposite direction and then helped Ellie-Mae.

'Thank you, Ethan, we are ready now,' said Samarah.

'One more thing,' Ethan said, as he lifted a couple of rolls and a bottle of water from his jacket pocket and handed them to her. 'It's all I could manage.'

Samarah began to sip the water but it quickly turned into a gulp. She handed the rest to Ellie-Mae who finished it in seconds, the water dripping from the side of her mouth as she drank. As she took a bite of the bread, Samarah could feel a semblance of strength returning. It was almost as though her body was saying thank you.

Together, they climbed the steps and at the top of the

spiral staircase, Ethan stopped.

'Be ready for anything,' he said, opening the door. 'The elite are moving in.'

Inside the main hall, figures moved in different directions. Many of them were dressed in civilian clothing and some of the mothers were carrying children and babies. As they slithered past each other, it was as though a family of snakes were gathering in the nest.

Head bowed, Samarah followed Ethan through the crowd but then one of the hatchlings, a child of around five-years-old, stopped in front of her. She had blonde-hair and friendly looking eyes and Samarah waved, smiled. The child waved back, only to be pulled away by a woman, whose face contorted with venomous intent.

'Scum,' the woman snarled.

Samarah wanted to say something. She wanted to tell the woman that both of them were caught in the same battle for survival, but the sheer hatred in the woman's eyes made her realise she was wasting her time. On the far side of the main hall, the latest batch of labrador puppies and juvenile pit bull terriers were gathering in their groups of greens, blacks and yellows.

A woman in camouflage uniform was standing amongst them. She was holding a baton above her shoulder as though poised to attack. One of the cadets came too close and Samarah recoiled at the dull thump of the baton striking the back of his head.

'How are you doing, Ellie-Mae?' Samarah said, under her breath.

'Better now,' she replied. 'The water and the food helped me a lot.'

The crumpled figure of a synthetic stood by the door to the bunker that opened from the outside. Although he was rooted to the spot and didn't offer any sign of life, his presence was a stark reminder of who was in control.

70

The group of cadets in green climbed the steps and went through the ironclad door. Samarah was in the second group, the ones in black, and she savoured the cool aroma of autumn as she headed onto the common. It was her first taste of natural air for almost a month and the sharp freshness caused her to take a short breath, then another until the tight sensation in her lungs receded.

Once she was past the walls that enclosed Clapham Common, Samarah noticed a row of armoured vehicles positioned at regular intervals. Like alligators on the banks of a river, they waited unerringly as though poised for attack. The soldier with the baton reappeared in front of her.

'Greens, this is your path,' the soldier said, her jaws snapping. 'The rest of you can follow me.'

Samarah looked to where Ethan and the rest of the cadets in green were being guided. The first of them was already heading along a high street laden with flags of The Shard and images of the Commandant that draped from every window. The soldier urged the cadets in black to turn right and Samarah looked over her shoulder to see that Ellie-Mae and the rest of the yellows were following closely behind.

'No slacking,' the soldier shouted.

Samarah kept her eyes in front as they headed into a street in which the doors were bolted and the windows barred. Midway along the road, they reached two black vans with darkened windows at the side of the road, their heavy engines throbbing.

The order came to *'Halt!'* The soldier stood beside her, kicking the mud from the bottom of her boots.

'Samarah, right?' she said. 'You're only going with them because you have to go somewhere. If the laws allowed him, Lucius would have got rid of you already, but he can't. Not yet.'

When the soldier finally stopped speaking and moved away, Samarah peered behind one of the vans to see that Ellie-Mae and the rest of the cadets in yellow had gone.

Chapter 13—Ethan

He turned into the high street to see a trail of red petals strewn across the road. Streamers fell from the rooftops, sirens blared and people stood at the open doors of houses, waving their flags.

'Keep to the left,' one of the soldiers yelled, pushing the cadets in green onto the pavement. 'Officials of The Entitlement Party, coming through.'

Ethan jumped out of the way to avoid the crush as an open-top bus made its way through the adoring crowd.

Painted across its windows was the symbol of the elite.

He recognised some of the faces at the top of the bus from the transmissions and others from pamphlets written by The Entitlement Party. One of the cadets beside him started to scream. At first, Ethan assumed she'd done something wrong and was being punished by one of the soldiers, but then he heard her whispered gasp.

'The Commandant.'

Ethan looked up at the roof of the bus and even though it was only a fleeting glance, it was enough to see a blurred, holographic image of the Commandant's moustachioed face. As Ethan looked again, he noticed a soldier who was using a hand-held camera to beam the 3D hologram amongst a group of actual, real-life party leaders. Each of them was making exaggerated attempts to wave and smile at the people below.

'Move along now,' a voice said. 'You've seen enough.'

A row of soldiers stood in front of the cadets, directing them into a street on their left. They hadn't gone far when Ethan's attention was drawn to the shop windows at the side of the road. He paused mid-step, unable to resist the branded clothing, designer labels and vivid colours that were impossible to obtain in the oppressed locations that housed the underlings. As he looked around, he noticed that some of the other cadets had stopped beside him, their eyes alight, their mouths agape.

Excited chatter began to spark among them, a mood already lifted by the sight of the Commandant's holographic image, was now rising into one of high excitement. It was only as he walked away that Ethan realised exactly what this was.

Even the most ambitious cadets were beginning to question what they were doing and why they were doing it, particularly after they'd seen the footage of the mock executions. This was nothing more than a deliberate act by the regime to remind them of what was on offer if they completed their contract.

They'd been walking for twenty minutes when they reached a tall building with a round tower at one of its corners. At the bottom of the tower was a white-faced clock that stated the time as twelve o'clock. The sound of shouting led him to a large area of tarmac and a sign to confirm they'd reached the station.

Clapham Junction.

The high-pitched shriek of a car horn announced the arrival of a stretched black limousine that made its way into the car park. The passenger door opened; the triumphant blare of *The Ride of the Valkyries* announced the presence of Lucius. As he stepped from the vehicle, a line of soldiers interlocked their arms in a protective circle

74

around him.

Standing next to Lucius was a shaven-headed cadet that Ethan didn't recognise and he adjusted his position to gain a better view. Both Lucius and the cadet were holding narrow champagne glasses filled with a liquid that sparkled in the midday sunshine.

'Congratulations,' Lucius said, 'and welcome to the elite.'

'Thank you, sir.'

'Let the cadets come closer,' Lucius continued, turning towards the soldiers. 'They deserve to see this.'

The line of soldiers moved to one side to allow the cadets in green to move forward. Ethan stayed where he was and watched from the back of the group.

'Tell me your name,' Lucius said.

'Daniel, sir. Daniel Quartz.'

'Tell me why you are here.'

'I have finished my quota of six eliminations and therefore my contract is complete,' he said, sounding as though he was reading from a pre-prepared script. 'I am very proud to say I am now part of the elite and living with my family inside the protected zone.'

Some of the cadets started to cheer and punch their fists into the air. None of them was as loud as the ginger-haired Josh who stepped towards Daniel and shook his hand.

'Nice one,' said Josh, and then turned to the other cadets. 'You know what this means, don't you? The boy who set himself on fire, the monk. He was the one who was lying.'

'Remind me of your name, cadet?' Lucius asked. 'The one who insists on interrupting me.'

'Josh, sir,' he said, pointing to the white band on his arm. 'I'm a platoon leader.'

'Today is not your day, Josh. You should know this,'

Lucius said, turning back towards Daniel. 'Tell the other cadets about your new accommodation.'

'It's nice,' he replied. 'I live in a penthouse, a top floor apartment. There's even a swimming pool in the basement.'

'You see?' said Josh. 'If he can do it, so can we.'

'You do like to get involved, don't you?' Lucius added. 'I like your spirit.'

Ethan wasn't so sure. There was something in Lucius's expression that told him Josh had overstepped the mark. Sure enough, as Daniel Quartz was helped back into the limousine, a soldier grabbed hold of Josh's arm and pulled him to one side.

'In a short while, you will board your train,' Lucius said, addressing the cadets. 'You will be given maps, accommodation details and the current location of those you have been assigned to eliminate. Any questions?'

One of the cadets lifted his hand. 'What about head-up displays? There's a rumour they aren't working.'

'This is correct. But they will do, in time,' said Lucius. 'In the meantime, you simply need to locate your target, point your weapon and pull the trigger.'

Ethan looked around him. The scared faces, the shuffles in their step and the sudden reduction in bravado.

'We haven't finished our training,' said a different cadet. 'I don't think I'm ready.'

'None of us is truly ready, are we?' Lucius said. 'But we must be brave and remember that being outside of our comfort zone is often the best way to grow.'

The soldiers moved forward and shoved the cadets into a single line.

'Follow me!' one of them shouted.

As the cadets began to disperse and head into the station, Ethan looked through a gap that opened, briefly. Lucius was speaking with Josh and at first, it seemed amicable. Moments later, the ginger-haired cadet was dragged away by one of the soldiers and separated from the rest of the greens.

'There's nothing to see,' said a soldier, closing the gap. 'Come along now. It is time to do your duty.'

Chapter 14—Ellie-Mae

They'd been taken to an underground station and told to wait on the platform. Ellie-Mae guessed their number as fifteen, but it was difficult to count as so many of the cadets were huddled together for warmth, their faces hidden in the yellow fabric of their uniforms.

She wasn't sure how long they'd been there. A few hours maybe? In the flickering candlelight, one of the soldiers hurried past and threw a bottle of water and some bread at each of the cadets. Bald, with a square-shaped head, he had a tattoo of the devil on the side of his face.

'Is this all we get?' asked a female voice.

Pierced lip, dyed pink hair, it was Clara and one of the girls who'd attempted to make Ellie-Mae sign the contract.

The soldier leant towards her. 'Do you know what my name is?'

'What?' Clara whispered, leaning back.

'My name is *Don't Care*,' he said, as he ripped the bread from her grasp. He then aimed his stare at Ellie-Mae. 'What about you, Landfill? Have you got something to say?'

She shook her head and when the soldier moved on, Ellie-Mae gave some of her food to Clara. She was about to take a gulp of water when the tunnel filled with a billowing cloud of steam.

'Time to go!' the soldier shouted.

Ellie-Mae peered through the gloom to see a grey steam machine positioned at the side of the platform. With the engine of a nineteenth-century steam locomotive and the body of a modern-day passenger plane it was similar to many of the so-called 'advances' championed by the regime. As resources dwindled, discarded concepts and materials were cannibalised at the lowest possible cost and then falsely advocated as examples of innovation.

Behind the steam machine was an oval shape container and the tattooed soldier clambered on board and climbed the ladder. Once he'd reached the top of the container, he unfastened a set of bolts and opened a hatch in the roof. On the side of the container was the sign of skull and crossbones above a single word.

TOXIC

'We can't get in that,' said Clara. 'It's a chemical truck. We might die.'

The soldier jumped to the platform and shoved his face into hers. 'Have you forgotten my name already?' he asked. 'I…Don't…Care!'

He grabbed at Clara's hands and placed them onto the rungs of the ladder that rested against the side of the container. 'Get on, or else I will throw you onto the tracks.'

Clara started to climb. Ellie-Mae went next as one by one the cadets lowered themselves through the opening of the chemical truck. As the last of them descended through the metal hatch, it closed behind them, their bodies tightening into a crush.

'I can't breathe,' said Clara. 'Get away from me and let me breathe.'

'I've got nowhere to go,' one of the cadets replied.

As the steam machine started to move, Ellie-Mae shuffled to the side of the truck and closed her eyes. Not that it made any difference. So many bodies amongst the pungent odour of chemicals ensured there was to be no escape. The endless journey continued fitfully. Just as the steam machine gathered pace, it shuddered to a halt.

'Where do you think they're taking us?'

Ellie-Mae opened her eyes to see Clara standing beside her. 'Somewhere horrible. The mines, maybe?' she said. 'Where's your friend, Scarlett? I haven't seen her.'

'They took her away. She did whatever Lucius wanted and became one of his favourites. I didn't see her again,' Clara replied. 'I refused. I couldn't do it and said no. It's why I'm here. It's why all of us are here. Because we objected in some way, like you.'

'You did the right thing,' Ellie-Mae said. 'I'm sure of it.'

The steam machine came to yet another halt. Instead of jolting forward, the metal hatch opened with a clatter of steel and the ladder was lowered from above.

'We've reached the end of the line,' said a voice. 'Get out!'

The bottom of the ladder fell beside her and Ellie-Mae did as the soldier ordered. As she climbed down the other side, she missed her step. Her feet trapped in the rungs, she stretched out her arms. Too late. The speed of the fall was swift and as she twisted her body, her head thumped onto the concrete platform. An arm grabbed the sleeves of her uniform and hauled her to standing.

'On your feet, Landfill.'

Her fingers trembling, Ellie-Mae examined the back of her head, but didn't find any evidence of blood. She looked back towards the carriage. One of the cadets, a boy with dark hair and a scared look in his eyes, stopped at the top of the ladder.

'This place,' he said. 'I know this place.'

The tattooed soldier stepped forward, grabbed hold of his arms and pulled him onto the platform. 'Move,' he said.

A staircase led away from the steam machine and in the darkness Ellie-Mae walked beside the cadet with the scared looking eyes. She wanted to ask him where they were. She wanted him to tell her why he was so terrified, but he kept his focus forward and offered her nothing.

When they reached the top of the stairs the air was thick with a greasy stench and, even in the gloom of first light, she could see clouds of mist rising from the mountains of waste. Black crows swooped amongst the piles of trash, screeching and fighting each other for scraps.

'The nearest town is that way,' the soldier said, pointing into the distance. 'If I were you, I'd get there before the sun rises.'

None of the cadets moved at first, but then the soldier opened the front of his jacket and lifted a handgun. 'This is for anyone who thinks about coming back down those stairs and getting into my carriage.'

His gun pointing at the cadets, the soldier backed away, his movement accompanied by the sound of a low intermittent cackle. One of the cadets gasped. Another turned and started to run in the direction the soldier had pointed.

Ellie-Mae didn't recognise the sound but started to realise why the dark-haired boy was so terrified. If she was right, they were about to be abandoned in one of the most dangerous locations in the country, because this wasn't just any wasteland. It was the one the regime had enclosed behind a wall to protect the rest of the country from marauding hogenas.

The long snout of a pig and the dark eyes of a hyena, it was the hybrid animal The Entitlement Party had purchased from abroad, then released into the wild to scavenge the wastelands and devour everything its razor-sharp teeth could slice into.

When their numbers increased and the attacks on people began, it was headline news on the national transmissions. As killings of underling workers became commonplace, the reports on the transmissions started to dwindle and become hidden behind arrogant claims of justification.

The cackle started again. It was joined by a second, then a third that grew in intensity.

'I would say good luck,' the soldier said, the speed of his backward step increasing. 'But these swine-bodied freaks sound as though they haven't eaten for days.'

Chapter 15—Samarah

Her hands resting against the concrete post, Samarah took a deep breath. In. Out. In. Out. The training runs alongside the wall that surrounded the city of Sheffield had become part of the routine as soon as the cadets arrived.

'You need to be ready for a war,' the lieutenant, Fabian, repeated on a daily basis. 'Most of you are ready for nothing.'

The cadets were dressed in black uniform. In a manner that Samarah considered as typically unsubtle, all of them appeared to have been chosen for 'special training' on account of their non-white ethnicity.

Samarah was treated as the biggest outcast of all. Anything she was allowed to get involved with seemed to happen at least ten metres behind the others and at night her wrists were handcuffed to her bed. If she stopped during a training run, even for an instant, one of the sentries on the wall would aim a rifle in her direction until she started to move once again.

Fabian seemed particularly keen to let her know what he thought.

'You need to speed up if you want to survive,' he said, as Samarah recovered her breath. 'If you don't sort yourself out, you'll be the first one to be targeted by the enemy.'

Samarah was trying, but there wasn't much else she could do. Those endless days of inactivity cooped up in a prison cell meant she was struggling to regain her fitness and as the lieutenant, Fabian, walked away, one of the cadets joined in.

'Hey, you're Samarah, aren't you?' he said. 'The Objector that Lucius said we could get rid of.'

'Shut up, Aaron,' said the girl beside him.

83

'He said we should take you to a forest,' Aaron said. 'A place where no one can hear you scream.'

'I said, shut up,' the girl repeated.

'Shut up yourself, Francesca. She's the reason we've been sent here. She's the reason they're treating us like kids.'

Both of them were playing the part that Samarah would expect. Francesca, the labrador keen to preserve harmony within her pack and Aaron, jostling for his position of alpha male amongst the pit bull terriers. A black van pulled up beside them and the side door opened.

'Where are we going?' Aaron asked.

'Just get in,' Fabian replied, then turned towards Samarah, 'and keep an eye on her.'

The pit bull climbed aboard. He lowered his hand towards Francesca and helped her into the back of the van.

'Maybe I can help you,' he said with a scowl, as he looked in Samarah's direction. 'Or would you complain about that as well, little Miss Objector.'

Samarah ignored him. Instead of replying, she propelled herself inside and took her place on the wooden seating. The door slammed closed, the roar of the engine confirming they were on their way.

Aaron sat opposite and lifted a packet of cigarettes from his uniform.

'You want one?' he asked. 'They keep giving me these for being so good at everything.'

After lighting its tip, he took a deep draw and blew the smoke into Samarah's face. Her stomach churning, she turned away. Convinced she was about to be sick, Samarah gripped at the edge of the seat, until finally, the van stopped and the side door slid open.

'Get changed and we'll see you in five,' Fabian said, pointing at a wooden hut on the far side of the car park.

84

Inside the hut were piles of khaki uniforms that lay on the rows of benches. As she moved towards them, Samarah noticed her name on the back of one of the jackets.

'They know our names, our sizes,' Francesca said. 'What else do they know?'

'Everything,' Aaron confirmed.

Samarah collected her pile of clothes from the centre of the bench and together with the rest of the female cadets, she headed towards the corner of the room.

'No peeking, boys!' said Francesca.

Samarah got changed and went into the washroom. She splashed a handful of cold water onto her face and looked at her reflection in the mirror. Dark rings surrounded her eyes and although she was tired beyond exhaustion, she knew she had to keep going.

Ever since she'd met them, something convinced her that together with Ethan and Ellie-Mae, the Objectors would come together in a manner she didn't yet know. Somehow, they would find a way to break the suffocating power of the regime and for now, all she needed to do was stay alive no matter what. She was so busy giving herself a pep talk, she didn't notice that Francesca was beside her.

'I think he fancies me, Aaron I mean. What do you think?'

Samarah didn't even raise her head. 'If that's what you want, it must be true.'

'You're just jealous,' Francesca replied.

Some of the cadets on the far side of the changing room had already left the hut. Samarah followed them outside to a field in which bundles of rifles lay on the ground.

'Basic drills today,' Fabian said. 'None of the weapons are loaded.'

Aaron picked up a gun, his eyes lightening as he

examined it from one end to the other. 'It looks like an SA80.'

'Someone knows their weaponry,' Fabian said. 'Standard issue service rifle of the British Armed Forces since 1987. They still do a job.'

Aaron handed the rifle to Samarah. 'It won't bite,' he said.

Samarah resisted the urge to punch him.

'Follow me,' said Fabian.

The group headed across the field until they reached a row of cloth bags hanging from upright frames.

'If anyone wants some proper training, they can have one of these,' said Fabian, opening a wooden box filled with rusted bayonets. 'How about you, Aaron? As big dog, you can show them how it's done.'

'Yea, that's for me,' he replied. 'I suppose I am the big dog, aren't I.'

'But where are you going to stick it?' said Francesca.

'Let me show you,' Fabian said, fixing the bayonet to the end of the rifle. 'They're blunt, so they should be safe.'

'Guns with no bullets, blunt bayonets,' Aaron said. 'How am I supposed to hurt anyone with these?'

'The first thing we need to check is that everyone knows what to do,' Fabian said. 'Not everyone is as good as you are. Not everyone can join the elite.'

Samarah looked at Fabian. Like a spider, he seemed intent on luring his prey just that little bit closer. There was no way that Aaron or anybody with the wrong coloured skin would be allowed into the bigoted, inner sanctum of the elite.

Then of course, there was the programme of supposed 'special training'. Surely even Aaron could see that this was nothing of the sort. A few runs, a few basic drills, but nothing that could be considered specialised in any way.

'Step to one side, Samarah,' Fabian said, pushing her

out of the way. 'When I think you're ready to get involved, I'll let you know.'

The rest of the cadets were already in position and Aaron was the first to reach the cloth-covered bags. Accompanied by the sound of laughter, he lost his balance and fell to the ground. His khaki uniform covered in mud, he pushed himself up. As he did so, he glanced in Samarah's direction. It was only a brief look, but enough for her to feel its power.

At first, she thought that Aaron had played some kind of mind trick, but then she realised that a vision was pushing its way into her imagination. She felt a sudden pain in her chest and closed her eyes, her mind reaching upward, outward.

As the image in her mind became clearer, she could see a group of cadets with their weapons held in front of their chests. Aaron and Francesca were among them as they ran towards a leaden sky. A mass of darkness gathered, approached and then smothered the cadets as though swallowing them whole.

For a few moments, nothing happened, but then came the screams, the cries for help and the yelps of pain as the cadets raced into the open. Some of them were holding their faces, others were covered in flames.

Their bodies splattered in blood, a few of the cadets moved forward as though trying to escape. For a moment, there was hope for all of them. For a few, fleeting seconds, it looked as though the cadets would make it to safety, only for the cloud to gather once again and engulf them in darkness.

Then the vision retreated and Samarah was back in the field with the rest of the cadets as they played at being soldiers.

Chapter 16—Ethan

Harvey Jones, thirty-four. Cheesemaker. Deemed as surplus.
Hannah Williams, forty-three. Scientist. Deemed as surplus.
Nigel Stevens, sixty-one. Journalist. Deemed as surplus.

Ethan stopped reading, his attention drawn to the second name on the list. He'd used the map they'd given him to locate where she lived. He'd worn his uniform as instructed and taken his gun as a symbol of who he was. Then, a few moments after he'd arrived on the doorstep, a face appeared at a window in one of the upstairs rooms.

'Leave me alone,' a voice pleaded. 'I've done nothing wrong.'

'You need to let me in. You have to do as I say.'

Eventually, the front door opened and Ethan stepped inside. Hannah would know why he was here. She would have seen the national transmissions to confirm that he was acting on behalf of the regime and within the law to complete her elimination.

'Please don't kill me,' she said, her voice faltering. 'Please let me go.'

'I'm not going to kill you,' Ethan said, closing the door behind him. 'But you need to leave this place today, find somewhere else to hide in the city and never come back to this house.'

He'd even been tempted to fire a shot at the wall to cover her escape and maybe even have taken a lock of hair or fingerprint. Ethan knew, however, that if he'd faked her death and registered Hannah as his first elimination, the regime would have sent a clear-up squad to her house to verify the kill. For now, the best thing he could do was to play their game and let them think he was doing the right thing.

Three hours later, he was back in his room, reading the names of the six people he'd been assigned to murder. He looked at the list again and then, using the tips of his fingers, he extinguished the candle and headed downstairs into the foyer. The platoon leader, Harrison, was amongst the circle of cadets who were sitting, waiting.

'Now that we're all here,' Harrison said, firing an accusatory glance towards Ethan. 'How's everyone else getting on?'

'I've found one of mine,' said a girl with short blonde hair and a badge inscribed *Amelia*. 'I think I might be able to do it on her way home from the mines.'

'It doesn't have to be one-to-one,' Harrison said. 'Just go straight in, speak to the foreman and tell them what you're there to do. He has to let you complete the elimination otherwise he'll be sent to the wastelands, or worse.'

'But without the head-up displays,' a different girl whispered. 'We can see their faces.'

'We're working on the H.U.D.s,' said Harrison. 'For now, do as Lucius commanded when you were standing at Clapham Junction station. You remember what he said, don't you? Locate your target, point your weapon and pull the trigger. It's as easy as that.'

Ethan sat back on his seat. He recognised Billy from the Elimination Centre and assumed some of the others were from the group of cadets who'd graduated in the first cohort. Harrison treated them all in the same, condescending way and every negative argument raised by the platoon was quashed by his aggressive positivity.

As the discussion continued, Ethan's thoughts turned to his fellow Objectors, Samarah and Ellie-Mae. Even though he'd helped them to escape their cells, he still felt guilty for betraying them and signing the contract. He hoped they were all right. He'd give anything to know where they were.

'Are you with us?' Harrison said.

'Yes,' Ethan replied. 'Of course.'

'Then tell us how you got on today?'

He thought back to the moment he stepped inside the house. The panic in Hannah's eyes as she pleaded for her life. 'I knocked on the door,' he said. 'There wasn't anyone in.'

'Did you knock on the window, go around the back, speak to a neighbour?'

'No,' Ethan said. 'Because there wasn't anyone in.'

'You need to go back tomorrow. You need to finish the job.'

'Give him a chance,' said Amelia. 'He's only been here a few days.'

Ethan looked towards her. He mouthed a 'thank you', but Amelia turned away.

'Maybe. But if people keep making excuses, we might have to start hunting in teams to complete the quota,' Harrison said. 'Hey, I don't want to, but if I have to go with you to make sure the job gets done, I will.'

'I thought this was supposed to be a rite of passage. That's what our training told us,' Billy replied, with more than a hint of sarcasm. 'It said this was our chance as individuals to prove our worth to the elite.'

'Fighting talk, eh? That's more like it,' Harrison said, looking at his watch. 'OK, seven o'clock, that's enough for tonight. Same time tomorrow.'

Chairs scraped across the wooden floor and Ethan made a deliberate attempt to move in Amelia's direction. She fired a stare in return. Not one of anger, but something else, something intriguing. Ethan waited a few moments then followed her through the glass door of the training centre and into the street.

It was already dark outside and he looked back, the bright, green sign of Wakefield One clearly visible in the gloom. Not that it needed any special lighting. The location that he and the other cadets had been sent to was inherently different to every other dilapidated building in Wakefield. Everything about it screamed an association with the elite. Tinted, reinforced glass windows offered an arrogant vision of opulence. The sharp angles at the peak of its structure, meanwhile, were reminiscent of The Shard in London.

He looked ahead at the red stone walls of the mill, his attention drawn by the sound of grinding machines. Inside, former teachers, engineers and refuse collectors worked alongside each other and recycled old clothes into new. All for the benefit of the elite.

A soldier appeared from around the corner and Ethan headed along Burton Street. He was about to return to Wakefield One when Amelia lifted herself from the shadows of a doorway. Billy was next to her.

'We know what you did today,' she said. 'We want to know why you let her go when you could so easily have killed the woman, Hannah, and moved on to elimination number two.'

'I don't know what you're talking about,' Ethan replied.

'Don't play games. If I wanted to, I could tell Harrison and the others everything, Ethan, the Objector,' said Amelia. 'What do you think would happen to you then?'

'We can't trust him,' said Billy. 'He's a turncoat, we saw that in The Elimination Centre. He probably works for the regime.'

'But we can use him,' Amelia said, 'and if he is one of the elite, we'll get rid of him.'

A crash of noise and a searing, brutal light broke the conversation. Ethan was sent catapulting in to the air. He landed in a crumpled heap and with his ears ringing, his head pounding, he wiped the dust and grime from his face. As smoke from the explosion began to clear, Ethan tried to stand, only to be weighed down by a blood-soaked body that covered his legs.

'Amelia,' he cried.

Hands grasped at his shoulder, heaving him upwards. 'She's dead,' Billy shouted. 'Come on!'

Clouds of black smoke blocked his view at first, but as he ran he noticed figures racing in every direction as the workers streamed from the exits of the mills.

'The uprising is here,' Billy shouted. 'The battle of the north has begun.'

'Where are we going?' asked Ethan but then, as he turned left and ran down the hill, he saw the sign for the train station he'd arrived at only days before.

Wakefield Westgate.

There were more of them now and all of them of a similar age to Ethan. He recognised some of their faces from the meeting room in Wakefield One and together they raced onto the station platform. Standing on the tracks was a battleship grey, wide-bodied XY7 steam machine. It was something he'd read about and, just like the ones he'd seen in the transmissions, it had the engine of an ancient locomotive and its shell had been reinforced by the oval exterior of a passenger plane.

'Where's Jake?' Billy asked, then turned towards Ethan. 'What have you done with Jake? I knew you were one of the elite.'

'Who's Jake?'

'Our driver.'

Ethan looked at the engine, determined to prove that he was on the same side as Billy and the other cadets. 'I know how it works. I used to drive something similar on the farm.'

Billy stared at Ethan. 'You'd better be telling the truth.'

'Get the rest of them into the carriage at the back,' said Ethan. 'Then follow me. I need a fireman.'

Ethan climbed the metal steps into the engine.

Although the layout on the dashboard was different to the steam machines he'd driven, the components were similar. He tapped the pressure gauge.

'The fire's going,' he said, as Billy joined him in the engine. 'Whoever Jake is, he's done a good job.'

'The soldiers are on the tracks,' Billy shouted. 'Come on!'

'We're almost there,' Ethan replied, lifting a pair of gloves from the dashboard.

'Where?'

'A hundred kilos per six and a half centimetres,' he said, pulling the main lever into gear. 'Just need to release the brakes.'

'It's Jake, he's behind us,' said Billy, leaning out of the window as the engine moved forward with a sharp tug. 'Come on, son, catch us up.'

Ethan looked into the side mirror to see a boy dressed in a brown boiler suit racing along the tracks. Behind him was a group of soldiers, their batons raised. At the front of the group was their former platoon leader, Harrison.

Moments later, Jake tripped. He pushed himself up and started to run. He almost made it to the carriage at the back of the steam machine, but then the soldiers reached him, and he disappeared beneath a torrent of bludgeoning fists.

Chapter 17—Ellie-Mae

His gun pointing at Ellie-Mae, the bald soldier with the square-shaped head retreated towards the steps that led to the chemical truck.

'See you never,' he shouted.

As the soldier disappeared from view, the howling, cackling calls of the hogenas grew louder by the second. Most of the cadets were already on the move and heading for the disused railway line that stretched into the distance.

'There's a cabin in the wastelands,' said the dark-haired boy, Alex. 'It's our only chance.'

Ellie-Mae decided to trust him. He seemed to know this place better than anyone and, with Clara alongside her, she followed him away from the tracks. With the mountains of waste towering above them, they ran along a deserted street of broken buildings.

'How much further?' Clara asked, as they headed into a concrete trench, the cackling cry of hogenas growing louder and closer.

'Not far,' Alex replied.

They reached a crossroad of trenches and Ellie-Mae looked along the left hand fork to see a huge pile of waste and fallen masonry. Although she didn't wait for long, it was enough time to witness an explosion of movement as the vast head and shoulders of a hogena burst through the rubble.

Blood dripped through its teeth and its menacing eyes fixed on Ellie-Mae. Bigger than she imagined it would be, more terrfying than she could have ever believed, the hogena stood completely still as though waiting for Ellie-Mae to make the first move.

'Run!' Alex shouted. 'We're nearly there.'

She turned and looked to the right to see a set of metal doors and the arched brickwork of a cabin. Although it was close, it still seemed an impossible distance away.

The sound of pounding feet echoed around the concrete walls of the trench as the hogenas raced behind them. Alex was first to reach the cabin. Ellie-Mae watched his trembling fingers twist the key that had been left in the lock. She then turned to see a group of five hogenas bounding in their direction.

One of the doors opened and the three of them fell inside. Ellie-Mae was the first to react and, together with Alex, she stood up, leant her shoulder against the door and shoved it closed. Just in time. Moments later, the first of the hogenas crashed against the outside of the cabin. As a second hogena smashed its head against the door, then a third, Ellie-Mae clasped her hands in prayer.

'Don't worry,' Alex said, as he turned the key in the lock. 'This place is made of titanium steel and built to keep them out.'

For the rest of the day and all through the night, the three of them took it in turns to keep watch as the hogenas circled, stared, threatened. Occasionally, one of the animals would charge and slam its torso against the doors of the cabin. Then it would retreat and move towards the others and the devious, menacing cackling among the hogenas would start again.

When it came to Ellie-Mae's turn, she sat on a wooden crate and soon developed a stiff neck from leaning forward to peer through the spyhole. As the hours passed and dawn approached, she was struggling to stay awake.

Forcing her eyes to stay open, she looked behind her to see that the others in the dome-shaped cabin were asleep: Alex, the boy who'd led them here after being dragged from the carriage by the tattooed soldier and Clara, whose face was hidden in the yellow of her uniform.

She wished it was her turn to rest, but then the calm of the moment, the soothing quiet in the cabin made her realise that something had changed. Almost too scared to look, she leant towards the spyhole once again for confirmation. Sure enough, for the first time since they'd arrived at the cabin, the hogenas had disappeared from view.

'Wake up. They've gone,' Ellie-Mae said, the palm of her hand pushing against Clara's shoulder, then Alex.

Clara stirred and rubbed her eyes. 'Are you sure?'

'See for yourself.'

'They might be hiding,' Clara said. 'They might be waiting for us outside.'

'It's not what they do,' Alex said, sprawled across the floor beside Clara. 'If they've gone, it means they've found something to feed on.'

Ellie-Mae shuddered at the thought. Now that she'd seen one for the first time, she fully understood their reputation. Jaws that crushed through wood and razor-sharp teeth that ripped through plastic and rubber, she knew they would stop at nothing to kill and devour everything they could.

'We don't even know where we are,' Clara said

'About seven kilometres from Worcester,' said Alex, 'and we should go before they come back. It might be our only chance.'

'Worcester?' Clara asked. 'Isn't it full of strange old people who talk about saving the King.'

'Monarchists,' Alex confirmed, 'and not all of them are strange.'

The three of them gathered what was left of the food and Alex pushed his shoulder into the door, its hinges creaking as it opened to reveal the cool dampness of morning.

'We should head for the railway,' he said, as they made their way through the concrete trench and towards a steel barrier. Some of its panels were covered in teeth marks and lacerations from where the hogenas had tried, but failed, to bite their way through.

'The underground network ends here,' Alex said, as they reached the location at which the square-headed soldier had left them. 'It doesn't start again until Worcester, but the remains of the overland tracks should guide us to the city.'

'How come you know so much?' Clara asked.

'I used to work here with my family,' he said. 'Until the elite shut it down and built an iron wall to keep the hogenas inside. Metal is one of the only things they can't eat.'

'What happened?' Ellie-Mae asked. 'I only know some of it.'

'Typical elite, they tried to raise some money and thought they could open a few trade deals at the same time,' Alex replied. 'Trouble is, the people in those other

97

countries were just as selfish as the regime and all they did was turn up, chuck out their waste and drive away.'

Ellie-Mae looked around at the giant piles of waste. She thought about her father. Somewhere, in a different part of the country, he was working in a place like this. Her fingers tightening at the crucifixes around her neck, she imagined his face and prayed she would see him again soon.

At the edge of the derelict railway line, Alex placed a finger against his lips and then climbed onto the broken line of tracks. He beckoned Ellie-Mae to follow him and the further they walked, the colder it became as the clouds obscured the early morning sun. Ellie-Mae closed the zip on her yellow jacket and when she looked up, Clara had stopped.

'What was that?'

'Just the wind,' Alex said. 'Don't worry.'

Ellie-Mae wasn't convinced. She thought she'd heard a noise too. Not the distinctive, intermittent cackle of hogenas, but an incessant high-pitched scream. Then it came again, the sound increasing as one scream intermingled with another.

'It's not a hunting call,' Alex said. 'It's the noise they make when they're feeding.'

Ellie-Mae winced at the thought. If his explanation was supposed to make her feel better, it hadn't worked. Their heads bowed, they carried on along the tracks until they reached the brow of a hill and a glimpse of Worcester that appeared to be no more than a kilometre away. Any semblance of hope was quickly extinguished as a shredded piece of yellow fabric drifted past on the wind.

'It might not be them,' Clara said.

Ellie-Mae wished it might be true, but as the tracks turned a corner, she saw a ragged mess of yellow uniforms covered in blood. She touched her forehead, lowered her fingers to her stomach and crossed her shoulders.

'Peace be with you.'

'We need to keep going,' Alex said. 'Now they've tasted human flesh, they'll be ravenous for more.'

The three of them started to run as the hogenas found their collective voice, their menacing cries echoing around them and their calls increasing in volume. For the second time in two days, Ellie-Mae was running for her life. Her lungs burning, she could feel the stamp of their pounding feet behind her and she looked towards the city, willing the stone walls to sprout gigantic wings and lift them to safety.

Nothing came and, instead, she ran like she had never run before. Occasionally, Alex or Clara would move ahead of her, then turn and shout.

'We've almost made it.'

'Don't give up.'

The deafening roar of the trembling ground and the snarling cackles confirmed that the hogenas were closing in on their feed. She could sense their desperate excitement and feel the warmth of their breath on the back of her neck.

'Please help!' Ellie-Mae cried, as she reached the city walls. 'Help!'

Her desperate plea was answered as the gates below the square turrets nudged their way open. Figures appeared at the top of the wall. Some of them were carrying rifles, others were holding crossbows and they scattered to their left and right along the ramparts. A crack of gunfire was followed by another, the whizz and scream of bullets and arrows firing into the hogena pack.

'Faster!' one of the figures at the city walls shouted.

As the gates started to close behind her, Ellie-Mae raced through the entrance of the city and into the courtyard. Alex stopped and turned. Clara was there too, her expression filled with terror and as Ellie-Mae looked behind her, she saw that a single hogena had made it through the gates. Its brown fur was peppered with gunshot wounds and as the hogena snorted blood through its teeth, it stumbled towards her.

'Move!' Alex shouted.

Ellie-Mae looked in both directions, then ran towards the city wall. As she did so, guns fired from the ramparts above her and then, with one final thump, the hogena fell to the ground. With her back resting against the wall, she looked through the cracked lens in her glasses to see the blurred image of Alex heading in her direction.

'Thank you,' she said. 'You saved my life.'

A second figure approached. A grey-haired woman with a stern expression who was walking in tandem with Alex.

'He didn't save you,' she said. 'I did.'

On the lapel of her jacket was a badge inscribed with a crown. She held out her hand and helped Ellie-Mae to her feet. 'Most people call me Maggie,' she said, 'and unless you do everything I say, I'll throw you out of my city and watch those hogenas tear you apart.'

Chapter 18—Samarah

'Hey, Objector girl,' a voice whispered. 'Someone wants to talk to you.'

In the semi-darkness, she lifted her head from the mattress to see the outline of Aaron's face leaning towards her. She attempted to lift her hands to protect herself, only for the chain of her handcuffs to tighten against the bed frame and restrain her. Aaron twisted a key and the handcuffs opened with a click. 'You can move now.'

'What do you want?' she asked.

'I'll only use this if I have to,' he replied, opening his jacket to reveal a six-inch knife.

Her head groggy, Samarah dressed into her black uniform. Even though the room was filled with cadets, none of them stirred as she made her way through the corridor of beds. Instead, their heads remained hidden beneath their blankets as though they were making a deliberate attempt to ignore what was happening. It had been the same since she'd arrived, and Samarah was getting used to being treated like an outsider by the other cadets.

Francesca stood at the top of the stairs. 'We need to be quick,' she said, closing the door behind them. 'He won't wait forever.'

'Who?' Samarah asked.

'I've already told you,' said Aaron. 'Someone.'

Samarah didn't trust either of them, but for now, her focus had to remain the same and to keep doing whatever she needed to in order to survive.

'The curfew,' Francesca said, as they reached the corridor at the bottom of the stairs. 'Do you think they'll enforce it?'

'I don't know,' Aaron replied. 'Just be watchful, OK?'

The previous day, truckloads of soldiers had left the

city to fight in the battle of the north. Within hours, the cadets were moved from their training camp on the outskirts of Sheffield and transferred to the barracks in the centre of the city. The warning they'd received from Fabian when they arrived in their new accommodation was clear and stark.

'Anyone found outside the training centre after dark will be dealt with severely,' he'd said.

Ignoring his words, they hurried across the cobbled paving stones until they reached the gate to Victoria Quay.

'We need to get to the bridge,' Francesca said.

Aaron unfastened the bolt on the gate and with their backs tight against the wall, the three cadets shuffled into the streets of Sheffield. In the shadows of the surrounding buildings, they headed right into Blonk Street until they reached a shattered tower block on their right, the few remaining windows in the upper floors glinting in the moonlight.

'Is that him?' Francesca asked, pointing at the silhouetted figure standing beside a vehicle with a raised back and a sloping bonnet.

'Must be,' Aaron replied.

A figure stepped away from the vehicle as they approached. Samarah tried to gain a closer look at the 'someone' who was apparently so keen to meet her. For a moment, she sensed the presence of the viper but as they headed across the bridge, she envisaged a different persona. A reptile, probably, but with his swaying gait and pinhole eyes, this man was no snake.

'Halt. Who goes there?'

The yell of enquiry was followed by the flash of a torch behind them. The man at the far end of the bridge raced back to the vehicle with its raised back and slammed the door. With a skid of its wheels, the car reversed, spun on its axis and sped away in the opposite direction.

'We've been caught,' Francesca said. 'I told you it was a stupid idea.'

Samarah flinched at the crack of gunfire and she looked to her left to see that Francesca had turned on her heels and was running towards a concrete path at the side of the river. She was about to follow her when a second shot fired, its bullet ricocheting from the metal railings on the bridge.

'Samarah,' Aaron shouted. 'Run.'

The pair of them sprinted past the shattered tower block, the rate of fire increasing in intensity, as though someone was shooting on full-automatic. More gunfire, frantic and coming from both sides to suggest that a street battle was taking place.

'This shouldn't be happening,' Aaron said, stopping for a moment. 'They said it would be easy.'

'What?' Samarah asked. 'Who?'

Aaron set off once again and Samarah raced after him into a narrow alley that was flanked by wooden panels.

'Why are you so much trouble?' Aaron said, as the alley came to a dead end. In front of them was a tree in the middle of a brick wall and he placed his hands into a cradle. 'I'll push you up.'

The branches of the tree grappled at the sleeves of her jacket as she reached the top of the wall. With the sound of ripping fabric, she jumped to the street on the other side.

'Aaaagh,' she shouted, her ankle twisting in the fall.

Aaron followed and thumped onto the concrete pavement beside her. 'We can't stay here,' he said. 'If they find us, the soldiers will kill us.'

'Before we go anywhere, you need to tell me what's going on,' Samarah demanded.

'Fabian, he gave me a message. He said that someone wanted to speak to you.'

'You keep saying the word "someone". What does that mean?'

'That's all I know,' Aaron replied, turning away from her. 'He promised us booze, cigarettes and food. All we needed to do was get you out of the barracks and take you to the bridge.'

'You shouldn't believe everything Fabian tells you,' she said, remembering the vision she'd seen when they were back at the training ground. She remembered how the cadets had run from the dark mass, their bodies covered with blood and their faces contorted with pain. 'The regime will use you and they will discard you.'

'Not me,' Aaron replied. 'They think I'm special. They think I'm the big dog and soon, I'm gonna' become one of the elite.'

He stood up. Samarah tried to do the same, but a stab of pain in her ankle caused her to slump back down. Aaron walked away from her and continued along the road, his outline clearly visible in a set of headlights as the vehicle with the sloping bonnet, the same one she'd seen on the bridge, came into view.

It stopped and Aaron leant through the window and pointed in her direction. A hand offered him a package of reward that the cadet placed underneath his jacket. Aaron glanced once again towards Samarah, smiled and then he was gone, his figure disappearing around the corner at the end of the road.

The lights of the vehicle brightened as it crept its way along the street. As it parked beside her, Samarah gained a closer look and recognised its sleek, but robust exterior as a Merlin 5 supercar. Championed by the regime with its titanium shell and battery powered engine, she remembered it from the transmissions in 2034. Before the synthetics, it was the human police who fought the war on terrorism, and this was the car they'd used to go into battle.

The door opened and a figure in an ankle-length coat stepped out. He was holding a gun that was clearly visible at the bottom of his coat sleeves. Samarah crawled along the pavement, her arms stretching, her hands grasping at anything she could find in a desperate attempt to get as far away as possible.

'It's time we had a conversation,' the man said.

She tried to stand once again. She attempted to propel herself forward but fell immediately, her twisted ankle unable to support her weight.

'Who are you?' she asked.

The man walked towards her. 'My name is Henry,' he said, lowering his weapon. As he came closer, she noticed the inscription of a white poppy on one of his lapels. On the other side of his jacket was the symbol of a white blade cutting through darkness, the image of the regime, to confirm her initial impressions. Swaying gait, pinhole eyes and a jutted jaw, he wasn't only a lizard, but one who was capable of altering his colours and allegiances to blend in with his surroundings.

'Come with me,' the chameleon said. 'You've been given a reprieve.'

Chapter 19—Ethan

'If anything happens, head along the tracks until you reach Manchester,' Billy said, as the steam machine continued its journey in the darkness. 'There are people in the city who should help you. If not, head for Birmingham.'

'Thanks,' Ethan replied. 'I'll do that.'

Only hours before, he'd been sitting in the candlelight of his room, reading the names of those he'd been contracted to eliminate. He remembered thinking that he would have given anything to escape the lies of working for the regime and here he was, away from their clutches and driving the engine of an XY7.

It had been a while since he'd applied the brakes to a steam machine and even then, the engines on the farm were basic models and must have been only twenty tonnes. This one, the XY7, felt more like fifty. It would be OK though, he was sure of it. All he needed was a decent length of track, some hefty persuasion on the brake lever and enough time to run the procedure through his mind.

Thoughts of regulators and pressure gauges were interrupted by a flash of light in the distance. He tried to pinpoint its position amongst the sea of blackness, but then it happened again, closer this time and Ethan was thrown backwards onto the floor as the steam machine screeched to a halt. Sparks flew into the cab of the engine and with his eyes stinging, he frantically wiped his gloves against his clothes to extinguish the flames.

'Ethan,' said Billy, amongst a cloud of smoke. 'We need to get out.'

He crawled along the floor and together with Billy, he leapt onto a grassy bank and tumbled down the slope.

'Over here,' shouted a cadet, pointing at a gap in the concrete wall at the side of the tracks.

Before Ethan could react, a beam of light struck the

cadet in the chest who screamed in pain, his body engulfed in flames. Ethan dived to the ground and propelled himself through the gap to find a group of cadets on the other side. One of them stood up and started to run, only to be struck down before she'd moved more than a few steps.

Ethan looked ahead to see the sanctuary she'd been aiming for, a wooded area at the other side of the field. It was so close, a sudden burst of adrenalin told him to go, certain he'd make it in a way the others couldn't.

'Get down,' Billy demanded, pulling him to the ground, 'and stay as low as you can.'

Using his hands and elbows to drag himself forward, Ethan slithered towards the edge of the forest. His elbows raw, his mouth filled with mud and grass, he crawled past the first row of trees. He was about to push himself up when he noticed a line of angular figures crashing their way through the branches.

Ethan looked again, his second glance confirming his greatest fear. The synthetic warriors were not only operational once again, they were also charging in his direction.

'We need to split up,' Billy said. 'It's our only chance.'

Ethan nodded and waited until Billy was out of sight before setting off in the opposite direction. Every now and then, he'd hear a scream of pain to confirm that a synthetic had located one of the cadets. He tried to block out the sound, he had no choice. Whatever happened elsewhere, right now, he needed to focus on himself.

'Do everything they say,' Samarah told him when they were about to leave The Elimination Centre *'and somehow stay alive'*. So far, he'd managed to follow the first part. Now he needed to make sure he gave himself the best possible chance of survival.

He stopped as a circular beam of light landed on the

tree in front of him. Without daring to turn, Ethan dived into a shallow trench and flattened his body against the cold dampness of earth. A mechanical stamp of feet confirmed that the synthetic warrior was close and then the beam of light moved from the tree and crept along the ground.

A fierce wind whistled through the branches of the trees and Ethan held his breath as the hulking synthetic came close enough for him to hear the whirring of its electronic eyes. Even in the darkness, he could see that the synthetic was bigger than those he'd previously encountered, its torso widened, and its heavy limbs embossed with its identification as *Mark II*. As it approached, Ethan tensed his body and waited, hoped, but then the heavy, mechanical footsteps moved on.

After a few, seemingly endless moments, Ethan looked up to see the outline of the warrior become hidden in the trees as it headed through the forest. Somehow, he hadn't been seen. Somehow, even though he'd been lying within touching distance, Ethan had escaped the glare of the synthetic.

He didn't have time to figure out the reason why because now, it was time to go. Crouching as low as he could, he edged away from the muddied trench and retraced his steps through the forest. He'd only moved a few metres when he found a cadet who was lying face down.

'Hey,' Ethan whispered, as he rolled him over.

Although his eyes were open, his stare was blank and Ethan rested the palm of his hand against the cadet's forehead and gently closed his eyes. He stood up, brushed down his jacket and headed through the trees until he made it to the place he'd started. When he reached the tracks, part of the engine was still burning, but apart from the hole in its side, the XY7 steam machine was largely intact. Amongst a squall of smoke, he climbed the steps and rummaged on the floor.

'Perfect,' he said, lifting his rucksack onto his shoulder.

He jumped back to the ground and looked into the darkness of the forest. As far as he could tell, the synthetics were nowhere in sight and Ethan could only assume they would be somewhere amongst the trees, hunting the rest of the cadets. He glanced to his left in the direction the XY7 steam machine had been moving when the synthetics attacked.

If anything happens, head along the tracks until you reach Manchester, Billy had told him and Ethan decided to heed the advice. As he walked along in the darkness, he thought back to what happened in the forest and recalled the moment when the synthetic had stepped within centimetres of where he lay.

His mind swirled as he remembered his time on the farm and the robots he'd operated to control the livestock. He'd used a basic radar sensor, powered by mobile phone technology, to detect for predators. Occasionally, if there was too much interference or background noise, the signal would break and he would alter the settings.

If the regime was using a similar system, it would explain why the synthetic had missed him in the forest. The utilisation of phone technology would also explain why the Buddhist Monk was able to launch such a critical cyber-attack on The Elimination Centre. The biggest question, however, was how the monk had managed to break through their wall of cyber defence and infiltrate their systems in the first place.

A flash of light broke his train of thought. He looked into the forest and sure enough, a narrow beam of light was scanning a clump of trees to confirm that a synthetic had changed direction and was now tracking his steps. As a few drops of rain started to fall, Ethan tightened the straps on his rucksack, pulled down his hood and started to run.

PART 3—Identities

Chapter 20—Ellie-Mae

25ᵗʰ October, 2042

The cracks of gunfire at the top of the battlements of Worcester continued, the occasional yelp of pain signalling that another hogena had perished on the other side of the wall.

With the speed of her breath reducing and her focus returning, Ellie-Mae looked at the corpse of the hogena that made it through the gate. It lay amongst a scattering of bullets and beside its blood-soaked torso was a royal crest imprinted on the ground in the centre of the courtyard. Beneath the crest was an inscription.

'*Civitas in Bello et Pace Fidelis*'

'The City Faithful in War and Peace,' the grey-haired woman, Maggie, told her. Worcester is loyal to King William, just as it was loyal to King Charles back in 1642. Although there may be darkness upon this land, a thick and palpable darkness, we pray that one day, the King will return from exile and deliver us from the evil of the regime.'

'Do we know where they are?' Alex asked.

'Safe and in hiding,' Maggie replied. 'The Entitlement Party may have stolen the palace, dissolved the monarchy and forced them out of the country but with God's will, the Royal Family will reclaim its rightful position as the head of our state.'

'Thank you for opening the gates and letting us in to your city,' Ellie-Mae said, as she drank from a bottle of water.

'Save your thanks,' Maggie said. 'There are better ways to show your gratitude and we could do with some young, strong bodies around here.'

'Did you want me to stay here and stand by the gate?'

Alex asked.

'No,' she replied. 'We need some hands in the kitchens. Ready?'

Alex was at the front of the group and Ellie-Mae at the back as they followed Maggie away from Battenhall Gate and into the heart of the city. The surroundings couldn't have been more different from London with its manicured buildings and landscaped parkland. Instead, entire rows of buildings had collapsed and those that remained were splintered with deep cracks. Elsewhere, piles of rubble and broken glass lay amongst tangles of rusted metal.

'Where are we?' Clara asked. 'It looks like a war zone.'

Ellie-Mae knew places like this from personal experience. At first glance, it appeared to be similar to the harshest of specialist towns provided by the regime to house the underlings. A place without livestock, fuel and sanitation and where outcasts of society were left to fend for themselves. Her chest tightened at the memory of the town that she and her family had been sent to and the location in which she'd lost her mother to the sickness.

The three cadets and their chaperones soon reached another wall and an arched doorway that was marked *Sidbury Gate.* Standing between them and the rest of the city was a metal grate of iron that rose from the ground to the top of the archway.

'The original defences to the city were built almost two thousand years ago,' Maggie said, as the portcullis lifted, its metal edges scraping against the stone grooves of the entrance. 'Not that it does any good. Not anymore. We can't defend against bombs and missiles.'

Once they were through the gate, Ellie-Mae could see the four peaks of a tower, its silhouette clearly visible in the clear blue sky.

'The Cathedral is where we feed the people,' Maggie

continued. 'I can offer you warmth, food and shelter. In return, I expect you to work.'

Standing at the entrance to the Cathedral was a knight in a chainmail suit and hood. At his side, he was holding a helmet and partly covering his metal suit was a blue cape decorated with a royal crest.

'Our very own knight,' Maggie said. 'In our position, we need all the help we can get.'

The knight pointed at Ellie-Mae. 'The miserable looking girl can come with me,' he said.

'Thank you, Arthur,' Maggie said, then turned to Alex and Clara. 'I have a different task for you two.'

Ellie-Mae followed the knight into the Cathedral and across the tiled floor. Beyond the cavernous arches were row upon row of wooden tables and accompanied by a rattle of wheels, a line of trolleys appeared from the far end of the Cathedral. Each of them was filled with metal jugs and being pushed by men and women who were wearing a mishmash of ragged clothing.

'Go to the kitchen and fetch the bread,' Arthur said, nodding in the direction the trolleys had come from.

Her legs heavy with fatigue, Ellie-Mae stumbled forward. She'd barely moved when she was handed a basket filled with loaves of bread. As she turned to distribute the food onto the tables, she noticed a group of elderly people entering through the main doors. Some of them were being helped by Clara and many of them leaned against walking sticks or pushed themselves forward in their wheelchairs.

Maggie hurried towards her. 'Help them sit down, serve them with food and drink. When they've finished, clear up after them. Can you do that?'

'Yes,' Ellie-Mae replied.

She lifted the metal jug on the table nearest to her. Her hands trembling in the cold air, she began to pour its contents into small cups. One of the ladies leant forward. She was wearing a red scarf that covered most of her forehead and the back of her head.

'Do I know you?' she asked.

'I don't think so,' Ellie-Mae replied.

Amongst a hum of chatter, the others on the table began to distribute the bread and plates between themselves. As Ellie-Mae moved from one table to the next, she noticed that Maggie was talking with the red-scarfed lady, who beckoned Clara to join them. Fingers pointed, mouths opened and nods of recognition appeared to confirm they'd agreed on whatever was being said. Ellie-Mae avoided them as best she could and headed in the opposite direction.

A roar of noise from above caused her to stop what she was doing. Cutlery rattled on the tables, the ground began to tremble and, immediately, the murmur of conversation ceased. Some of the people left their seats and made their way to the side of the Cathedral. On the central table, they slapped and banged their hands and started to sing.

'God save our gracious King, long live our noble King, God save the King.'

The singing of the national anthem continued and Ellie-Mae glanced at Maggie, then towards the main door of the Cathedral where Alex was staring upwards. She raced in his direction and followed his gaze to see a white stream that followed a grey object in the sky. At first, Ellie-Mae thought it looked like some sort of jet, but then it started to descend.

The singing on the central table increased in volume. Others in the hall began to scream as a hand clasped hold of Ellie-Mae's forearm.

'Get down,' said Alex.

A deafening, thunderous crash shook the building, the

jolting force of the explosion causing Ellie-Mae to lose her footing and fall onto the steps below. Then silence. A still, nerve-shredding silence that continued for a few seconds as a cloud of dust drifted above her.

'It's all right,' Alex said. 'The rocket missed us.'

She looked up to see a spiral of grey smoke rising above the windowless building opposite. 'Who's attacking the city?' Ellie-Mae asked, but then realised the answer to her question was a simple one.

Unlike the place in which she and her family had been housed, this was a different type of specialist town. Although she'd heard rumours of such a place, she didn't believe them and couldn't comprehend how the regime could be so evil.

The people inside these walls were trapped and unable to leave because of the hogenas that roamed the wastelands. Instead, the old, the infirm and those the regime considered as useless were gathered in a single location, then annihilated for fun. She placed her hands over the crucifixes that hung from her neck.

'Lord, give them hope,' she whispered.

'The Lord might be able to give them hope, but so could you,' Maggie said. 'Ellie-Mae, the Objector.'

Behind them, a group of people had left their tables and were now gathered at the entrance to the Cathedral. Clara led the red-scarfed woman by her hand as she came closer. 'I knew I recognised you,' she said.

Others followed, some of whom shook Ellie-Mae's hand. Arthur, the knight in the chainmail suit, knelt on one knee beside her.

'I am at your service,' he said.

Others hugged her so tightly, Ellie-Mae could barely breathe. When the last of them finally pulled away, she lowered her gaze.

'You'll have to get used to that,' said Maggie. 'They've

seen the transmissions and think you're a hero.'

'A hero? Why?'

'Because of what happened at The Elimination Centre and the way you stood up against the regime.' Clara added.

'All I did was survive,' Ellie-Mae protested.

'Exactly. To the people who live in this city, survival is everything,' Maggie said. 'We can build walls; we can even feed and look after each other. But when they took away our beloved monarchy, we lost any semblance of hope. Do you feel strong enough to speak to them? They'd love to hear what you have to say.'

Alex and Clara stepped into the background as the group continued to gather around. 'But I am nobody. I am just Ellie-Mae.'

'You are not just Ellie-Mae and in their eyes, you are definitely not a nobody.'

Three women came towards her. They were holding a white dress that had been stitched with a crown.

'We knew you'd come,' one of them said.

Reluctantly, Ellie-Mae accepted the dress and nodded a thank you.

'We have suffered more than most,' Maggie said. 'Will you help us?'

'I can try,' Ellie-Mae replied. 'I don't know what I can do, but I can try.'

Chapter 21—Samarah

'Stay down and keep hidden,' Henry said, as he helped Samarah into the back seat of the Merlin 5 supercar.

'What was all that about?' she asked. 'Who is shooting at who?'

'It's complicated,' Henry replied and then handed her a blanket. 'Use this and don't show your face until I tell you.'

Samarah did as he'd asked and lay down across the back seat. Even though she was buried beneath the fabric, she could tell by the gentle rhythm of the engine that progress was slow. They'd only been moving for a few minutes when there was a screech of brakes and the car came to a halt.

'I'll be back soon,' Henry said.

The door slammed behind him, the jolting click of the latch confirming to Samarah that she'd been locked inside. From where she lay, she heard the muffled sound of conversation, but then the voices ceased. As the silence lengthened, her sense of uncertainty increased. She had no idea where she was. She also knew nothing of the man who'd locked her inside his car and worst of all, she had no idea where he was taking her.

An image of her twelve-year-old sister, Annalise, filled her mind, reminding her of how alone she was in the world. It was an image she'd forced to one side on many occasions but as she lay in the back of the car, seemingly powerless to control her own fate, she decided that this was the time for acceptance.

She thought back to the night she'd seen her family for the last time. They'd left the sanctuary of Exeter Cathedral, each of them filled with the hope of a new life. It had been planned as their moment of escape. The boat was supposed to take Samarah, her mother, her father and her younger sister to a safe place away from the sharpening claws of the elite. But then the sky in the English Channel closed in a swirl of darkening cloud. As the storm approached, it gathered the waves of the sea and assembled them into towering monsters of death.

Her mother was smiling the kind of endless smile she always seemed to manage in times of crisis and like a bear protecting her young, she gathered Annalise in her arms. Samarah was alongside her father, his face etched in haunting grey as the power of the storm struck at the side of the boat like a giant fist and catapulted them into the depths of the sea.

At first, Samarah struggled to find her bearings and was dragged below the surface by the power of the current. She tried to force herself free, only for the talons of the sea to grab her ankles and drag her into the depths. Just as it felt as though her chest was about to explode, the pull of the current relented and the talons released their grip.

In the gloom of the sea, she looked up to see a faint light. Samarah lifted her arms and kicked as hard as she could until she burst through the surface, gulping at the air. The next thing she knew, she was lying on the beach. The storm had passed over and the gentle waves were sweeping over her feet then retreating across the sand in the direction of the sea.

Weak to the point of exhaustion, she vomited the contents of her stomach and as she wiped her mouth, she remembered looking up to see a dark figure in soft clothing, like fur.

'Come with me,' he said. His voice was strong, yet gentle and he bore the enquiring eyes of a wolf.

'But my family is still out there,' Samarah said. 'I need to help them.'

The wolf lifted her up and placed her over his shoulders. It was the same wolf who'd invited her into his pack and offered her refuge in his cellar when the elite were searching for her. He risked everything to keep her hidden, he knew the penalty for protecting one of the Objectors. When they finally located his lair, the wolf had no choice but to flee with his pack as the huntsmen smashed down the door and lifted Samarah from the shadows of the basement. An hour later, she was on her way to The Elimination Centre and about to begin the next part of her journey.

The click of the lock and the opening of the car door brought Samarah back to the present.

'Stay down,' Henry said.

Again, Samarah did as he'd asked and attempted to return to the memories of her family. Instead of her mother, her sister and her father, however, Samarah's mind filled with a different group. The ibex whose soul was hidden inside the body of Ellie-Mae and whose inner strength would fight back against even the fiercest of predators. The cub, Ethan, who would soon be a lion and find his moment to roar. Then of course there was herself, the wolf who would guide the pack in the right direction.

'Goodbye, Mother, goodbye, Father, goodbye, Annalise,' she whispered, as the tears streamed from her eyes onto her cheeks. 'I have a new family now.'

'Who is Annalise?' said Henry.

'Someone I will always love and never forget,' Samarah replied, brushing away the tears and then pushing away the blanket. 'Where are we going?'

'Away from here. Unless you have any better ideas.'

She peered through the back window to see that the Merlin 5 was parked in the shadows of the city walls of Sheffield. A flash of headlights and the deep growl of an engine caused her to duck beneath the window. When she felt safe enough to look for a second time, she saw a line of armoured trucks. They were heading towards the city gates that opened as the vehicles approached.

'The cadets are inside the trucks,' Henry said. 'They're being taken to the battle of the north.'

'What about me?' Samarah asked. 'Why aren't I going with them?'

'I'll explain later.'

The trucks drove past them and towards the exit to the city. The Merlin 5 stayed where it was until the last of the trucks was out of sight and then edged slowly towards the exit. The electronic gates started to close, and Henry kicked his foot onto the accelerator and raced through the gap.

Samarah looked over her shoulder to see a pile of upturned vehicles on their left. On their right, the remains of a building hung from its iron frame, its dome tower having fallen to the ground beneath the remains of the motorway flyover that lifted towards the darkness of the sky. Lying amongst a carcass of tangled steel was a battered sign in tall white letters.

"*Meadowhall*"

'Is it later, now?' Samarah asked. 'You said you'd explain everything later.'

'This will tell you more,' he replied, handing her his phone. 'It's something we intercepted and the reason you're not heading into battle with the other cadets.'

The screen on his phone flashed the venomous image of the viper. Lucius. He was standing in the foreground of The Elimination Centre at Clapham Common.

Beside him, the doors to an armoured vehicle opened and a squad of synthetic warriors climbed aboard.

'The uprising is failing, the rebels are fleeing and the so-called Objectors will not be with us much longer,' 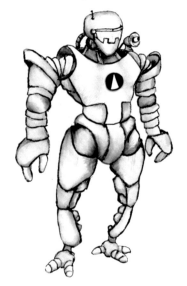 Lucius said, his mouth widening into a smile. 'Underlings, you must surrender, and you must do it quickly. In the meantime, we will send an army of superior troops into battle, the Mark II synthetics, each of whom is programmed to destroy everything you care about, house by house, town by town and city by city.'

The screen on Henry's phone panned away from Lucius and focussed on rows upon rows of warriors that marched in perfect rhythm towards the camera.

Twice the girth of the Mark I synthetics, they paraded in front of Lucius. One of them stepped forward and lifted its silver weapon. A narrow beam of light discharged from its tip and fired into a concrete wall that glowed, then disintegrated into dust.

'This is how we will destroy your defences,' Lucius said, 'and once we are close to your cities, we will have an even bigger, nastier surprise for you all.'

The synthetic that fired the laser clicked its silver weapon back into its holster, turned and joined the others as they marched towards the gates of The Elimination Centre. Moments later, the images on Henry's phone flickered, and the screen darkened.

'This was recorded a few days ago. Only some people have seen it. Most people haven't, but I'm sure Lucius will release it to everyone soon,' Henry said. 'The Mark II synthetics are already involved in the battle of the north and the fact he mentioned the Objectors makes you important. It is why I was sent to find you.'

'He's a bully, plain and simple, who hates the thought of people standing up to him,' Samarah said. 'Get the Objectors together and we can beat Lucius, the elite, all of them.'

'Just like that,' Henry said. 'How can you be so sure?'

'I just know,' Samarah replied. 'Somehow, I've known it all along.'

Chapter 22—Ethan

No matter how fast he tried to move, it was soon obvious that Ethan couldn't outrun the giant strides of the synthetic. Instead, he chose to test his theory of how the Mark II synthetics were programmed with only the most basic of sonar settings.

Crouching low to the ground and keeping absolutely still, he watched its hulking frame smash through the trees in the forest and its whirring eyes search the undergrowth. As before, the synthetic came close enough for Ethan to feel its stamp on the ground beside him, only for the mechanical footsteps to bypass Ethan's location and head further along the tracks.

As a result, progress was slow going. The requirement for stop-start manoeuvres to avoid detection meant that it was almost light when he reached a steep bank and a damaged sign for Manchester.

The walls of the city were only a few hundred metres away and he could see the outline of the viewing towers that were located on the battlements at regular intervals. Between Ethan and the city was an area of open land. No trees, no bushes, no buildings, no life, and it meant that any attempt to reach the city wall would be in full view of anyone or anything that could be watching.

He edged his way up the bank and, at first sight, the figures at the top of the ridge looked innocuous enough but as the image became clearer, he could clearly make out a menacing line of synthetic warriors. Twice the girth of the Mark I synthetics, it was obvious that these were the same type as those that attacked the XY7 steam machine.

A series of trucks stopped beside the synthetics and a huddle of human figures in black uniform jumped to the ground. Ethan scanned the cadets. He counted fifteen, maybe twenty, but as far as he could tell, Samarah wasn't among them. They were quickly organised into groups of five by the synthetics, the cadets pointing their rifles in different directions as though they were expecting immediate contact.

The ground shook to the pounding rhythm of stamping feet and as the synthetics approached the city, flashes of gunfire indicated the position of the defenders. In response, a group of warriors stepped to the right in perfect, mechanical formation and fired their lasers into a single section of the wall that glowed in the brightest of light.

A different group of synthetics moved to the centre of the advance. They opened their mouths and lifted their heads upwards, each of them emitting a dark mass that combined into a single cloud.

A shout of battle grew into a roar as the cadets charged past the synthetics and into the line of fire. Faster they ran, their screams of battle echoing in the morning air and as they reached the city wall, the dark cloud lowered from the sky and engulfed everything in its path.

In the ensuing silence, Ethan held his breath.

The dark mass continued to drift forward. As the last of its menacing tendrils edged into the city of Manchester, a huge gap appeared in the stone wall as though a giant fist had punched its way through. His heart thumping, he watched the line of synthetics stomp through the gap.

Ethan was about to turn from the city and go when he noticed a figure in black uniform creeping from the darkness. His head bowed, the cadet was carrying something in his arms. Then, like a puppet whose string had been cut, he crumpled to the ground. Ethan left the cover of the bank and crossed the open ground. As he approached, he realised that the something the cadet was holding was a girl.

'What can I do?' Ethan asked.

'They used us, man. All that training and they used us as cannon fodder.'

'I'm sorry,' Ethan said, as he knelt beside the cadet. 'What was in the cloud?'

'Hell, death, the end of the world. Take your pick and times it by twenty,' the cadet replied. 'Hey, do I know you?'

'Maybe. I was at The Elimination Centre.'

The cadet sat forward and grabbed hold of Ethan's jacket. 'I can see that from your uniform and the three stripes on your badge, but you ain't just some cadet. You're one of the Objector people like that girl, Samarah,' he said, his eyes narrowing into a stare.

'D'you know where she is. Samarah, I mean?'

'Somewhere else. If you see her again, tell her Aaron says sorry.'

Ethan looked down at the girl that Aaron was holding. Her eyes were glazed, her stare unfocussed. 'You know she's gone, don't you?'

'Her name is Francesca. We were friends. Real good friends if you know what I mean and yea, I know she's gone.'

Ethan lifted a bottle of water from his rucksack. 'Thirsty?'

Aaron snatched the bottle from Ethan's hands. 'Thanks, man.'

As he tilted the bottle, the ground shook from the weight of pounding feet from within the city walls.

'This is to say sorry for what I did to Samarah,' Aaron said, lowering Francesca from his grasp and lifting a circular, metal object from his pocket. On its front was the emblem of the elite, the white blade cutting through darkness to symbolise The Shard. 'The soldiers gave it to me. They said I was the "big dog" and it would keep me safe.'

Ethan knew what it was straight away. He'd seen it often enough in the last few years to recognise its origin. 'It's from a synthetic warrior, isn't it? Something they wear on their chest.'

'It stops them from shooting at each other. It stopped them from killing me as well,' Aaron said, picking up his rifle from the ground. 'Take it and run. I'll cover you.'

'No way,' said Ethan. 'You're coming with me.'

'Waste of time. I got shot by my own team. No more "big dog" for me,' said Aaron, a grimace appearing on his face as he lifted his black uniform to reveal a deep wound below his rib cage.

'One more thing,' Aaron said, handing him a knife. 'Just in case.'

'Thanks,' Ethan said, taking it from him.

He placed the knife in his jacket and headed across the open ground. He'd only moved a few metres when he heard the snap of a rifle. Exposed in the chill night air, he turned to see that Aaron was pointing his gun at the advancing synthetic.

He didn't even get the chance to fire.

Instead, a beam of light fired from the synthetic's silver weapon and scanned the cadet from head to toe. The wide beam then narrowed into a laser aimed directly at Aaron's heart and Ethan pressed his hands against his ears to escape the scream of pain that followed.

The synthetic altered its line of vision, its green eyes scanning its surroundings. Ethan's instinct told him to go. Even if he stayed absolutely still, if its sensor picked up on his human outline, it would trigger the setting inside the synthetic to fire. Instead of running, therefore, he opened his hand and lifted the circular image of The Shard that Aaron had given him above his head.

The synthetic pointed his weapon at Ethan. A beam of light crept its way across the ground and onto his arms, his chest and his face. Ethan forced his eyes to stay open, daring not to blink until finally, the light extinguished. The synthetic warrior lowered its weapon, turned its head and then stomped its way back towards the city. Ethan waited a few moments before heading across the open ground, just in case the synthetic picked up on his movement.

Clouds of smoke lifted from the streets of Manchester and Ethan looked through the gap in the wall to see a line of people. For a moment, it looked as though the prisoners were about to be marched out of the city, only for a synthetic to step forward and execute them one by one, their bodies exploding into flames.

In response, Ethan turned and started to run.

Chapter 23—Ellie-Mae

The missile destroyed an entire block of houses in the northern sector of Worcester. When Ellie-Mae asked if anyone knew how many had perished, Maggie simply replied *'Too many, it is always too many.'*
Although she'd been given keys to an apartment, she didn't want to be on her own at a time of such misery. Instead, for two nights, she'd found some space to lie on the floor amongst the others in the crypt of the Cathedral. On each occasion, she spent much of the night staring into the darkness, her mind filled with the expressions of the scared looking people she'd promised to help.

'Maggie wants to talk to you,' a voice said. 'She's waiting upstairs.'

At first, Ellie-Mae thought she was dreaming, but then realised the voice belonged to Clara. Bleary eyed, she stood up, climbed the stairs and shuffled towards the main entrance. As she walked towards Maggie, Ellie-Mae smiled at a group of people who'd gathered at the side of a stone pillar. They smiled back, then blew into their hands as though trying to keep warm.

'You need to go out into the city, past the inner wall, and into the area affected by the recent attack,' Maggie said. 'The first few days are always the worst.'

'What do you want me to do?'

'Let them see you,' Maggie replied, handing her a map and a loaf of bread. 'If you meet anyone, let them know where we are. Tell them we can offer food and comfort to anybody who wants it.'

'Come on,' said Clara. 'I'll go with you.'

Alex was waiting for them on the Cathedral lawn. He was leaning against the concrete base of a darkened statue. On top of the base, an angel looked down towards a soldier who was crouched below.

'That's you, Ellie-Mae,' he said, with the hint of a grin. 'All you need to do is grow some wings.'

'No,' she replied. 'I have too many scars.'

Their yellow uniforms discarded, and dressed in ill-fitting clothes, the three of them crossed the road. Ellie-Mae lifted one of the sleeves of her tartan coat and stopped to look at the map she'd been given. In the centre of the map, a pencilled line directed her towards St Martin's Quarter and on to the northern part of the city marked as *'The Foregate'*. Using the city walls to guide her, she reached the gatehouse and glanced towards a set of steps that led downwards.

'The underground station is our only link with the outside and we still receive supplies from the cities in the north,' said Alex. 'For how long, we don't know.'

The wooden entrance to The Foregate was open and once she was through to the outer section of the city, the sense of destruction was immediate. The air was filled with a grey mist and the streets littered with chunks of concrete and masonry. A man stumbled towards her, his eyes gazing and unfocussed. Ellie-Mae's instinct told her to step back, but then she noticed a gash in the side of his head.

'Spare any food?' he asked.

Ellie-Mae ripped a chunk of bread and handed it to him. 'Peace be with you.'

'Bless you, young lady.'

She watched him waver then fall in the middle of the road. She wanted to stay with him and make sure he was all right, but as she turned around, she noticed that the knight, Arthur, was heading towards the man. He was complete in his chainmail suit and holding the reins of a chestnut-coloured horse that walked beside him.

'Don't worry, Ellie-Mae,' Arthur said. 'I'll look after him.'

She nodded. Although it was difficult, she knew it was right to keep going and catch up with Clara and Alex who were waiting for her at the side of the road. As she looked at the map once again, she noticed an arrow that directed them to a bridge.

Avoiding the shattered glass and fractures in the ground, Ellie-Mae clambered over the broken trunk of a fallen tree and stopped at the wall that looked over the canal. She glanced down and took a sharp intake of breath at the sight of the bodies that floated on the surface of the water.

'So much suffering,' she said, and grabbed at the wall to keep her balance.

Her composure regained, she carried on towards the remnants of a crumpled building. Dust and smoke rose from inside and a group of men and women were lifting a body from the rubble. One of the men interlocked his fingers and pressed his hands onto the chest of the body to commence cardiopulmonary resuscitation. A few seconds later, the group began hugging each other to confirm that one life, at least, had been saved.

'The bombing,' Ellie-Mae said. 'How long has it been going on?'

'Five months, maybe six,' Alex replied. 'The White Poppy movement attacked the missile launch pad in Brize Norton. It worked for a while, but they soon tightened security. Now, even the guards are guarded.'

'I can't believe I listened to Lucius and the regime,' Clara said. 'How could I have been so naïve?'

'It's what they do,' Ellie-Mae replied. 'They make it seem as though everything they do is for the right reason. In reality, the elite are as evil as any group of people in history.'

As if to prove the point she'd made, every step took Ellie-Mae further into desolation and as she continued to

131

climb the slope that led away from the city, she reached an area of charred earth. Only one building remained. '*The Rainbow Hill Centre*', it said, its colourful emblem standing like a beacon of hope and compassion. Hanging from the wall was a set of makeshift posters and each of them was inscribed with the word '*MISSING*'.

'*Sandra Williams, aged 73,*' one said

'*Have you seen this man?*' asked another.

Ellie-Mae lowered herself to her knees and placed her head in her hands.

'It's not your fault,' said Clara, helping her back to her feet. 'Whatever Maggie says, you can't be expected to help them.'

'I promised I'd try,' Ellie-Mae said.

A man stood in the road opposite, his ragged clothes falling from his shoulders. 'Is it safe?' he asked. 'Has the bombing stopped?'

'Yes,' said Ellie-Mae. 'You can come with us if you like. We have food and water.'

A wooden hatch opened in the ground and a different man appeared from the depths below. Others started to appear. Figures lifted themselves from the basements of fallen houses, their faces covered with the blackness of earth.

'She's the girl we've been told about,' one of them said. 'The Objector.'

'I've heard she's a descendant from royalty,' said another.

A woman came closer as though she was trying to gain a better view. 'Yes,' she said, smiling. 'It's her. It's really her.'

As Ellie-Mae retraced her steps back to the Cathedral, the numbers of the group increased to ten, then twenty. She had no idea how she'd managed it, but in spite of her doubts, Ellie-Mae started to believe that something amazing could be possible after all.

She walked past the darkened statue of the angel and thought about the glimpses of hope she'd witnessed. Arthur and the sight of his horse that clopped its hooves along the road. The person lifted from the rubble and helped back to life, the rainbow in the middle of a shattered street and the looks in the eyes of the people as they rose from the darkness of their basements.

As she stepped through the arched doorway of the Cathedral, the mood changed completely. Maggie was partly hidden amongst a crowd that gathered by a screen and she beckoned Ellie-Mae towards her.

'We've received another transmission,' she said. 'It's not good.'

Ellie-Mae winced at the sight of the image in the centre of the screen. It was filled with the face of the man she wished she'd never see again, his jagged scar moving in rhythm with his words.

'Do you know what day it is?' Lucius asked. 'Make a note because the 28th of October, 2042, will always be known as the day the battle of the west began. The battle of the north is complete. We have destroyed Durham, Newcastle, York, Manchester and wherever you are, your city will be next.' Lucius paused, as though allowing his words to sink in. 'Unless you hand them over.'

Ellie-Mae winced at the sight of her face that flashed onto the screen, next to the word that the regime used when they were looking for her. Judas. The images and descriptions of Samarah, Immigrant, and Ethan, Traitor, came next.

'It turns out we were wrong,' Lucius continued. 'The so-called Objectors are being helped by others. This is treachery against the state and anyone guilty of protecting them will be dealt with in a very special way. We should never have let them leave The Elimination Centre and because of them, the fight continues. Somehow, the Judas, the Immigrant, and the Traitor, are seen by the uprising as a symbol of optimism. Therefore, to save yourselves from total annihilation you need to give them to us. Alive or dead, it doesn't matter. Just do it quickly, for all of your sakes.'

The screen flickered. The image fading to black and then returning to the beginning of the message.

'Do you know what day it is?' Lucius repeated. 'Make a note…'

Ellie-Mae turned away.

'Don't worry, we're not going to hand you over. But there's something else you should know,' Maggie said. 'The regime has discovered a new weapon. A deadly, chemical weapon that's killing thousands and can you guess where they're sending the injured and the sick?'

Ellie-Mae placed her hand against the top of her chest. 'Here?' she whispered.

'Where else?' Maggie said. 'Come with me. There is much to do.'

Chapter 24—Samarah

Henry handed his phone to Samarah, who listened to the transmission for a second, then a third time. The fact that Ethan and Ellie-Mae were *'being helped by others'* was a good sign. It meant they were still alive. Her biggest concern, however, was that Lucius had made it even more dangerous for all three of them by heightening their identities.

'Be ready,' Henry said, taking the phone from Samarah. 'We could leave at any moment.'

They'd spent the previous night in a barn. Henry slept on the floor and Samarah amongst the hay in the rafters. Although he didn't tell her where they were, the silence of her surroundings suggested it was one of the forbidden locations. She guessed at somewhere in the Derbyshire Dales, a place in which outlaws from Sherwood Forest were known to roam the landscape. Exactly the type of place that a chameleon like Henry would thrive.

The *'any moment'* he'd suggested, turned out to be several hours later. Under the cover of darkness, Samarah filled her bottle with ice-cold water from the outside tap and sat in the passenger seat of Henry's car.

'Ready?' he asked, and then pressed the ignition button and lowered the headlights of the Merlin 5.

'We should take the back road,' he said. 'There are too many eyes on us to even think about using the main gate.'

With the sound of tyres crunching on gravel, he drove away from the barn into a narrow road. Occasionally, the jagged teeth of the walls would take a bite from the sides of the car and the overhanging branches would tap and scrape their fingers on the roof.

Henry stopped the Merlin 5 at a junction. Maybe it was the dark playing tricks with Samarah's vision, but for a moment, his eyes appeared to move independently and look in both directions at once. Like a chameleon who was able to watch an approaching object and scan the rest of his environment at the same time, Samarah was sure that Henry had achieved the same feat.

Any thoughts of what she'd seen, or hadn't seen, were interrupted by a light in the distance that flashed, then extinguished. She looked over her shoulder to see a different light and this time its beam was aimed at the place they'd recently departed. Shadowed figures appeared on the roof of the barn, their voices raised into shouts as they smashed their way inside.

'Bounty hunters,' Henry said, as he drove in the opposite direction. 'To people like them, you're worth a lot of money.'

'Can I ask you something? Who exactly are you?'

'Like I said before, it's complicated,' Henry said, as he leaned forward and opened the glove compartment. 'There's an envelope in there. It might explain a few things.'

Inside the envelope was a letter. It was headed with the image of a white blade that cut through a circle of black.

Underneath the logo of The Shard, was a single paragraph.

Henry Slater

We confirm that you have been accepted into The Entitlement Party. You are now validated as an official member of the elite and we look forward to your loyalty.

'Where did you find a million pounds?'

'I didn't,' he replied. 'They invited me as a recognition of service.'

'A police officer, I assume. That explains why you have the car,' Samarah said. 'Did the White Poppies invite you too? I saw the symbol. It was on your jacket.'

'I have a helicopter, too, not that I use it,' Henry said, as he kept his eyes on the road ahead. 'People think there's only two sides to this. The elite on one side, White Poppies on the other, evil against good, devils against angels and all that, but there's a whole lot more going on.'

'Like what?'

'Do you know how many different factions there are in the uprising?' Henry said, lighting a cigarette. 'Some of them want the former government to return, the ones who legged it to Switzerland when it all went sour. Others want a new regime and the restoration of the monarchy. Some people want it all to stay exactly as it is. Me, I just want to be friends with the strongest team.'

'I think you're better than that. I think you're a good man.'

Henry laughed. 'Better than some, worse than others.'

The journey continued in silence. Samarah's instinct about Henry had been correct. A chameleon, definitely, and yet beneath his scaly exterior she could sense the fragments of uncertainty and the sadness of an incomplete life.

'Another city destroyed,' Henry said, as a blanket of fire lifted into the sky. 'The uprising continues to fight, no matter what Lucius says, but it won't be long until the synthetic army moves south as he promised.'

Samarah looked at the place he'd referred to. As she opened her mind to the inhabitants of the city, she could feel their suffering and hear the screams of the dying. She could also sense the loss of those who'd already died. She tried to reach out to the survivors. She wanted to offer them hope and comfort but, in response, she heard nothing but silence.

In the transmission, Lucius had promised to use the Mark II synthetics to carry out his mission of annihilation. He'd sent them into battle with the intention of destroying everything house by house, town by town and city by city. There was no doubt in Samarah's mind that they would also have been programmed to wipe out the population.

Henry slowed the Merlin 5 to a stop at the side of the road. Above them, the underside of the motorway flyover stretched its great wings in both directions. The car door opened and Samarah watched him walk in the direction of the slipway. A few minutes later, he came back and restarted the engine. Headlights dimmed, Henry drove the Merlin 5 at walking pace to avoid the clumps of rubble and cracks in the road.

'Question for you,' he said. 'How well do you know Lucius?'

Samarah clenched her hands together. 'We had a few conversations. Why?'

'He wants to see you again. In fact, he'd do anything to speak with you.'

The speed of the car increased, and Samarah gripped at the handle beside her as the Merlin 5 swerved through a gap in the central reservation. Jolted from one side to the other, she glanced into the side mirror to see the headlights of a vehicle that was gaining with every second. Closer, closer and she tightened her core as the brakes of the car screeched and the wheels skidded. Samarah was thrown forward in her seat, the seatbelt tightening around her shoulders as the Merlin 5 shuddered to a halt.

Doors slammed and Samarah glanced into the wing mirror to see a parked van only metres away. Beside the van was a group of figures in black balaclavas striding towards them.

'These people will take you to Lucius,' Henry said, his eyes appearing to move independently once again to confirm his chameleon persona. One of them looked towards the men who were striding towards the Merlin 5. The other one fixed on Samarah. 'Still think I'm a good man?'

The figures came towards her and a masked face appeared at her window.

'How can you live with yourself?'

'I've been dead for a long time,' he replied, the image of his scales thickening, the fragments of uncertainty smoothing together into a single, continuous shade of black.

The car door opened and Samarah was pulled from her seat. Her arms were grappled behind her and she was hauled onto the road.

'How much do we owe you?' asked a gruff voice.

'Nothing,' Henry replied. 'But I need to come along.'

Her ankle twisted in agony as Samarah was lifted towards the van and thrown on board. She watched the chameleon slither into his Merlin 5 and then the door to the black van slammed closed behind her.

Chapter 25—Ethan

He was hiding in a makeshift hut of steel panels and corrugated iron when he heard the noise. The high-pitched scream and rumbling thunder sounded like a pack of hogenas at first, as though they'd escaped from behind the iron walls of the wastelands and ventured north.

The smell of sulphur convinced him otherwise and Ethan went out of the hut and descended the slope that led away from the railway line. It was his first chance of contact with people since Ethan had left the burning city of Manchester. In the hope of putting distance between himself and the synthetics, he'd continued to follow the tracks of the railway as quickly as he could and the effects had taken their toll.

Ethan was tired beyond tiredness, his energy spent in the constant movement at night and broken sleep during the day. To gain a ride, therefore, would be his only chance of heading south with any measure of speed.

He'd already discarded his green uniform and changed

into the civilian clothing he'd found in the hut. A heavy woollen jacket, a ripped pair of jeans and a hunter's hat. It wasn't perfect, but after what he'd witnessed in Manchester, it was far too dangerous for him to be seen in the uniform of the elite.

A swathe of vehicles approached. Steam-powered cars, cattle trucks and go-carts manoeuvred their way past the debris and piles of earth that littered the road. Standing at the side of the carriageway, he lifted his thumb and hoped until, eventually, one of the trucks stopped beside him.

'Get on,' shouted a bearded man. 'The elite are close behind.'

Ethan hid his face in the hood of his jacket to reduce the possibility of recognition and climbed on board. On each side of the truck, men and women were huddled together, their belongings piled on top of their knees. As the truck started to move, he widened the gap between his feet to improve his balance and grabbed at one of the horizontal metal bars above him.

'Joseph,' said the bearded man standing next to him, offering his hand.

'Jake,' Ethan lied. He had no idea who these people were and decided his safest option was to trust no one. 'Is anyone left in the north?'

'Not many. The mines are shut, the cities are being demolished and people are getting sick,' Joseph told him. 'The uprising is fighting back where it can, but everyone else is on the move.'

'Where are you going?' Ethan asked.

'South Wales. We've been told of a crossing point at Chepstow Castle,' Joseph replied. 'You?'

'Birmingham,' Ethan replied.

Joseph raised his eyes. 'Watch yourself. I've been told they've adopted a new policy. It's called shoot first, ask questions later.'

'Thanks,' said Ethan. 'I will.'

The truck continued its journey. The occasional battered sign for Stoke, Stafford and Cannock offering him a sense of location. Soon after, an overhead banner for Wales and the M54 indicated it was time for him to find his own way. The truck stopped at the side of the road.

'Good luck, Ethan,' Joseph said, shaking his hand.

'You too,' he said. 'Hey, how do you know my name?'

Joseph smiled. 'Everyone knows who you are, Ethan, the Objector.'

He looked around, wondering if the people in the truck would display any feelings of resentment at his decision to join Lucius and the elite when he was back in The Elimination Centre. Instead of hatred, however, each of them offered him a sense of warmth and encouragement.

He jumped to the ground and watched the truck re-join the convoy. For a moment, he wished he was back on board. Too much time on his own hadn't helped his fragile state of mind. Even so, he knew he needed to head towards Birmingham and the location Billy described as *'if all else fails'*. He also believed it would give him the best chance of meeting up with the two people who now meant more to him than anyone. His fellow Objectors, Samarah and Ellie-Mae.

Tightening his rucksack to his shoulders, Ethan trudged his way past the open sewers of the Black Country. Once a location of ironworking foundries and forges, its workers had been relocated to the mines, the mills and the specialist towns in various parts of the country.

Instead of people, its streets were filled with the threatening call of wild dogs and the scurrying feet of rats. It meant that Ethan was forced to keep going until he made it to the sanctuary of the forest in Sandwell Valley.

It was here that he decided to stop for a single night, camp and set the snare to catch the occasional animal that came too close. If he could, he'd have built a fire to keep warm, but the ground was too sodden from the recent rain and the branches of the trees too wet to ignite. Instead, he ate the raw flesh of his quarry in a way that he and his family would often do in the harshest of winters on the farm.

The next morning, cold and fatigued, he continued his enforced march through the increasingly broken world. He'd almost given up on finding civilisation ever again, when the square turrets and imposing walls came into view to confirm he'd reached the place he was aiming for.

The rogue city of Birmingham.

Everyone knew its reputation and how, for a price, the city leaders had agreed an uneasy peace with the regime to let its people do as they pleased. Merchants, tradespeople and jacks of all trades: as long as they paid their taxes, they were allowed to live in a way that nowhere else could.

Ethan looked ahead. In many ways, the city was structured in a similar manner to Manchester only on a far bigger scale. There had always been walls, most cities had them to protect the people who lived inside the defences. Some, like fortress Birmingham, were huge and built with the clear intention of keeping people out.

The sight of the guns, fifty metres apart, was a reminder of Joseph's warning. The alleged policy of '*shoot first, ask questions later*' meant that his decision was an easy one. He would wait amongst the trees at the edge of the expanse of open ground in front of the walls until it was dark enough for him to move without detection. Even then, it would be down to fate, he'd need luck in finding a way into the city.

An increasing wind announced the onset of a storm the gathering clouds had threatened. Water dripped from the branches, the rain seeping into every part of his clothing, but still he waited beneath the trees until he was sure the time was right to move. As the last of the day's brightness descended to gloom, he set off across the expanse of open ground and in the direction of the city.

After ten, maybe fifteen metres, he was immersed in the circular beam of a spotlight. His heart racing, he turned and ran back towards the forest. Within a few strides, Ethan stopped and with his breath rasping in the damp night air, he bent double and coughed a lungful of phlegm onto the ground.

Once he'd recovered, he peered through an opening in the trees and towards a group of figures in white who were running towards him. Looking like space travellers, their faces were hidden behind tinted visors and they were clothed in surgical body suits.

'Only the guilty run,' said a woman, pointing a rifle in his direction. 'You have ten seconds to show yourself.'

Ethan moved from beneath the trees. 'Who are you?'

'That's the question I need to ask,' she replied, her voice muffled behind her visor,' so you'd better start talking.'

His thoughts scrambled with exhaustion, Ethan

lowered his hand towards his bomber jacket, edged his fingers towards the handle of the knife and lifted it from the inside pocket. *'Just in case'* Aaron had said. In response, the woman lurched forward and kicked the blade from his hand.

'You had your chance,' she said, lifting her rifle and aiming its muzzle at Ethan.

'Sophia, stop!' came a shout. 'Don't shoot.'

Ethan turned in the direction of the voice and even though the face was partly hidden behind a visor, he recognised who it was.

'This is the Objector,' Billy said. 'The one from the transmissions.'

Sophia lowered her gun. 'Whoever he is, you know what to do,' she said. 'If the sickness has got to him, he'll be dead by the morning.'

There were others beside Sophia, each of them wearing tinted visors and keeping their distance from Ethan as he stumbled his way back through the forest. His hands covered in black, rubber gloves, Billy gave Ethan the knife that Sophia had kicked from his hand and he placed it back into its leather sheath.

'She would have shot you,' Billy said. 'What were you thinking?'

'I don't know,' Ethan replied. 'I haven't got the strength to think anymore.'

In the pouring rain, they headed across the area of open land that surrounded the towering city defences. A set of wooden gates opened to reveal a courtyard on the other side of the walls. On one side of the courtyard was a windowless steel building.

'Quarantine,' Billy said, tightening the visor to his face as he led Ethan down some steps and opened the first door they came to. 'I'll see you tomorrow. Try not to die on me.'

145

'I'll do my best,' Ethan said, 'and thanks.'

The door closed and he sat on the bed. Now that he was alone, Ethan's mind turned to Sophia's words about the sickness and he thought back to the moment in Manchester. The synthetics, the dark mass they fired towards the city and how he'd knelt beside Aaron. He looked at his shaking hands and then closed his eyes to relieve his pounding head.

'I'm not ill, I can't be. It's been too long,' he assured himself. 'I'm just tired, I just need some sleep.'

He took a sip of the glass of water at the side of his bed, lay down on the mattress and buried himself beneath the blankets. Any sense of comfort was quickly replaced by anxiety as his entire body started to shake and his throbbing headache grew in intensity.

His mind swirling with fear, he thought about Samarah, the girl who'd given him the strength to keep going. He visualised Ellie-Mae, the fragile looking girl with the crucifixes around her neck and whose faith he wished he could replicate.

'Please let me live,' he shouted, as tears poured from his eyes.

Chapter 26—Ellie-Mae

The steam machine rumbled its way into the underground station of Worcester Foregate Street, the doors clattering against the sides of the steel carriages as they opened from within.

It was the fifth arrival that day and, as before, the front carriages were filled with those who'd become infected in the recent chemical attacks. The carriages at the back were loaded with soldiers of the uprising and people who'd escaped the cities before the synthetics arrived and obliterated everything. Ellie-Mae searched through the billows of steam to see the first of the stretchers being lowered to the platform.

'Sick to the Infirmary. Injured to the Cathedral,' she shouted, her voice echoing in the oval shaped tunnel, 'and keep your face masks on.'

A man fell into her, a bloodied bandage covering part of his face.

'This way,' she said, edging her way through the crowded platform.

'Thank you,' the man replied. 'Where are we?'

'Worcester station.'

'Worcester? That's not far enough,' he said, his voice rising into panic. 'They're on their way to us. They'll kill us all.'

Ellie-Mae took hold of his arm and helped him towards a concrete bench at the side of the platform. A woman shoved past on her right, then a child on her left. 'Stop pushing. Let the stretchers go first!' Ellie-Mae said, then turned back to the man.

'Tell me again, please. What is it you would like to say?' she asked.

'Everyone's dying. It's the synthetics. They're spraying this stuff from their mouths.'

'The chemical weapon,' Ellie-Mae said. 'It's making people sick.'

The man nodded. 'We tried to fight back, but they attacked us again. The army at the front were decimated in seconds and I ran like a coward.'

'If you hadn't, you'd be dead too,' Ellie-Mae said, as she helped him to his feet. 'We'll get you checked over, to make sure you're all right.'

'Thank you. I'm sorry for losing it,' he said. 'My name's Paul, by the way. Paul Worthington.'

Ellie-Mae waited for most of the crowd to disperse from the platform. Eventually, a gap opened in the melee of bodies and, after tightening the straps of her facemask, she climbed the staircase that led away from the underground station. Sheets of freezing rain splattered against the inner-city wall and forced her to shelter beneath the iron roof of The Foregate.

She looked across the road to see the last of the stretchers disappearing into the narrow walkway that led to the Infirmary. The weak and the injured were already on their way to the Cathedral, their twisted, zombie-like shapes being helped by others as they fought their way along the high street in the pouring rain.

'Like a scene from the apocalypse,' said Paul.

'Not yet,' Ellie-Mae replied.

They made their way past the hollowed buildings and windowless shops until they reached Elgar's statue at the end of the high street. Alex and Clara were waiting at the door to the Cathedral. Even though their masks covered their expressions, Ellie-Mae could see that both of them were struggling to stay calm as they ushered the injured inside.

'There's not much space,' Clara said. 'If I were you, I'd head for the crypt.'

'I'll do that,' Ellie-Mae replied, taking hold of Paul's

hand to guide him through the rows of patients strewn across the stone floor.

'Thank you again,' Paul said. 'How old are you?'

'Sixteen.'

'Same age as my daughter. You have an impossible life ahead of you. My generation has well and truly messed things up for the years and decades to come.'

'Where is she now? Your daughter.'

'The elite took her. She was one of those selected to go to The Elimination Centre.'

'I was there too,' Ellie-Mae whispered.

Paul slowed down, his hands gripping into her arm. 'I thought I recognised you,' he said. 'You're one of the three we've seen on the transmissions, the Objectors, the ones they're after.'

'I am Ellie-Mae,' she replied, as they made it past the final row of bodies on the floor. 'I did what I thought was right.'

'We should all do more of that, I guess,' Paul said, relaxing his grip. 'Tell me about Lucius. I want to know what he's like.'

'Vile,' she said, trying to calm herself at the mention of the devil in the night.

'My daughter, Scarlett, she used to speak highly of him. When she first arrived at The Elimination Centre, she used to send us messages telling us how happy she was. She told us the regime wasn't as bad as people made out,' he said, his head bowed, but then he lifted his face towards hers. 'Do you know her?'

Ellie-Mae winced at the mention of Scarlett's name but was saved from replying as Paul appeared to lose his balance. She tried to help him as he stumbled backwards, his hands catching at the side of her mask and ripping it from her face.

'Tell me everything,' he implored, phlegm spitting from

his mouth. 'She's all I have left.'

'Try and get some rest,' Ellie-Mae said, lifting the blanket over his shivering body. 'I'll come back soon.'

She headed across the Cathedral floor and out of the exit. Although she felt guilty about not telling him anything else about his daughter, she needed time to think it through. After all, how could she tell him that Scarlett had submitted to Lucius in a way that other girls refused? Her pace increasing, she headed along the high street and towards the steps that led to The Foregate underground station.

'Can I help?' she asked.

'Put your face mask on!' Maggie shouted.

Ellie-Mae had barely lifted the straps of the mask over her ears when the bars of a stretcher were placed into the palms of her hands. She looked over her shoulder at the man who lay on the canvas. Similar to most of the people she'd seen with the sickness, his expression offered only emptiness, as though he was oblivious to all that was happening.

'Quickly now,' said Maggie, who stood at the opposite end of the stretcher.

Avoiding the puddles and the cracks in the stone path as best she could, Ellie-Mae hurried into the narrow alley, along the road and through the western gate of the inner-city wall. A set of steps led them into the main reception of the Infirmary. She was partly through the door when a man in a white coat squeezed past.

'Spare bed?' she called out.

'Maybe,' he said. 'Head to the wards.'

She followed the corridor until she came to a room on her right, only to be waved away.

'Next one,' said a voice.

The same response happened again and again until the rattle of a trolley caused her to turn. Behind her, a patient was being wheeled away. A different man in a white coat pushed past, his clothing splashed with blood and as Ellie-Mae looked at the trolley for a second time, she noticed a dark blanket was being lifted over the head of the corpse below.

'That's our bed,' said Maggie.

Ellie-Mae headed into the ward, tilted the stretcher and lowered the man onto a blood-soaked mattress. Together with Maggie, she then squeezed herself out through the door and back towards The Foregate. The rumble of wheels on the tracks in the underground station announced the arrival of a steam machine and another consignment of desperate people. Ellie-Mae focussed her thoughts on what she needed to do and headed down the steps.

She soon lost count of how many trips they'd made between Foregate Street station and the Infirmary. The ache in her shoulders increased with every trip and as darkness finally descended, she stood on the steps that led into the hospital and waited for instructions.

'Are there any more trains? Should we go back to the station?'

'Not tonight,' Maggie said. 'Go to your lodgings and get some rest. There'll be plenty to do tomorrow.'

Even though she was tired, she still had one more errand to run. In the rain, she lowered her face mask and headed through the western gate. As she reached the path alongside the inner-city wall, the words of psalm twenty-three repeated in her mind to offer her comfort.

'Yea though I walk through the valley of death, I will fear no evil, for thou art with me, thy rod and staff to comfort me.'

Many of the candles in the Cathedral were extinguished by the time she reached the main door. Even so, there was enough light to guide her through the bodies that sprawled across the floor. As she reached the top of the crypt, she

151

glanced around. For a moment, Ellie-Mae wondered if she was in the right place but then a wooden cross told her everything. It was lying on a mattress that was separated from the others and covered in a plastic sheet. Written in the centre of the cross was an inscription dedicated to the man she'd helped from the station.

Paul Worthington, died 30th October 2042, of the sickness

'The one who endures to the end will be saved,' she said, her knees buckling, and she clasped at the crucifixes around her neck. 'We come from dust and to dust we shall return. Peace be with you.'

After tightening her collar, she stood up and headed across the Cathedral floor and out into the damp night air. The further she walked, the less she was able to control the shuddering cold in her chest and a feeling that she was about to fall. A sense of dizziness caused her to lean against the wall behind her.

As the world continued to swirl, she closed her eyes. Dark, demonic images reminded her of the illness that killed her mother and that Ellie-Mae had once fought and survived. This time, however, the onset of delirium was more sudden, the loss of perception more acute.

Her hands shivering, her mouth dry, Ellie-Mae climbed the steps to the lodgings she'd been allocated at the edge of college green and beside the Cathedral. She forced her key into the lock. Panicking at the memory of how she'd removed her face mask in the Cathedral, she ran to the bathroom. Surely this was happening too quickly.

'Lord have mercy,' she said at the blue colouring on her face.

She leaned forward, her hands gripping the cold edge of the sink as a rasping cough was accompanied with a mouthful of blood.

PART 4—Fugitives

Chapter 27—Samarah

1ˢᵗ November, 2042

Samarah's knees rested against the opposite wall. A black hood covered her head, it was claustrophobic; she thought she might suffocate. Her wrists, bound with string, were chafed and sore; she looked through the gap at the bottom of the hood to see specks of blood and a deep red dribble trailing down her left hand.

The journey in the black van had been no longer than an hour. When it ended, Samarah was led into a building that echoed with the sound of footsteps. She was guided through a narrow corridor and forced into a space the size of a broom cupboard.

Once again, the wolf was incarcerated against her will and even though she wasn't sure how long she'd been there, it was long enough for her neck to ache and her injured ankle to throb like crazy.

'These people will take you to Lucius,' Henry told her at the moment he'd handed her over and Samarah was thrown into the van. Although she was filled with the most incredible anger at the way she'd allowed herself to be conned by the chameleon, she knew she needed to hold her nerve no matter what happened next and where they might take her.

The sound of voices on the outside of her cell preceded the rattle of keys in the lock. Air rushed onto her face as the door opened and a hand snatched at her arm, lifting her from the floor. Her hood removed, Samarah's elbows bumped against the walls of the corridor as she was pulled forward into a room.

A chair nudged into the back of her knees and she fell into a seat. As the door to the room slammed behind her,

Samarah looked around. The walls were covered in darkened glass and opposite her a television monitor was mounted on a wooden frame.

On the screen of the monitor, an intermittent black arrow turned in a circle chasing its tail. It continued to circle, its speed increasing and then the arrow vanished as the screen lightened to confirm an internet connection had been made.

'It's been a while,' Lucius said, from the centre of the screen. 'The last time we spoke, you told me I'm a waste of a human being. Do you remember?'

The viper had her precisely where he wanted. It was the same place that any snake would choose to have its prey. Trapped within the coils of its tail and caught in its glare. In the car, Henry asked her how well she knew Lucius. If she was right, then this was the time to blunt his fangs and offer him nothing.

'What's that, I can't hear you?' Lucius continued. 'I suppose it must be quite a shock to see me again. How lucky for you. Anyway, as I'm sure you've worked out, you have been betrayed, again. Maybe it's you who is the waste of a human being.'

Even though the effort of retaining control was causing Samarah's hands to tremble, she remained silent. On the surface, Lucius offered his customary arrogance. Nevertheless, she could sense something else in his persona, a brittleness to suggest that this was definitely the time to test the patience of his ego.

'Maybe I can speak for you,' Lucius said, leaning towards the lens of the camera so that only his rage-filled eyes and the snarl of his mouth were visible. 'You don't have a plan, you don't have any allies and soon, people will have forgotten you even existed. In the meantime, you will be brought back to The Elimination Centre,' he said, then moved his face away from the camera, slightly. 'Don't

155

worry, we've kept your room exactly as it was. Your friends, the little black creatures with hungry mouths and gnashing teeth, are waiting to welcome you home.'

The flare in his eyes and the increased desperation in his voice were clear indications that the time was almost right for her to disturb his rhetoric.

But not yet.

'In a day or two, you will have your very own private execution party,' Lucius continued, the speed of his words increasing into something less audible. 'When I say private, don't worry, the entire country will be given the opportunity to watch you die. That will be nice, eh? Something to look forward to. Your trial has already taken place and the verdict of guilty returned unanimously by the jury. The punishment has been confirmed and sanctioned by the regime to allow juvenile decapitation. Just think, Samarah, for a few seconds, you may even be as famous as I am.'

This was the moment. The exact moment when his bombast of condescension had transformed into vanity.

'Why have you gone to all this trouble? If I'm such a waste of a person, why are you so determined to bring me back?'

'I should never have let you go. That was my error,' Lucius said, his words accompanied by a cascade of spit. 'Each one of the Objectors was sent to a place from which you should never have returned. Dying in the line of duty has always been acceptable, but then what happened?'

He stopped speaking, lifted a bottle of whisky, emptied the last of its contents into his mouth and threw the bottle over his shoulder.

'Everything I'd arranged was destroyed,' Lucius said. 'People helped you and the belief in the uprising grew in strength. This is why all of you will be eliminated as enemies of the regime. The Traitor, whose family we supported, the Judas who cares more about her God than she does about carrying out her duty, and the Immigrant, a symbol of poisonous foreign blood that we allowed to pollute our country.'

'It won't work,' she said. 'When we die, there will be ten more Samarahs, a hundred Ellie-Maes and a thousand Ethans. You will never win because in the end, evil never does.'

It was the turn of Lucius to be quiet for a few moments. 'Hardly,' he said, stepping back from the camera. 'We were wounded by the cyber-attack and we weren't ready for a war back then, but now we are.'

'What about the scheme of elimination?' Samarah asked, probing an area he may not have been expecting. 'What about all those killers fulfilling their contracts?'

'The elimination scheme was flawed from the start. It was never going to reduce the population in the numbers we wanted, but it soon became the perfect smokescreen for our purposes,' he said, his face reddening. 'I would have thought that a clever girl like you would have been able to work this out.'

'Purposes? Samarah asked, probing a little deeper. 'You make it sound as though you have it all worked out.'

'Only the glorious members of the elite will survive this war and soon, there will not be a single underling left. When we have cleansed this country of the incapable, the worthless and the ineffective, we will keep every remaining resource and asset for ourselves.'

Bingo.

With the correct, careful manipulation, the viper had struck at exactly the moment she anticipated. Samarah knew which buttons to press all right, and in the lengthening hush, Lucius's image on the screen froze, faded, then extinguished.

For a few moments, Samarah stayed exactly where she

was, leaning forward in her seat. As the seconds lengthened into minutes, she leant back, wondering if she'd done the right thing and whether she'd be left on her own as punishment. But then the door to the room opened.

'I knew it,' Henry said.

'Knew what?' Samarah asked, as the string was cut from her hands.

'That you could find the truth,' Henry said, the hint of a smile betraying a semblance of mischief. 'Some people suspected, others refused to believe it but now, everyone knows exactly what Lucius and the regime are planning.'

Samarah was incredulous, her stomach flipping over and over. 'So this was just some set up? Chuck me in with Lucius and make him tell me everything.'

'Not exactly,' Henry said. 'But your reactions needed to be real and authentic. Otherwise, he'd have known something was wrong.'

'I still don't get it. You need to explain what's going on, properly, or else I'm getting out of here and you will never see me again.'

'Like I tried to explain when we were in the car, the uprising has always been divided in their thinking,' Henry said. 'Not anymore. Once the different factions have seen the recording of Lucius's admission, and his plans for the annihilation of the underlings, there won't be a single person who'll believe his lies.'

Samarah stood up and looked around the room, suddenly aware of the people who were partly hidden behind the darkened glass. 'What do you intend to do?'

'That's up to you, Samarah. I'm in your hands now.'

'You heard what he said. He's scared of the Objectors and what we represent,' she said. 'All you need to do, is get us together and hope it's not too late.'

'Let's go then,' Henry said, opening a door at the

opposite end of the room.

'What do you care?' Samarah asked. 'Once this is over, you can go back to being the chameleon you always were.'

'Chameleon eh? I like the analogy,' Henry said. 'But here's another one. Like the leopard that doesn't change his spots, I always like to stay on the side of the team with the best chance of winning.'

Chapter 28—Ethan

He woke in the middle of the night. Dazed and confused, it took a few seconds to remember where he was. After a few moments, the recollection of Billy escorting Ethan into a room at the bottom of some steps came flooding back, along with the memory of uncontrollable shivering. His sheets covered in cold sweat, he pushed away the blankets. As he sat at the edge of his bed, he rubbed his clammy palms together and exhaled deeply from within. Another deep breath helped him to push any thoughts of dying from the sickness to one side and focus on trying to gain the rest he needed.

It didn't take long for his eyes to droop and his head to spin and Ethan laid back down and searched for a dry space beneath the blankets. He thought again about Samarah and Ellie-Mae and remembered how, at the moment he believed he'd contracted the sickness, it was his fellow Objectors he'd turned to for comfort. If he could, he'd have entered their minds and wished them protection and hope.

Sleep came quickly, his conscious thoughts drifting into a dreamless slumber that was interrupted, sometime later, by the scrape of footsteps and the outline of Billy standing in the doorway.

'Looks like you made it,' he said.

Ethan stirred, then pushed away his blankets. He rubbed his eyes and took a gulp of water from the glass at the side of his bed. 'Have I really been asleep for eighteen hours?' he asked, checking his watch.

'No idea, but that's how long you've been in quarantine,' said Billy, as the two of them left the room and climbed a metal staircase until they were in the courtyard. 'We haven't seen much of the sickness here, yet, but they say it's pretty quick. Sometimes only a few hours before people start dying.'

'They're using the synthetics to spread it.'

'Yea,' said Billy. 'We've heard that too.'

'How did you get to Birmingham?' Ethan asked. 'Last time we saw each other, we were both on the run.'

Billy paused at the top of the steps. 'The next morning, I met up with the others. There were only five of us left and we hid in a cave until the synthetics moved on. Then we hitched a ride.'

'I hitched a ride too,' Ethan replied. 'I was lucky, I think.'

The shadow of the fortress stretched across the courtyard in the early morning sun. Layers of sandbags surrounded the buildings closest to the city wall but, otherwise, Birmingham resembled the kind of bustling town that populated the country before The Entitlement Party came to power.

At the edge of the courtyard, he noticed a parade of shops. At the far end of the high street, a flutter of canopies sheltered the market stalls below. People scurried between shop and stall, their heads bowed as they gathered supplies.

'They know what's coming,' Billy said, 'and they know it's coming soon.'

Ethan lowered his head to avoid a coil of barbed wire that hung from the entrance of a cabin in the far corner of the courtyard. Inside the cabin, an open fire blazed and crackled, the drift of wood smoke thickening the air. At the fringes of the room, people sat on stools, chairs and some on the floor. Of those he could see, Ethan and Billy were by far the youngest.

A woman stood by the fire, her hands outstretched towards the flames. Even though she was no longer dressed in the white suit and visor, Ethan recognised her as the woman who'd threatened to shoot him in the forest.

'We're risking a lot in having you here,' Sophia said. 'What can you tell us?'

'They're destroying the cities,' he said. 'The underlings are fighting back where they can, but the rest are heading south in their thousands.'

'We know this already,' Sophia said. 'What about their weapon?'

'The Mark II synthetics are bigger than the previous ones. They have a laser that cuts through walls and a black cloud that follows on behind,' Ethan said. 'I saw it in Manchester. I wasn't close enough to see everything, but a cadet described it as being like the end of the world.'

'If they find out we're helping an Objector, it might be the end for all of us,' Sophia said.

'Do you know where they are?' he asked. 'The other Objectors? I need to find them.'

Sophia didn't reply. Her attention was drawn to a man who'd entered the room. 'Synthetic patrol,' he said, his breath hurried as he spoke. 'About a mile away and closing.'

Sophia stared at Ethan. 'As I thought,' she said. 'You've led them to us.'

The chairs and stools scraped across the floor as the room became crowded with bodies. Ethan was the last to leave the cabin and when he did make it into the courtyard, he was almost knocked over in the rush of people heading towards the ramparts.

'Come with me,' said Billy.

Ethan did as he was asked and reached the top of the city wall to find a machine gun pointing towards the open ground surrounding the walls. On his left, a cannon moved into position and one of the gunners rammed a cast-iron shot into its muzzle.

'Here they come,' Billy said, gazing ahead.

A row of synthetic warriors charged across the open

land. In the same way as they'd done in Manchester, they approached in perfect formation. The gunners on the city ramparts waited until the first of the warriors were no more than two hundred metres away.

'Fire!'

Along the line, there was an explosion of gunpowder as the projectiles leapt from the cannons and Ethan jumped to his right to avoid the violent recoil of the gun.

'Reload,' Billy shouted.

The dense cloud of smoke made it difficult to see whether the first wave of fire had been successful. Then it began to clear. Instead of opening their mouths and directing a black cloud towards the city, the remaining Mark II synthetics came together into a single group and formed the shape of an arrow. They quickened their step, the point of the arrow moving, swaying until it aimed directly at Ethan.

Billy grabbed at the sleeves of his woollen jacket. 'They're after your blood. You need to GO!'

After one more glance at the synthetic army, he ran down the staircase. He'd only just reached the bottom step, when Ethan heard a second wave of cannon fire, followed by a second shout of *'Reload'*. An intense heat caused him to turn. A glow of light appeared in a single area at the bottom of the city wall that intensified and then, with a shattering of stone, a section of the ramparts collapsed.

The air was close and choking and Ethan ran across the courtyard. He hid in the doorway of the building opposite and was about to move once again when he heard the clatter of metal. A faint outline appeared in the dust. It was crawling towards him like an animal and as the cloud of dust began to clear he could see the upper torso of a synthetic. Its legs were shattered below the waist and it was using its broken hands to scamper along the ground.

It was clear the synthetic knew where he was and that any hopes of avoiding detection by remaining still would be ineffective. Instead, Ethan searched the pockets in his jacket until he found the synthetic badge that Aaron had given him. Any hint of human movement would give Ethan away to the synthetic's sensor and in one continual manoeuvre, he lifted the badge of The Shard above his head.

As the synthetic warrior clambered towards him, its green eyes brightened and Ethan realised his mistake. This wasn't a slave unit like the one in Manchester. Instead, it was a master synthetic, set to individual attack mode. A shock of pain sent Ethan hurtling to the ground and his fingernails scraped at the dirt as the synthetic dragged him beneath its shattered torso.

The fierce glow of its eyes continued, and Ethan punched its mechanical chest. In response, the brightness of its stare faltered for a few seconds and then returned as the warrior lifted its silver arm, as though poised to strike.

Trapped beneath the synthetic, Ethan punched his fists against its chest for a second, then a third time until, finally, the grip of the synthetic loosened and the colouring in its eyes faded into darkness. One last punch and the metal remains fell to one side.

Exhausted, Ethan lay on his back and looked at the synthetic warrior. As he looked again, he noticed a jagged crack at the front of its skull. His heart racing, Ethan lifted the leather sheath from his jacket and used the tip of Aaron's knife to prize open its forehead. Inside, was a knotted mass of electronics that fizzed and sparked. Ethan waited for the last of the circuits to burn themselves out and then pushed and jabbed at the wires until he found the item he was looking for.

The control box.

Its thin metal casing was similar to the ones he'd seen on the farm. He squeezed the nail of his thumb inside a small indentation at one end and the lid of the control box opened with a click. In its centre was a printed circuit board. Partly concealed beneath a metal clip at one end of the control box was the second item he was hoping to find.

A SIM card.

'Mobile phone technology,' he said, unable to control the grin that lengthened across his face. 'I knew it.'

Ethan panicked at the sound of pounding feet. His alarm quickly subsided at the sight of Billy emerging through the dust and smoke.

'Are you all right?' he asked.

'Better than I've been for a long time,' Ethan said, but as he closed the control box, a sudden realisation dawned.

The synthetic had been sent to kill him. The fact that the regime was utilising resources to send individual, programmed assassins to track him down meant they would stop at nothing until he was dead.

Chapter 29—Samarah

'We move tomorrow,' Henry told her, as they left the room in which Lucius had outlined his agenda of extermination.

Samarah was given a key that locked a room from the inside. Blackened sheets were nailed to every surface, wall and window. A night of fitful sleep was interrupted by a knock on the wall. Her eyes bleary, she glanced at the padlock on the door to make sure it remained closed and bolted.

'Samarah, it's me, Henry.'

'Give me a minute,' she replied.

At the side of the room was a sink and she washed, dried her face and dressed into a set of clothes she'd been given the previous night. She then opened the padlock to the door. Henry handed her some food and water and together they headed through a corridor until they reached a high-ceilinged warehouse. As she lowered herself into the passenger seat of the Merlin 5, she glanced in Henry's direction.

'Are you definitely on the right side, this time?' she said, 'because other than you, Mr Chameleon, I still have no idea who I am dealing with.'

'If I can't be a good man in your eyes anymore,' he replied, 'let's just say I'm filled with good intentions and yes, I am definitely on your side now.'

The Merlin 5 rolled its way through the warehouse. A trio of steam-powered cars stood on one side of the car park. Like a pack of Doberman pinschers waiting for instructions from their owners, their engines were running, and their bonnets pointed in the direction of the exit. Samarah glanced through the tinted windows of the vehicles to see that the identity of the drivers and passengers was concealed with balaclavas.

'So many secrets,' Samarah said.

'It's safer this way. For everyone,' Henry replied, as he drove through the car park towards a sign at the side of the road. *'Macclesfield.'*

'The uprising are gathered for the battle of the west and for now, we're heading south,' said Henry. 'Other than that, it's up to you.'

Samarah closed her eyes and allowed her mind to reach upwards, outwards. She thought about the boy with the anxious blue eyes, the lion who was not yet fully grown. Although she could see his outline, there was something of a crossroads in his pathway to suggest that his destination was unclear.

She envisioned the ibex and although the image of the girl with the long, brown hair was faint, she visualised a bridge that stretched across a river and the tips of a Cathedral tower. Then the vision altered. Instead of buildings and landscapes, the image faded into two, golden crowns, one larger than the other.

'We should head for the faithful city with two walls,' she said, opening her eyes. 'Worcester.'

Like Dobermans protecting their young, the steam-powered cars flanked the Merlin 5 for the remainder of the journey and every now and then, a billow of steam would rise from their bonnets. Henry kept to the back roads and although the route was mainly hidden by trees and buildings, Samarah managed to catch a glimpse of fortress Birmingham in the distance.

Although it was only a fleeting look, she was sure she could see smoke lifting from one of the turrets. Within the smoke, she could feel the presence of the lion cub to indicate he'd been involved in a battle. Samarah was tempted to suggest a detour to check if Ethan was all right, but then something told her that her presence was required elsewhere. A sense of anxiety increased the further they went until, several hours later, they made it to the northern outskirts of Worcester.

The Merlin 5 stopped.

'Why are we waiting?' Samarah asked.

Henry opened his window. 'First, to check for hogenas. They don't tend to roam this side of the city, but you never know. Secondly, in case the people of Worcester decide to attack,' he said. 'No one likes unexpected visitors. Especially now.'

Samarah looked towards the battlements and, as far as she could see, the city was deserted. As the seconds lengthened into minutes, the first of the steam-powered cars that guarded the Merlin 5 supercar in its journey to Worcester, crept away. The rest of the pack of Dobermans followed, and Henry re-started the Merlin 5.

'I think we should be all right,' he said, as he negotiated the cracks in the road and drove the last few hundred metres towards the gate.

As they approached the city wall, and the one that represented the larger of two crowns that surrounded Worcester, Samarah's sense of apprehension grew in strength and concentrated on Ellie-Mae. The vision that Samarah had seen when she'd searched for direction had led her to this place and yet, the closer they drove, the weaker the image of the ibex became.

At the top of the gate, a knight in a suit of armour rose like a meerkat standing to attention. He was wearing a blue cape decorated with a royal crest. As the Merlin 5 edged closer to the city, the knight lifted his arm and thrust his hand forward as a signal for them to stop.

Henry leaned his head through the window of his car. 'You need to let us in,' he shouted. 'It's important.'

The meerkat barely even twitched. 'This is a royalist city,' he said, eventually. 'You are not welcome here.'

Samarah could feel the disdain in his voice and it didn't

take long for her to realise why. The Merlin 5. Only the privileged and members of the elite would be allowed to drive a car like this. She undid her seatbelt and stepped into the road.

'I've come to see Ellie-Mae,' she said, making sure she was in full view of the meerkat. 'I'm an Objector like her, and she is my friend.'

The knight looked down and offered a hint of recognition. He then turned and shuffled out of sight. At first, Samarah was convinced she'd been ignored, but then he appeared on the ground beneath the archway and beckoned them forward.

'Head for the Cathedral,' the knight said. 'If you hurry, you might just get there in time.'

'Thank you,' Samarah replied.

Beyond the wall, the first of the streets looked eerily unscathed as though untouched by conflict.

The further they went, the image of a broken city became clearer. Roads were pitted with craters, vehicles stood like twisted skeletons, their windows shattered and the steelwork covered in rust. Of the buildings that remained, the brickwork was choked with ash. As the sun became hidden behind clouds in the darkening sky, Henry turned his car and drove through a gap between houses.

'I'll try a different way.'

The main road was easier to navigate, and they soon reached a series of tall archways. Beyond the arches was the second of two walls that represented the smaller, golden crown that Samarah had envisaged. The road came to an end. Unable to drive any further, Henry stopped at the side of the road.

Samarah opened the car door. Something told her to look towards a zig-zagged path on her left that led to a red-bricked building. Ellie-Mae's image flashed in her mind. Samarah closed her eyes. She started to visualise the fragile girl with the cracked lens in her glasses. As she did so, a dull ache deepened in her stomach as the ibex appeared, its horns tangled and its head tight against its chest.

She was about to move towards the zig-zagged path when she remembered the words of the knight. *'Head for the Cathedral. If you hurry, you might just get there in time.'* Beyond the tall archways, Samarah could see the four peaks of the Cathedral tower. Determined to get there before it was too late, she unfastened her seatbelt.

'Wait here and look after the car,' she said. 'I'll come back soon.'

Using the perimeter of the inner wall to guide her, Samarah nudged her way towards the bridge that stretched across the river and climbed the parapet at the side of the gatehouse. Cold rain pricked against her cheeks and with her hands resting on top of the concrete wall, Samarah peered across the heads of the crowd to see a procession of people, each of whom was wearing a face mask.

The dull thump of a drum began to echo and Samarah

170

followed the direction of its beat. At the front of the crowd, she noticed the distinct shape of a coffin on the back of a horse-drawn cart. The procession continued; the crowds of people who'd gathered at the bridge began to join the trail of mourners who made their way through the streets of Worcester.

Samarah lifted the sleeve of her shirt to cover her face and trudged the slow march into the masked crowd in front of the Cathedral. At the edge of the grounds was a series of photographs in upright frames. Many of the images were filled with regal poses of the royal family before the dissolution of the monarchy. They were sitting in the throne room in what used to be known as Buckingham Palace. Others were from former King William's coronation in Westminster Abbey.

Then she noticed the images of Ellie-Mae. In one of them, she was wearing a white dress with the stitched image of a crown as she knelt beside a hospital bed. In another, she was handing out food and water to people whose arms were outstretched. The dull ache in Samarah's stomach returned as she read the words beneath one of the photographs.

MARTYR TO THE PEOPLE. HER CREMATION WILL ALLOW HER SPIRIT TO LIVE AMONGST US ALL

'She's not dead,' Samarah said, pushing through the crowd. 'She's dying, but she's not dead.'

A woman in a black dress moved towards her. 'Let her through,' she said.

Like cows at a feeding station, the crowd grumbled a discontented murmur but allowed a gap to open.

'It's great to see you, Samarah, but I'm afraid it's too late,' the woman replied. 'Nobody survives the sickness and tomorrow, her spirit will become part of everyone.'

'No,' Samarah shouted. 'You're wrong.'

The gap closed as the muffled singing of the national anthem filled the skies. Pointed elbows and lowered shoulders pushed Samarah away from the woman in black. She tried again, her feet anchored to the ground as she pushed and shoved against the wall of bodies until she lost her balance and fell. Legs and feet started to trample her into the ground, but then a hand lifted her upward and away from the stampede.

'Samarah,' Henry said. 'Let it go.'

'These people are mad,' she screamed. 'I keep telling them that Ellie-Mae is still alive and no one is listening.'

'How can you be so sure?'

'Because she's my friend,' Samarah said, looking at the attempt at compassion on his face. 'And because she's told me.'

Chapter 30—Ethan

Ethan looked at the gap in the wall of the previously impregnable fortress Birmingham, the place the lasers had targeted. An entire section of the ramparts had fallen and amongst the wreckage, synthetic limbs and metal skulls were scattered between chunks of stone.

'We managed to stop most of them,' Billy said. 'Only one of them made it through.'

'It was the Master Unit. Programmed to come after me,' Ethan replied, opening the control box and showing him the printed circuit board.

'Can you get it to work?'

'I'd need a few things,' Ethan replied. 'A USB cable, a computer that talks directly to the mainframe and an internet connection if you have one.'

'Not here, the regime took most of the electrical gear for themselves,' said Billy. 'Maybe in the wastelands, but you'd need a guide. There are hogenas everywhere.'

Ethan started to walk, only for a shock of pain to cause him to stumble. He lifted the bottom of his jeans to find a line of blood on his knee where the synthetic's fingers had gripped into his skin.

'I hope that hurts,' Sophia said, from across the courtyard. 'We've lost ten good people because of you.'

One of the men beside her stared in Ethan's direction, then shook his head and muttered under his breath as he started to move the crushed parts of the synthetics to one side. Others arrived at the scene and Ethan paused, his heart sinking as the body of one of the human defenders was lifted from the remnants of the wall.

'Some of them might not agree, but it was obvious the elite would attack us sooner or later,' Billy said. 'Come on, we need to finish our conversation. Sophia wants to send you on your way.'

'You know that wasn't a full attack, right? When they strike this city properly, you won't be able to stop them,' Ethan replied, but Billy had already gone inside the cabin before he'd finished his sentence.

Ethan ducked below the barbed wire at the entrance and followed Billy into the cabin. Sophia came next and handed Ethan a bandage that he wrapped around his knee.

'You need to leave Birmingham today,' she said, 'If you do, it might just give us enough time.'

'Where should he go?' Billy asked. 'You saw what happened. That synthetic came after him. It almost killed him.'

'But it didn't,' Sophia said. 'The most destructive predator we've ever known came after him and yet he's still alive.'

'He only survived because he knows stuff,' Billy said, looking at Ethan. 'Go on, tell her what you told me.'

Ethan was about to show her the control box but decided not to. The last thing he wanted was to give her a reason to force him to stay in Birmingham. 'I think they're using basic electronics to control the synthetics. I might be able to access their systems.'

For a moment, he thought he'd said too much. But then her expression hardened into annoyance. 'I admire you, Ethan. I admire anyone who stands up to the regime, but you are too dangerous. You turn up here and they follow you. One of them attacks and you fight him off. Now you seem to know all about their technology,' she said, and then directed her attention on Billy. 'Let him leave with the other boy, because right now, I have a city to protect.'

'Don't worry about her,' Billy said, as she left the cabin. 'Sophia is just scared like the rest of us.'

'I get it,' Ethan said. 'I'd be angry too.'

The truth is, he would have loved to have said

174

something back. He'd met too many people of Sophia's age who seemed to blame everyone but themselves for the mess. Who was it that broke the world? Even if it wasn't entirely the older generation's fault, the fact remained that the rise of The Entitlement Party and the collapse of society had happened when they were supposed to be on lookout. Now, apparently, it was up to people of Ethan's generation to put things right.

In the courtyard, figures continued to move in all directions. As quickly as the debris from the attack was taken away, a different cartload of stones and rocks arrived to rebuild the wall. Sophia was standing in the middle, shouting, pointing. She stopped as Ethan walked past.

'Good luck,' she mouthed and went back to her work.

In the streets at the edge of the courtyard, the doors to the shops were closed and the windows boarded to confirm that the city of Birmingham was closing down. The market stalls were being dismantled and it was only as Ethan walked past them that he noticed the variety of items. Clothes, blankets, food and guns, all of which were being loaded into boxes.

'We need to head for the south underpass,' Billy said. 'Hopefully, we'll find you a ride.'

'Who's the other boy I'm supposed to be leaving with?'

Billy smiled. 'You'll see.'

The southern section of the city was in complete contrast to everything he'd seen so far. If the northern wall was set for a battle, the area in front of the southern underpass looked as though it was getting ready for an evacuation.

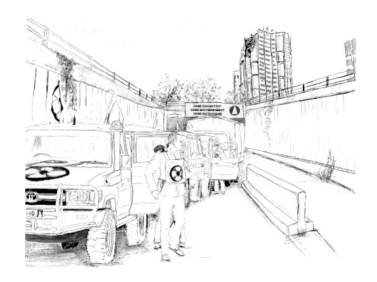

Plastic bins were filled with cabbage leaves and wooden crates of meat were piled on top of one another. Next to the food, a convoy of vehicles stood in a line, their engines firing. Steam poured from their bonnets emblazoned with images of white poppies.

'Since the uprising started, we've been sending supplies to some of the places that are really struggling.'

'Not so much a rogue city anymore?'

'We've been paying protection money to the regime for years,' Billy replied. 'When the regime doubled, then tripled it, we had a rethink and started helping others. It's why Sophia wants you to leave. She knows they'll punish us sooner or later for what we've done and with you here, the regime will hit us even harder.'

'They're coming anyway,' Ethan said. 'They're on their way.'

'Yea, I know. But if we're lucky, they might leave Birmingham until the end and give us time to prepare.'

People rushed about, filling the vehicles with as much as they could carry. Ethan's attention was drawn to one person in particular. Acne-filled face, ginger hair and an annoying, self-satisfied expression, it was someone he'd last seen on the day he'd left The Elimination Centre.

'No way,' Ethan said. 'What's he doing here?'

'You know me,' Josh replied, as he lifted one of the plastic bins onto the back of his car. 'It's how I roll.'

'Together again, eh?' Billy said. 'I'm sure you'll make a great team.'

Ethan couldn't believe it. Of all the people he'd choose to spend time with, Josh would always be bottom of the list. As he looked around to see if there was space in any of the other vehicles, the gates to the underpass opened.

'The steam machines in the underground railway between here and Worcester are filled with the sick and the injured. Once you're through the underpass, you'll have to stay above ground and take your chances on the road,' Billy said, as he lay a final box onto the back of the vehicle. 'Keep a look out for hogenas and whatever happens, don't stop unless you have to.'

'Shall we?' Josh asked, as some of the other vehicles started to move.

Ethan covered his mouth at the choking smell of sulphur and stepped inside the car. Beside him, Josh released his foot from the pressure gauge. He drove the steam car into the underpass beneath the wall and then up towards the road on the other side. They hadn't gone far, when some of the vehicles left the main procession and headed right along a different road.

'They're heading for Chepstow,' Josh confirmed, 'and the towns in the west.'

'Last time I saw you, we were in Clapham,' Ethan said, determined to change the subject. 'Lucius didn't seem happy with something you said.'

'I got a kicking all right,' said Josh. 'Then for punishment, I became a security guard at the penthouse.'

'The penthouse?'

'Yea, the one where they sent that cadet, you remember, Daniel Quartz.'

Ethan recognised the name, but it took a few moments to remember why. 'The guy at the station?' he said, finally, as the memory stirred. 'The one who'd finished his quota of eliminations and was drinking champagne with Lucius.'

'That's the fella,' Josh replied, his mouth biting down on the knuckles of his hand that he'd lifted from the steering wheel. 'They gave him his penthouse all right. He was even given a fancy room with plasma screens and a Jacuzzi. A few days later, they threw him out of the window. They said he wasn't good enough to join the elite.'

'What about his family?' Ethan asked, even though he already knew the answer.

'Yea, them too, and I was given the job of clearing up the bodies,' Josh said. 'Those bastards said it was an accident, but it wasn't. That's when I saw the regime for what they were and I knew I had to get out.'

'And join the uprising?'

'That's right,' Josh replied. 'Anything to stop the elite.'

Ethan was tempted to push it further, but as the steam-powered car continued its journey, he decided that for now, he had no choice but to let it go. Josh appeared to be committed enough in what he'd said. Ethan had even seen him being pulled away by the soldiers at Clapham Junction station when Josh had interrupted Lucius's flow.

Nonetheless, and almost as though he was feeling one of Samarah's premonitions, his instincts screamed that something wasn't right.

Chapter 31—Samarah

The coffin was lowered from the horse-drawn cart and carried into Worcester Cathedral. As the wooden doors of the entrance slammed close, Samarah stood back from the crowd.

'What now?' Henry asked.

Samarah scanned the outside walls of the Cathedral. 'We find a way in.'

Candlelight flickered in the upright windows and as the mourners began to step away from the building, Samarah closed her eyes, her mind reaching upwards, outwards. She could sense the delicate beat of Ellie-Mae's heart to prove that the ibex was still alive. She could feel her warmth, but as Samarah opened her eyes and glanced towards the Cathedral, a realisation dawned.

'Ellie-Mae isn't in there,' she said. 'The coffin is empty.'

Even though she could sense that the ibex was hidden elsewhere, the feeling was too weak for Samarah to place her exact location. She looked behind her to see the crowd begin to disperse. Some of them were heading back towards the bridge. Others made their way along what was left of the high street. The largest group headed right towards the stone wall that enclosed the eastern side of the city.

'This way,' Samarah said.

Their heads bowed, their bodies slumped, the people in front of Samarah and Henry dragged their way through the opening of a gatehouse and into the broken streets behind. Dust and smoke rose from the smashed-up houses and Samarah watched as the last of the people disappeared into various holes in the ground and through the doors of the buildings that remained.

'Someone must know where she is,' Samarah said.

The cold bite of the wind offered the inhabitants of

Worcester the perfect excuse to keep themselves hidden. Nevertheless, Samarah wasn't in the mood to give up and moved from street to street, wrapping her knuckles against the windows, doors and the wooden covers of basements. Occasionally, someone would appear at a half-open window, or rise from one of the holes in the ground. Instead of offering any hope, they'd simply shake their head and usher her away.

'How many more do you want to try?' Henry asked.

'All of them,' Samarah replied. 'Someone will help us to find her.'

'What about the other one, Ethan, can't we concentrate on him?'

Samarah looked away and focussed her annoyance on thumping her hands against another front door. There didn't seem much point in shouting at Henry or trying to explain. How would a chameleon, and one who was capable of changing his characteristics at any moment, fully understand the roles of the Objectors? The inner strength of the ibex, the roar of the lion and the guidance of the wolf. Each of their individual qualities were needed to join as one and create a single collective power.

First though, she needed to find Ellie-Mae.

A door opened on the opposite side of the street and Samarah saw a face at one of the downstairs windows that quickly ducked out of sight.

'It doesn't look good,' Henry said.

'I don't care,' Samarah replied. 'It's contact.'

She crossed the road. The door was partly open and Samarah pushed her way inside. She was about to beckon Henry to follow her when a girl with a pierced lip and dyed pink hair appeared in the hallway.

'Just you,' the girl said, closing the front door behind them. 'My name is Clara. I was at The Elimination Centre at the same time as you.'

'You may not believe this,' said Samarah. 'But Ellie-Mae is still alive. Can you tell me where she is?'

'They will have taken her to the Infirmary. It's where they keep the bodies,' Clara said, as she tightened the buttons on her coat and lowered the hood to cover her face. 'I will take you there.'

'Thank you,' Samarah replied. 'Before we go, can you tell me what's going on? The people of Worcester move around as though they are already dead and from what I heard earlier, they want to cremate Ellie-Mae's body.'

'Too much death has sent them bat-shit crazy,' said Clara. 'The bombings, the sickness and the transmissions from Lucius have convinced them that the world is about to end. For some reason, Ellie-Mae seemed to give them hope.'

Samarah nodded. 'Now I understand. She would have given them strength they didn't know they had.'

In the chill November evening, they headed through the front door and into the road. Samarah glanced over her shoulder to see that Henry was following but keeping a safe distance.

'We'll use the back streets,' Clara said, 'and head for the bridge.'

Their senses alert, they hugged the shadows of the buildings and moved from one hidden alley to the next. The moon had disappeared behind darkened clouds by the time they reached the bridge and Samarah glanced in the direction of the gatehouse.

'Where is everyone?'

'Keeping dry,' Clara replied, as the first of the raindrops started to fall.

The gate was open, and they headed onto the bridge and reached the metal bars of the ladder on one side. It was the route Samarah had followed only hours before when she'd shadowed the procession. With the river on

181

one side of them and the inner-city wall on the other, they made their way towards the row of steep archways that Samarah had seen only hours before. Henry's Merlin 5 was parked at the side of the road and she looked up at the jagged path that led to a red-bricked building.

'Ellie-Mae is in there, isn't she,' Samarah said, remembering the feeling she'd sensed when they'd first arrived in the city.

'Yes, in one of the rooms at the top,' Clara replied. 'They'll be getting her ready for the cremation tomorrow.'

The door on the ground floor of the Infirmary opened and a pair of white-coated figures headed down the zig-zagged path. They were holding a stretcher and midway along the path they stopped, tilted it to one side and threw away the body as though they were getting rid of the trash.

'The death pit,' Clara said. 'Still think she's alive?'

'Yes,' Samarah replied. 'I'm sure of it.'

'Wait here. A friend of mine, Alex, works in the Infirmary.'

Samarah watched her go, Clara's silhouette disappearing into the shadows as she made her way up the path. As the seconds lengthened into minutes, Samarah tried to gain an inkling of her inner identity. In a similar way to the moment in which she'd doubted Henry's reliability, she wondered if Clara was about to betray her, especially when the vision of sharp claws and the sheen of white fur came into view.

However, as the image cleared to reveal the shining green eyes and sleek frame of a panther, Samarah recognised Clara's persona as the embodiment of loyalty.

Finally, there was movement. The door opened at the ground floor entrance and a trio of figures in white uniforms headed along the path towards the death pit.

'I'll get the car,' Henry said, from behind her.

Once they reached the pit, the trio of figures stopped.

Instead of tilting the stretcher, they held their position. A smash of glass diverted Samarah's attention and she looked up to see a chair falling from a broken window at the top of the building.

The figures in white moved away from the death-pit. The stretcher was lying on the ground behind them as they raced towards Samarah and Henry.

A boy in dark glasses came first. He was holding the body of a girl with long-brown hair.

Behind the boy, was a woman with red hair that was too vivid to be natural. Samarah guessed her to be in her late thirties and on her badge was an inscription 'Dr Patterson'.

Clara came next, her green eyes shining in the gloom of evening. 'This is Alex,' she said, as the door to Henry's Merlin 5 opened. 'He's coming with us. He's the one who organised the diversion on the top floor of the Infirmary.'

'If Ellie-Mae is still alive, I need to come with you as well,' the doctor said, handing a face mask to Samarah and Henry. 'She shouldn't be infectious anymore, but just in case.'

Already, there was movement at the entrance to the building. A set of guards was racing down the slope and as Samarah looked to her right, she saw a different group of people standing in a line across the road.

'They don't want her to leave,' Clara said. 'We'll never get her out of Worcester.'

The ground began to tremble, a sound that was drowned out by a roar from above. Samarah looked up to see a white stream rushing across the sky. She looked again towards the road on which the line of people had already broken and started to disperse. Then, with a soul shrivelling howl, the missile descended. Samarah held her breath, clasped her hands, but then a shock of light and a thunderous crash on the other side of the wall confirmed its target elsewhere in the city.

'Come on,' she said, as a bank of black smoke lifted into the sky. 'This is our chance.'

Clara and Alex went into the back of the Merlin 5 with Dr Patterson and the blanket-covered Ellie-Mae was carefully laid on top of their knees.

'Keep your heads down,' Henry said, as he started the engine. 'This might get rough.'

Samarah jumped into the passenger seat. 'Too right. We still need to get through the gatehouse.'

As the car approached the northern sector of the city, a convoy of trucks and cars, all loaded with wooden crates and plastic bins, was waiting at the open gates. The knight was standing in the centre of the road, the royal crest clearly visible on his blue cape as he held back the approaching convoy of steam with a wave of his hand.

Henry swerved the Merlin 5 out of his way and stopped. Samarah was about to duck beneath the dashboard when she recognised the face of a boy who was leaning against the gatehouse. Fair complexion, light brown hair and blue eyes that flicked from side to side.

'Ethan,' she said, opening the door to the Merlin 5 and stepping outside.

'He can't come with us,' Henry said. 'There's no room.'

'Yes, he can. He has to,' Samarah said, opening the boot of the Merlin 5 as Ethan ran towards her. 'Get in.'

'What about me?' asked the ginger-haired boy beside Ethan. 'I need to go with him. They told me to go wherever he goes.'

'Whatever you decide to do,' Samarah said, as the gates to the city began to close. 'Just do it quickly.'

Chapter 32—Ethan

There was barely enough room in the boot of the Merlin 5 for one of them. There was definitely not enough space for two and Ethan's spine contorted, as though his back was about to snap. He was also struggling to breathe and with his face tight against Josh's knees, he knew he couldn't last much longer.

'Stop moving, will you?' Josh said.

'I can't stand it,' Ethan replied, banging his fists against the metal roof. 'I have to get out. Now!'

Within moments, the speed of the car reduced and his panic receded. As it stopped, the boot of the Merlin 5 opened and Ethan levered his way to the edge of the trunk and threw himself onto the ground.

'Sorry,' Samarah said, kneeling beside him. 'We had to keep going. We needed to get as far from Worcester as we could.'

His breath returning, Ethan noticed a man with pin-hole eyes and a jutted jaw walking towards him. Next to the man was a dark-haired boy that Ethan recognised as Alex from the Elimination Centre.

'We can't stop for long,' the man said. 'Otherwise, the hogenas will pick up our scent.'

Ethan looked at the mountains of waste on the opposite side of the road. It was a place in which he could sense an opportunity.

'I've had enough of hiding and running from Lucius. It's time to fight back.' he said, his thoughts returning to his conversation with Billy. 'I need to get hold of a computer that connects to the regime's mainframe. Someone said I could find one here.'

'Why do you need a computer?' Samarah asked.

'To see if I can access their systems,' Ethan replied, lifting the silver control box from his pocket. 'It's how they're programmed. I pulled it from a dead synthetic's skull.'

'Can't you just use a phone?' Samarah asked.

'No,' Ethan replied. 'It needs to be an antique computer, one that speaks to the hard drive directly.'

The dark-haired boy appeared from behind Samarah. 'I might know a place,' Alex said, examining the control box. 'As long as it's still there.'

Samarah moved towards Ethan. 'I always knew this would happen. I always knew you would find your moment, but if you have to stay here, keep safe,' she whispered, hugging him tightly and kissing him on the cheek. 'It's all I ask.'

Ethan's heart began to race at the feel of her body against his and as she moved away, he retained eye contact for as long as he could. She seemed to offer him something back, something real and more than a simple goodbye.

Samarah turned to the man with the jutted jaw. 'How long should we give them, Henry?'

'I'll come back in two days' time,' he replied. 'If you're not here, I'll assume you haven't made it.'

'Two days,' Ethan replied. 'See you then.'

Henry walked to the car. Samarah followed him into the Merlin 5 that skidded back onto the road, its rear lights glowing in the rain that was beginning to fall. Ethan stayed where he was. He didn't want to move in case the moment with Samarah was lost too quickly.

'I don't blame you. She's beautiful and I've always fancied her myself,' Josh said. 'Come on, lover boy, we need to get out of here.'

Ethan allowed himself one more glance at the blurred lights of the Merlin 5, then followed them as they hurried into the mud-soaked streets. With the shrieking, cackling call of hogenas behind them, they quickened their step through a maze of concrete buildings until they reached a cabin that was covered with a plastic tarpaulin.

'We need someone to keep guard,' said Alex.

'I'll do it,' Josh replied. 'It's how I roll.'

Maybe it was because of how quickly Josh had offered to help. Maybe it was because he simply didn't trust him. Whatever the reason, Ethan felt the same sense of foreboding about Josh's allegiance as he'd experienced when they were driving on the outskirts of Birmingham.

'You okay?' Alex asked.

Ethan nodded. 'Yes,' he said. 'Let's do this.'

Alex untied the knots at the side of the plastic sheet. 'If you see anything or if they get too close, make sure you bang on the door.'

'Don't worry,' said Josh. 'I get it.'

Ethan and Alex ducked beneath the steel beam at the top of the entrance and went into the cabin. Inside was a single room, filled with boxes of electrical equipment and in the centre of the cabin was a computer.

Ethan looked around, 'Where did you get all this gear?'

'When they built the wastelands, the regime gave us the materials to make a few places like this. We were supposed to keep watch on the hogenas and measure the toxic fumes,' Alex replied. 'It ended when the hogenas started eating people.'

'You must have been young.'

'About nine when they opened the wastelands,' Alex said, 'and fourteen when I was reassigned to Worcester. I haven't been back since.'

'How long have I got?' Ethan asked, as he searched the equipment until he found the lead he was looking for.

'At best, I'd say about ten minutes before the auxiliary power runs out.'

Ethan lifted the control box from his rucksack and connected the plug at one end of the lead into one of the laptop's USB ports. He clicked open the silver control box and fixed the other end of the lead into the female connector. Immediately, the power LED at the side of the SIM card flickered a faint red.

'We're in business,' Alex said.

'A good start, that's all,' Ethan replied, adjusting the position of the SIM until the power light brightened.

Ethan looked at the computer screen and tried to recall the sequence he'd used when he worked with the robots on the farm. First, he needed to install the operating system. After that, it would be a question of searching for cellular signals. His shoulders slumped at the request for a password.

'It's encrypted,' Ethan said.

'That's no surprise,' said Alex. 'Any ideas?'

He added a few dates, starting with 1/03/2035, the day The Entitlement Party came into power. REJECTED. Names followed, such as leaders of the party. Once again, he received the same response and with each rejection, the level of auxiliary power reduced.

'It might be simpler than you think,' Alex suggested. 'Something a bit closer to home.'

Ethan tried using the name Lucius.

REJECTED.

Then he remembered something he'd once said when they were standing on Clapham Common and he tapped his fingers at the keyboard.

LUCIUSISGOD

'No way,' Alex said.

Ethan shrugged and pressed enter. Nothing happened for a few moments but then the screen flickered and changed from black to green.

'I think he truly believes it, Lucius I mean,' he said, connecting a mouse to the side of the computer and allowing the cursor to hover across a grid of boxes, files and images.

He clicked on one of the files that opened to reveal the face of Lucius. Although most of his features were hidden below the brim of a cowboy hat, his narrow eyes remained visible. Ethan clicked the mouse for a second time and the scene fast-forwarded to the image of the Wild West town and the simulation Lucius used to encourage the cadets to complete their training.

Ethan clicked inside a separate group of files and found a series of Xs that shimmered as they moved across a map. He hovered over the central X. He recognised the construction of its distinct coding as the master unit. Immediately, the image of a synthetic warrior appeared alongside a set of co-ordinates and a scroll of text.

OBJECTOR LOCATED .. ETHAN.. DISTANCE TO TARGET - 20 KILOMETRES.

Ethan moved the mouse, but instead of following his instruction, the cursor remained where it was as though frozen on the screen. He moved it again, hurriedly, but still it wouldn't budge. Instead, the grid of files constricted into the shape of an eye.

'What is it?' Alex asked.

'They know we're watching and they're coming for us.'

The electric cables fizzed and sparked to confirm that a fire code had been sent to burn out the RAM in the CPU processor. Ethan pulled the control box from the USB port on the laptop and stepped back. Just in time. Within moments, the laptop burst into flames. He stood up, opened the control box and removed the SIM.

'Will it still work?' Alex asked.

Ethan placed the SIM in his pocket. 'I hope so.'

His rucksack over his shoulder, he left the cabin.

Josh was waiting outside but instead of keeping guard, he was leaning against the doorframe, the annoying smugness having returned to his face.

'You lose,' he said, lifting a gun from his jacket. 'I said I'd get you back, didn't I? Now, you need to give me the control box.'

Ethan had been right to question Josh's supposed change of allegiance. Determined to try something devious of his own, he tapped his fingers against the SIM in his pocket. He then opened his rucksack, checked inside and decided to roll the dice. 'It's in here,' he said, throwing the rucksack onto the ground.

Josh took the bait, picked it up and lifted the control box from inside. 'See you later, suckers.'

As Josh went one way, Alex set off in the opposite direction. Ethan followed him as they ran through an alley of concrete and into a widened road. He was about to dive behind a wall when something cracked against the side of his skull.

Ethan lifted his hand to his forehead, his eyesight fading and then everything turned to blinding white.

Chapter 33—Samarah

The rain created star-shaped blotches on the windscreen of Henry's Merlin 5. Even though Samarah kept her eyes on the road, her mind was filled with the boy she'd left in the wastelands.

'Keep safe,' she'd said at the time and now, all she could do was wait for the lion cub to grow into maturity as she knew he would.

She also remembered his look of desperation as she let him go. She'd felt a connection too and one that crossed the boundaries of friendship. The intense feeling of attraction wasn't something she'd expected and as Henry drove towards the outskirts of Exeter, she was struggling to think about anything else.

The sight of the city defences drew her attention back to the present. Its reputation as the forgotten city of Exeter was well deserved and instead of high stone walls, its perimeter was protected with a hotchpotch of overturned vehicles. It didn't need much. Other than those with nowhere else to go, no one came to the hurricane belt of the south west anymore.

'This is the place,' Samarah said, as they reached the iron bridge that led to the centre of the city.

'Here?' Henry asked.

Samarah nodded. This was the exact location she'd visualised, an elevated section that rose above the rooftops of the houses below.

'Did you want to stop?'

'No. Keep going,' Samarah replied. 'I'll come back.'

The Merlin 5 crossed the elevated bridge. With a wall on one side and open ground on the other, it was the perfect funnel for the ongoing hurricanes to gather their strength. As Samarah looked to her left, she could see the effects of their impact. The buildings were bleached and colourless, windows were smashed and roof tiles clung precariously from the rafters. The Merlin 5 followed the trail of the storms through the streets until they reached the Cathedral.

Here too, the damage from the storms was obvious.

Part of the roof had fallen into ruin and its walls were covered in mottled algae. Samarah stepped from the Merlin 5. As she approached the building, she smiled at the realisation that the Chapter House was fully intact.

'I suppose you know this person?' Henry asked, as a figure appeared at the doorway.

'Yes. Please ask her anything,' she replied. 'She will help you in any way she can.'

'What about you?'

'I need to head back to the bridge.'

Samarah watched the others help Ellie-Mae from the Merlin 5 and lift her towards the Chapter House. Although she wanted to go with them, now that she was back in Exeter, Samarah wanted to make sure that everything remained in the position she'd envisaged.

Avoiding the pools of stagnant water at the edge of the Cathedral lawn, she headed past the war memorial and back into the ruined streets.

In front of her, the road descended towards the bridge. A few years before, she'd climbed to the top of the multi-story car park that overlooked the road and taken some photos. It was only now that she realised why.

She imagined the synthetic warriors marching across the bridge. She could see them charging up the hill, only to be pushed back by the roar of the lion. This was always going to be Ethan's time to shine his most brilliant light. Ellie-Mae would be there too and although her part was yet to be written, Samarah was convinced that the ibex would play the most significant role of all.

The sound of hurried footsteps broke her concentration. She turned to see Henry running down the slope towards her. 'Samarah,' he said, pointing at the screen of his phone. 'We've received a transmission. It's personal. It's for you and you need to see it.'

As the connection settled, Lucius appeared on the screen of the phone. He was standing in front of The Elimination Centre and the iron gates emblazoned with the image of The Shard.

'Hey, Samarah. I hope you're not missing me too much,' he said. 'I have some news for you.'

The screen altered. Instead of Lucius, it was filled with the image of a military truck with the metallic frame and nozzle of a cannon fixed to each side.

'We've been buying some toys,' Lucius said, as the screen showed the image of a line of armoured trucks, each of which was driven by a synthetic warrior. 'Thirty-nine calibre barrel, these beauties have a range of 30km. We have designed them to be particularly effective in open ground. We've also knocked a few gaps in the iron wall that contains the hogenas to allow them to feast on some of the underlings.

The image moved back to Lucius. 'But you could save them all, Samarah. All you need to do is sacrifice yourself and let me know where you are. You and your dead friend, you know, the one who caught the sickness.'

The image on the phone altered once again. It focussed on an area of wasteland and the remnants of a stone cabin. In amongst the debris, was Ethan's rucksack.

'By the way, we've located your other friend,' Lucius continued. 'One of our spies tracked him down and he perished in the pathetic little hutch he was hiding in. You're on your own now, the last Objector alive and that means I need the rest of the country to see you, briefly, in the moments before your execution. See you soon, Samarah.'

The transmission ended as quickly as it began.

'They didn't show us his body,' Henry said. 'If he's dead, they'd have shown us everything, you know what they're like.'

Samarah didn't answer. The way in which Lucius had spoken with such delight at finding Ethan. The sight of his rucksack and the ruins of the stone cabin was enough to make her believe that it might be true. Her breath shallowed, quickened, and she placed the palm of her hand against her quivering lips.

'I'll leave tonight and see if I can find him,' Henry said. 'You can come with me if you like.'

'No,' she replied, as the speed of her breathing slowed. 'I need to stay with Ellie-Mae.'

Henry placed his phone in his pocket. 'There's something else,' he said. 'She's in a coma, I'm sorry. It doesn't look good.'

Samarah gazed around her. The bridge. The broken windows. The battered buildings. Only moments before, she'd felt the euphoria of everything coming together in the way she'd anticipated. Without Ethan and Ellie-Mae at her side, however, everything seemed lost. Henry placed his arm around her shoulders and together they climbed the hill and headed towards the Cathedral.

Samarah stopped at the entrance of the Chapter House. 'It was my decision to bring her here,' she said. 'If I have to say goodbye, let me do it on my own.'

Inside the Chapter House was a single row of beds, their frames tight against the wall. Ellie-Mae was lying beneath a white sheet in the centre of the room and Samarah knelt at her bedside.

'Don't leave me,' she said, clasping hold of her hand. 'Not now.'

In terms of the uprising, the transmission hadn't changed much. The elite were evil, everyone knew that, and with Lucius directing their forces, they would continue to destroy everyone and everything that stood in their way. Nothing would stop them and if she truly believed it would save the lives of the underlings involved in the uprising, she would do as Lucius asked and sacrifice herself for the sake of others.

Dying didn't scare her, it never had.

Nonetheless, for Samarah, the most frightening thing was the possibility of losing a family for a second time. As she rested her forehead at the edge of the bed, she reached out to Ellie-Mae in an attempt to locate the inner soul of the ibex. She tried again, then a third and fourth time, but something prevented Samarah from reaching her.

Instead, the longer she waited at Ellie-Mae's bedside, the deeper the feeling of loss became. She looked up at the stone figures in the arched alcove that adorned the wall of the Chapter House. A woman sat with an infant in her lap. Beside her, the statue of a bearded man clasped his hands in desperate prayer. Samarah looked towards the stone figure and begged him to find some space in his

196

thoughts for Ellie-Mae.

Still nothing, and it meant the only thing that Samarah had left was her love. She moved closer to the bed and laid her head on Ellie-Mae's lap. She then tightened her grip and wished for her life to be taken away and given to her friend.

Her eyes closed, Samarah appeared to enter a world of darkness. At the edge of the darkness, a circle of light grew wider, brighter and then disappeared as quickly as it arrived.

'Where am I?' a voice whispered.

Samarah remained where she was for a few moments. She didn't dare to move from Ellie-Mae's lap in case it wasn't true, but then she felt the faintest press against her fingers. Slowly, Samarah lifted her head to see that Ellie-Mae was back, her inner spirit having fought back against the fiercest of predators.

PART 5—Gathering Storms

Chapter 34—Ellie-Mae

5th November, 2042

'Are you real?' asked Ellie-Mae. 'Or am I still dreaming?'

The girl at her bedside, smiled. 'I am real, and you are definitely awake.'

Ellie-Mae sat up. 'I know you, don't I?' she said, as a faint recognition grew into something stronger. 'You're Samarah.'

'That's right,' she replied, 'and don't forget to breathe.'

Ellie-Mae leaned forward. She pressed the plastic visor onto her face and took a breath from the cold, steady feed of oxygen. She took another one, deeper this time, and then leaned back against her pillows. Opposite her, a shaft of sunshine glowed through the windows and spread its angel-like wings across the room.

'What is this place? Am I still in Worcester?"

'You've been moved,' Samarah replied. 'You're in Exeter now.'

'What about Maggie? What about the man who'd lost his daughter? Paul, I think he was called. Paul Worthington…' Ellie-Mae stopped speaking, as she remembered the wooden cross that lay on his mattress in Worcester cathedral.

A door at the far side of the room opened. People approached and some of them stood at her bedside. One of them was the doctor that Ellie-Mae knew from the Infirmary in Worcester. A woman of about forty with dyed red hair, she wore a white coat with her name '*Dr Patterson*' inscribed on a metal badge. Clara was beside her.

'You've made it,' the doctor said. 'I can't believe it.'

'Made it?' Ellie-Mae replied.

Samarah moved closer and took hold of her hand. 'You

contracted the sickness and as far as we know, you're the first person to survive. Are you able to tell us what happened?'

'I remember being on the platform at the underground station in Worcester,' Ellie-Mae said. 'We took some of the people to the Infirmary and some to the Cathedral. Paul was Scarlett's father, the girl from The Elimination Centre.'

'Concentrate on the sickness, please,' the doctor said. 'Even the smallest thing might help.'

'It's like you've been injected with a nightmare. It traps you in this place full of demons. There's this intense heat too. It feels like a blowtorch burning your skin and pushing you forward.'

'Pushing you,' Samarah said. 'To where?'

'A way out,' Ellie-Mae said. 'There's a light and it's trying to push you towards it.'

'But you didn't go,' Samarah asked. 'Why not?'

'I don't deserve to be saved. None of us do,' Ellie-Mae said, lowering her gaze. 'Just like the last time, I refused to give in to temptation.'

Dr Patterson rested her hands at the edge of the bed. 'The last time,' she said. 'Are you saying you've experienced this before?'

'I think so,' Ellie-Mae replied. 'When they threw us out of our home in London, they sent us to a specialist town in the east. It killed my mother, our neighbours and so many more.'

'Were you the only one to survive?'

'Others did too,' Ellie-Mae said, suddenly reminded of the bodies in the street and the choking smell of funeral pyres. 'Not many, but some.'

'This sickness you had, is it the same one?'

The room darkened and Ellie-Mae stopped speaking at the sight of a shadowed figure at the end of her bed. Its demonic shape was engulfed in flames and for a moment, Ellie-Mae was back in the world of nightmares.

'Stay with us,' Samarah said. 'Breathe deeply and slowly. Try to stay calm.'

Ellie-Mae felt the squeeze of a hand against hers. Sunlight returned to the room, the radiant glow of angels dissolving the shadowed figure into dust. 'Not the same, but similar,' she said. 'This time it was much worse.'

'An early strain,' Dr Patterson said, turning towards Samarah. 'I knew it. Those bastards have been nurturing this one for years. They probably made it in one of the wastelands.'

'Is that why she survived?' Samarah asked.

'I think so. It's likely the sickness they created has mutated over time, but she must have created enough antibodies to give her a chance,' the doctor said, then turned back to Ellie-Mae. 'Where was this? Can you remember the place and the dates you were there? If so, we can get the word out to those who were with you.'

Ellie-Mae took another deep breath of oxygen and removed the plastic visor from her face. 'I can write down as much as I remember.'

'That would be really helpful. No detail is too small,' Dr Patterson said. 'Can you remember why some of you survived and others didn't?'

'We prayed,' she said.

'I'm sure you did, good for you, but there must have been something else, something practical. Can you remember?'

'After my mother died, we took communion every day.'

'Communion,' Dr Patterson said. 'With pasteurised wine? We already know your blood group is O Negative and maybe there's something in the wine too, something to neutralise the chemicals they're using.'

'You have your science and I have my faith,' Ellie-Mae

said, 'and it was my belief that saved me.'

She lay back down and looked in the opposite direction. She was exhausted and no longer had the strength to talk to the doctor. It was also obvious that she didn't have some of the answers the doctor was searching for.

'Let her be,' Samarah said. 'Come back later, when she's feeling better.'

'One more question,' Dr Patterson said. 'Ellie-Mae. It's possible that you and others like you are carrying the properties for an antiserum that could save hundreds, thousands, maybe even hundreds of thousands. Would you mind if I took some blood?'

Ellie-Mae continued to look in the opposite direction. 'No. That's fine.'

'Thank you,' the doctor answered.

As Dr Patterson walked away, Samarah placed her hands against Ellie-Mae's shoulders. 'You did brilliantly.'

'That's kind of you,' Ellie-Mae replied, 'and thank you for helping me to escape my nightmares.'

'I did what I could,' Samarah said. 'You did the rest.'

'You saved me,' Ellie-Mae said. 'You appeared in my dream at the end and offered your life. It seemed to break the spell and I owe you everything.'

'You owe me nothing,' Samarah replied. 'Now get some sleep.'

Ellie-Mae closed her eyes and instead of a return to darkness, she saw the faint image of the boy with the fair complexion. Opening her eyes, she rolled back to face Samarah.

'Where's Ethan?' Ellie-Mae asked.

'I thought he was gone, but now you've come back to us, I'm not so sure,' Samarah replied. 'It's what you do. It's what you always do, Ellie-Mae, you give people hope.'

Chapter 35—Ethan

Ethan woke to the cackling call of hogenas. His shirt was damp and reeked with the stench of clinging dirt. A thin blanket covered his legs and he sat up, only for the hammer of pain to strike at his temple.

'You're back with us,' Alex said, from the opposite side of the cabin.

'I guess so,' Ethan replied. 'How did I get here?'

'On my shoulder,' Alex replied. 'You were out like a light. A rock, I think, and probably fired from a synthetic. It smacked you on the forehead.'

'Josh?'

'Don't know,' Alex replied. 'Don't care.'

Ethan pushed the blanket to one side and glanced around him. The cabin was enclosed by rutted walls and sparsely furnished. There were a couple of shelves and a steel cabinet next to a spyhole, but not much else. A shuddering thump smacked against the iron door and a cloud of dust fell from the ceiling.

'Should I be worried?' he asked.

'Probably. It won't hold forever,' Alex said, as a second hogena crashed against the door, its rusted hinges buckling at the force of the attack. 'This cabin was one of the first we built. It's a call station made from low grade steel and not as strong as some of the titanium ones.'

'What about the synthetics?' Ethan asked, as he peered through the spyhole.

'No sign,' Alex replied. 'At one point they were behind us, but then we headed into the tunnels and they disappeared.'

'They would have lost the signal. When we went underground,' Ethan said.

His head pounding, he rested his hand against his pocket. The SIM card was still there. 'Remember what he said, the man with the Merlin 5? We need to get back to where he left us. Any ideas?'

'I can find it. No problem.'

Ethan looked around the cabin and started to search the shelves. 'This call station. Does it have a phone? An old one I mean, anything except an iPhone. They were too secure and now I've logged into their system once, I shouldn't need a computer anymore.'

Alex opened the door to the steel cabinet and handed Ethan a couple of devices. 'Nokia any good? Android?'

Ethan took the Android phone, removed its leather casing and clicked open the back. The metal sleeve was damaged and he carefully removed the existing SIM card and exchanged it with the one from his pocket.

'Will it have any power?' he asked, closing the back of the phone.

'Battery, maybe. Wi-Fi, not a chance and anything you do find will be full of bugs.'

'That's what I'm hoping,' Ethan said, glancing through the spyhole to see the menacing eyes of a hogena staring back, its angled torso pointing towards the cabin. 'It might be our only chance of escape.'

'If we're going outside,' Alex said, lifting a golden horn from the steel cabinet. 'We'll need a distraction.'

'What is it?'

'A mating call,' said Alex, buffing its sides with the sleeves of his fleece. 'It attracts the bull and makes the rest of them go a bit weird. We used it sometimes to help us get clear of the cabin.'

'This is getting better and better,' Ethan said, with a grin, as the screen on the phone offered him the image of a keyboard. He winced as he added the login details *LUCIUSISGOD*. 'Doing something irrational is often the only way to cheat fate.'

'So you're hoping for chaos?'

'Kind of,' Ethan replied, 'and a bit of luck.'

The grid on his phone opened in mobile view and allowed him sight of one file at a time. He scrolled through the files until he located the series of Xs that shimmered and hovered over a central X. The master unit. He pressed his thumb onto the screen and slowly increased the pressure until it constricted into the shape of an eye.

'They're on their way,' Ethan said. 'It's time to make some music.'

Alex pressed his lips to the mouthpiece of the golden horn. The sound was muffled at first, but grew into a deep, intermittent hum. Ethan looked through the spyhole and just as Alex predicted, the demeanour of the hogenas altered. The one closest to the hut started to retreat, its legs unsteady. The others did the same and as they moved in the opposite direction, Ethan opened the door to the cabin.

Outside, the lanes were enclosed in a labyrinth of concrete alleyways and Ethan stepped forward, slowly at first, his eyes on the hogenas that continued to withdraw.

'Go!' Alex shouted.

They started to run and hadn't gone far when they reached a junction of passageways. Ethan looked left, then right, his attention grabbed by the sight of the biggest and most ferocious looking hogena he'd ever seen. 'Don't tell me.'

'Yep,' Alex said. 'It's the bull.'

'What now?'

Alex was already on the move and Ethan followed him through the opening of a concrete tunnel. Once they were inside the tunnel, Alex slammed a door behind them and dived into the entrance of a wide metal pipe.

'In case it gets bad and the synthetics don't turn up,' Alex said. 'Just remember to find your way back to here. Metal is one of the only things the hogenas can't eat.'

'Noted,' Ethan replied, and slithered along the pipe until he reached a burrow at the other end that was just about big enough for the both of them. At one side of the concrete burrow was a thin, post-box-sized window and Alex crawled towards it.

'Whatever it is you're planning,' he said. 'Do it quickly.'

The first of the hogenas had already arrived, its razor-sharp teeth chopping and slicing at the concrete above them. As the stench of its breath thickened the air, Ethan lifted the phone from his pocket and pressed his thumb against the eye in the centre of the screen. He pressed it again and a scroll of text moved from left to right.

DISTANCE TO TARGET – 500 METRES

The teeth of the hogenas continued to crunch through the concrete and drips of spittle fell from their mouths as they screamed in expectation of a feed.

'Tell me when,' Ethan said.

'When what?'

'When the synthetics have killed most of the hogenas,' Ethan replied, as he tapped in the command code he'd found.

A series of networks opened at the top of the screen and as the first of the hogenas squealed and thudded onto the roof of the burrow, Ethan searched through the networks until he found the item he was looking for. The symbol of a wooden horse. Ethan was tempted to launch the program straight away, but he knew he had to wait until the system was at its most vulnerable.

'Now,' Alex shouted. 'There's only one of them left alive.'

Ethan clicked on the image of the horse. Nothing happened at first and he clicked again. Still nothing. A thud followed, the bloodied head of a fallen hogena covered the window and blocked out the light. Not for long. A green, mechanical hand appeared and pulled its carcass away. The burrow shook to the rhythm of thumping synthetic fists fighting their way into the burrow. In the chaos of noise and trembling movement, the phone slipped from Ethan's grasp.

'Kill the Objector. Kill the Objector,' an electronic voice cried, as Ethan picked up the phone to see a jagged crack on its screen.

For a moment, he was sure it was broken. As he slid his fingers along its side, however, a twelve-digit code confirmed that the Trojan virus had embedded itself. His fingers trembling, he scrolled back to the central X, clicked on the master unit, and allowed the virus to smash open the doors of its operating system.

Immediately, everything stopped.

The crashing of synthetic fists ceased in an instant as though someone had turned off the power. Ethan checked the phone to make sure that the system was still closed, waited a few moments and then crawled through the metal pipe. Part of the tunnel had been destroyed completely and he climbed through the dust and rubble.

Outside, the air was filled with the sickly smell of burnt flesh. Hogena carcasses were scattered and lying in pools of blood. Beside them, synthetic warriors stood in a series of contorted, broken shapes as though replicating their appearance at the time of the cyber-attack.

'Is that it?' Alex asked. 'Is it over.'

'No,' Ethan replied. 'All I did was introduce a spoofing programme. They'll soon work it out and the synthetics will be up and running in no time.'

He was about to explain the basics of networks and viruses, when a skid of wheels and a puff of dust alerted him to the approach of a vehicle. The sound of the engine and the shake of the ground made him believe it was an armoured truck at first, but then the sloping bonnet of the Merlin 5 came into view.

Chapter 36—Samarah

It was decided that Exeter would become the test centre for the sickness. The first of the cases had already arrived and it was hoped that the set-up would provide an understanding of how to treat the infected. Each of them was isolated into a makeshift cubicle and carefully laid out in a single row inside the Chapter House.

So far, only two of them had been cured of the sickness. For the others, Samarah had witnessed their suffering to the accompaniment of screams and a desperate wish to be released from their nightmares. Struggling to cope with so much despair, she climbed out of her protective suit, removed her face mask and sat amongst the ruins of the Cathedral.

'It's better than you think,' Dr Patterson said, perching against the wall beside her. 'As well as the people who've survived this awful sickness, they've found some others from the specialist town that Ellie-Mae was sent to.'

'What about a cure?'

'An anti-serum seems weeks away,' she replied. 'But we're close to a vaccine.'

A girl with a ponytail of long, brown hair walked towards them. Complete with an armful of towels, she skipped towards the Chapter House like an ibex clipping its feet on a mountain path.

'Shouldn't you be resting?' Dr Patterson asked.

Ellie-Mae turned, offered one of her shy smiles and kept going. Samarah was about to ask the same question as the doctor, but knew there was little point and anyway, as well as her immunity to the infection of the sickness, there were other attributes that the ibex offered.

'She will give them hope,' Samarah said. 'Her warm smile and gentle touch will offer them more than anything they've ever experienced.'

'Yes, you're right,' Doctor Patterson said. 'I can feel it every time she walks into the room.'

The doctor followed Ellie-Mae into the Chapter House and Samarah was about to go with them when she heard someone shout from behind her.

'Samarah. He's made it.'

She looked across the Cathedral lawn to see a boy with a fair complexion, his blue eyes flicking from side to side. She'd heard rumours that Ethan was on his way to Exeter but didn't want to fully believe it until she saw him with her own eyes. As she looked towards him, she allowed herself a few moments for her thoughts to settle and then ran across the lawn and threw her arms around him.

'Hi, Samarah,' Ethan said.

'Lucius told me they'd found you. He said they'd buried you in a concrete grave.'

'Found me, yes,' Ethan replied, with a grin. 'But you know Lucius. Everything else was lies.'

As she let him go, Samarah looked over his shoulder to see the shimmering black bonnet of the Merlin 5 that was parked in the shadow of the war memorial. Henry leaned against the side of the car, his eyes staring at his phone.

'This doesn't look good,' she said.

Since they'd met, Henry's ability to alter his persona had made it difficult for her to read him at times. As she walked towards him, any sense of ambiguity had been replaced with an expression of unmistakable dread.

'We've received a transmission,' he said, holding out his phone. 'Everyone needs to see this. It's bad.'

They gathered in a circle. Samarah, Ethan, Alex and Clara as they linked hands and waited for the circular arrow to turn and release the frozen image in the centre of the screen.

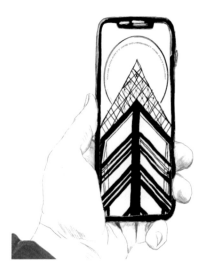

'Hey there,' Lucius said. 'You know I like to keep you updated, right? So this is what's happening. Because the Objector, the immigrant Samarah, hasn't given herself up to me, we have put some measures into action.'

The screen altered from Lucius to display images of armoured vehicles and columns of synthetic warriors pointing their weapons towards city walls.

'Worcester is about to be annihilated and our friends in Birmingham are surrounded,' Lucius continued, as the image altered to the top of a hill on which a separate column of synthetics were marching towards the border between England and Wales.

'There's also a group hiding in the grounds of Chepstow Castle who think there might be an escape route. Well, guess what? There isn't and they will soon know the meaning of what it is to defy me. The end is coming, people, and when it comes, it isn't going to be pretty. See you all, very soon. Or not, maybe.'

Henry lowered his phone. 'It isn't over yet,' he said. 'There's not much we can do to help the people in Worcester or Chepstow, but Birmingham will hold for a few days, I'm sure of it. It should give us enough time to mobilize what is left of the uprising.'

Samarah waited for Ethan or Clara or Alex to say

something. She wondered if any of them would suggest something better than the plan she'd envisioned for some time, but nothing came.

'Fighting isn't the answer,' she said.

Henry looked at the others, then back at Samarah. 'Please don't mention anything about peace talks and treaties. You heard him, it's too late for that. Objection cannot win this battle. Not anymore.'

Samarah took a deep breath and savoured the smell of salt in the air and the hint of a cold breeze that brushed at her neck. The change in wind direction, the increase in its strength was something she'd experienced on many occasions to indicate the onset of a storm.

'We need to tempt them to come here,' she said, looking towards the accumulation of dark clouds in the distance. 'Even if they send their whole army, we need to convince them to come to this place at the precise moment we want them to.'

As she finished her sentence, she broke the linking of hands as Ellie-Mae joined the circle. 'They won't send their whole army. Not when there's a chance they might get infected,' Ellie-Mae said. 'It's why they built the synthetics in the first place. To go into places that are too dangerous for living things to go.'

'She's right,' Alex said. 'They won't send human soldiers, it's too dangerous. They'll send synthetics and armoured vehicles, that's all.'

'And when they find out that Ethan and Ellie-Mae are still alive,' Clara added. 'They'll stop the destruction of the other cities until the Objectors are captured and taken back to The Elimination Centre as trophies of victory.'

Samarah looked at the members of the circle. Each one of them offered the same positive demeanour, except one. 'What is it Henry? What don't you like?'

'It's good to have an idea. It's great to hold hands in a

circle, but everything you've said relies on two major factors,' he said. 'One, that we can tempt them here at the exact moment we want them to arrive and secondly, what the hell are we supposed to do when they get here?'

'I can get them here,' Ethan said, 'and even if every single one of their synthetics does turn up, I should be able to break their circuits. How do you think we survived the wastelands?'

'I've seen it,' Alex said. 'It's amazing.'

Samarah gripped the hands of Ethan and Ellie-Mae beside her as she aimed a smile in Henry's direction.

'Happy now?'

Chapter 37—Ethan

At Samarah's request, in the first instance, it was only the two of them who would show their face to the regime.

'Ellie-Mae will be the biggest surprise of them all,' she told him. 'Imagine how Lucius will feel when he realises she's survived the sickness.'

The sky had darkened in anticipation of the oncoming storm when Samarah told Ethan the time was right to go ahead. As the gusts of wind grew in strength and concentration, Ethan stood beside her on the lawn at Exeter Cathedral. Henry was in front of them, the lens of his phone aimed at Samarah.

'Hey, Lucius, you know how we like to keep you informed,' she said, mimicking the words he'd used in previous transmissions. 'I have someone here who would like to speak to you.'

Henry's phone pointed at Ethan. 'Hi, Lucius,' he said. 'I'm still here and together with an army of underlings, I am waiting for you in the city of Exeter.'

The message was saved and sent to an all-England transmission channel. Once it was on its way, the phone was handed to Ethan and with the SIM card enclosed, he used the passcode *LUCIUSISGOD* and logged into the system.

'Are you sure this will work?' Henry asked, as they headed away from the Cathedral and descended the slope towards the bridge.

'Yes,' Ethan replied, walking beside him. 'Now let me concentrate.'

There were more Xs than before, more files to examine, and it took a while for Ethan to locate the master unit. When he did, the image of the eye emerged through the darkness of his screen, its demonic appearance accentuated by its bloodshot gaze.

'How much time have we got?' Samarah asked.

'As long as it takes them to get here,' Ethan replied, showing her a line of text that scrolled across the screen.

OBJECTOR LOCATED
.. ETHAN ..
DISTANCE TO TARGET
-
50 KILOMETRES.

The barricade that stretched from one side of the bridge to the other was as complete as it could be. Rocks, bricks and sheets of corrugated iron were all piled on top of each other. Although it wasn't as big as the Objectors wanted it to be, they hoped it would be enough to compel the synthetics to stop on the bridge and give Ethan the opportunity to do the rest.

'No pressure,' Samarah said, as they climbed over the barricade, 'but when they get here, I'm expecting big things from you.'

'Get them close. Then it should work.'

'Should' was about as certain as he could be. He had no choice but to attempt a similar technique to the one he'd used in the wastelands and hope it produced the same result. This time, however, he needed to find a deeper hole in their defences, one that replicated the method the Buddhist Monk had used in the attack on The Elimination Centre.

If it worked, Ethan was sure that he'd be able to deactivate the synthetics indefinitely. The only question he had, and the one that swirled in his mind, was whether he would be able to find the programme he needed in time.

'Steam machine approaching,' Henry shouted, as he jumped into the Merlin 5. 'Get in.'

As the Objectors expected, Lucius had chosen the fastest possible method to reach Exeter and instead of marching overground, the synthetics were utilising the railway.

Ethan opened the passenger side door and before he'd even fastened his seatbelt, the car was on the move and speeding away from the barricade. As they raced past the blue sign for The Imperial Hotel, Henry turned the wheel and the Merlin 5 swerved into the station forecourt.

Alex was already waiting on the platform and Ethan stepped out of the car. The rain was falling in clumps, and he peered below the peak of his cap to see a billow of white smoke in the distance that rose from the engine of the XY7 steam machine.

'What can you tell me, Ethan?' Samarah asked.

'Yes,' he said as he checked his phone. 'It's the synthetics all right.'

Once they arrived, he had to make sure he was in plain view of the warriors. That way, the sensors in the individual units would transmit their message to the master unit who would then confirm the sighting with the main, diagnostic controller. In short, it would mean that the synthetic warriors would follow him to the bridge.

Behind the bloated shape of the engine was a row of five steel carriages. If each of them was filled with fifty synthetics, it meant that Ethan would need to immobilise almost ten times the number he'd deactivated in the wastelands.

As the XY7 approached the station, the reduction in speed was accompanied by the high-pitched shriek of brakes clamping on the wheels. Ethan caught a glimpse of the human driver. Red face, his eyes wide, he looked as though he was straining to bring the engine to a halt. The engine was still moving when the driver jumped from the cab.

'They forced me to bring them. They threatened my family if I didn't,' he shouted, as he stumbled on the platform. 'Get away from here as quickly as you can.'

As the steam cleared, the first of the hulking synthetics stepped from one of the steel carriages. Its silver weapon pointing forward, its eyes whirring, the synthetic scanned the platform as though searching for a victim.

'Don't run,' Ethan whispered. 'It will see you.'

Too late. The green eyes of the synthetic focussed on the driver to verify its target had been found. Moments later, it fired its laser from the silver weapon and the driver froze, burst into flames, then fell to the ground.

Instead of moving, the huge frame of the synthetic warrior remained on the platform and towered above the burning body. Its green eyes scanned its surroundings once again, its mechanical head shifting from side to side until it stopped and fixed on its second target.

'Ethan,' Samarah shouted.

He turned to see the others waiting in the car and he climbed into the back. As the Merlin 5 turned on its axis and set off, Ethan glanced through the window to see that a group of at least fifty synthetics were charging towards him, their weapons lofted above their heads.

In response, Henry manoeuvred his way out of the car park and past the signs for The Imperial Hotel, just as a single synthetic warrior appeared from an alleyway on the right. Ethan looked down at his phone that confirmed the lone synthetic was the master unit. Even though his heart was racing and his mouth dry at the sudden weight of expectation on his shoulders, Ethan allowed himself a moment of optimism. At least the first part of the trap had been set.

The Merlin 5 raced towards the barricade and as the car doors opened, Ethan glanced over his shoulder. Behind the Merlin 5, and gaining with every step, was an army of angular synthetics, their shoulders forward, their green eyes glaring as their feet clattered against the tarmac.

When Ethan turned back, he noticed a group of human figures in front of the barricade. He recognised them as people from the city of Exeter who'd helped to build the obstruction across the bridge. Each of them was holding a rifle and aiming it towards the synthetic army.

'You need to leave,' Ethan shouted. 'If they fire their chemical weapon, they'll kill you.'

'We've heard that Lucius is with them,' said one. 'We want to kill him.'

'Lucius?' Ethan asked.

'It's true,' Samarah said, beside him. 'The viper is here. I can sense it.'

Ethan looked again towards the army of synthetics. They'd stopped running and were standing in formation as though awaiting orders. All of them appeared to be three metres high and there was no immediate sign of the smaller figure of Lucius. Then again, Ethan knew that as the great powerful leader he believed himself to be, Lucius would only appear when the battle was won.

'Please take them with you, Alex,' Ethan said. 'Let us finish this in the way we agreed.'

Alex beckoned the others to join him as he climbed over the barricade. It was obvious from their reluctance to move that none of them wanted to go. Once they were on the other side, however, they kept their eyes ahead and followed Alex up the slope in the direction of the Cathedral.

It meant that only two of them remained on the bridge and the more that Ethan thought about it, the more likely

219

it seemed that Lucius would definitely be with the synthetic army. What a moment of triumph it would be for him to stand in front of Samarah, the Immigrant, and Ethan, the Traitor, as he proclaimed his victory.

Samarah dressed into her protective suit, then covered her face with a visor. His hands trembling, Ethan did the same. As he lifted the suit over his shoulders, the wind rattled the iron railings at the side of the bridge.

It was time for the second part of the plan. As the synthetic warriors approached and the thunder roared in the distance, he searched through the programmes on his phone. Now that Lucius was here, Ethan was sure he could use his personal attributes to heighten the damage on the regime's internal database.

His fingers flicked at the screen; his eyes darted through the files until he found the item he was searching for. Ethan looked again, checked its detail for a second time and then realised that for this to work, Ellie-Mae was going to have to place herself in the most incredible danger.

Chapter 38—Ellie-Mae

The sound of a hard wind rattling the windows and the distant echo of thunder confirmed it was time to leave the Chapter House. Ellie-Mae let go of her patient's hand, stood up from the side of the bed and took off her face mask. Once outside, she looked up to see a yellow tinge in the blackened sky and as the cold rain splashed onto her face, she tightened her elbows to her side and squeezed through the oncoming crowd.

'They're here,' a man cried, his eyes wide with terror. 'The synthetics are here.'

She rounded the corner and descended the slope towards the bridge. Alex was leading a group up the hill and he stopped, briefly.

'Good luck,' he said, and then joined the others who were fleeing the scene and running in every direction except for the one that Ellie-Mae was aiming for.

On the far side of the barricade, she could see an army of synthetic warriors standing in perfect formation and each of them aiming their silver weapons at Ellie-Mae. Even so, she forced herself to keep going, to climb the barricade and descend the steps on the other side. Samarah was waiting for her, covered from head to toe in protective clothing.

'You have got the power,' she said, through her visor. 'Go, girl!'

Ethan stood beside Samarah, his gasmask removed.

'Make him mad, Ellie-Mae,' he said. 'I need him to shout.'

'I'll try.'

As she stepped forward, the column of synthetics split into a series of rows. The first row remained in position, a hundred metres from the barricade. Metallic boots pounded the tarmac, the ground trembling from the weight of their feet, as a second row lined up behind the first. A third row formed, then a fourth, each of them glaring across the shoulder of the warrior in front.

Ellie-Mae didn't break her stride and as the rain fell like golf balls and soaked her hair, her face and her shoulders, she drove herself into the swirling wind. A gap opened in the first row of synthetic warriors to allow a human figure in a H.U.D. to manoeuvre his way through. As he lowered his H.U.D, his dark eyes became visible, along with the scar that ran down his cheek.

'Well, well, well,' Lucius said. 'They told me you were dead. Those liars told me you'd been infected and we all know that no one survives the sickness, don't we?'

Ellie-Mae stopped and focussed on the top of his forehead. No matter what happened, there was no way she was going to offer him even a semblance of fear. Instead, she wanted to show him that she was different to the terrified girl he'd visited in the night with his threats and inappropriate touch.

She wanted him to know that she would no longer be affected with the name, Judas, the shameful label he'd given her. Most of all, she was determined to repay the trust that Samarah had placed in her.

'Every city is surrounded,' Lucius said, as he drew his finger across his throat. 'Every opportunity destroyed, and every hope has been extinguished. What do you say to that, Ellie-Mae?'

'We accept your surrender,' she said.

Lucius paused for a moment, then leaned back and screamed his laughter into the pouring rain. He placed the H.U.D. back on his head and stared through the visor. 'In which case,' he said, in an electronic voice. 'You can be the first to die.'

With a clatter of mechanical feet, the first row of synthetics moved towards her. Ellie-Mae stood firm. As a dark mass poured from their opened mouths and engulfed her within seconds, she knew that she could rely on something far stronger than Lucius could ever imagine or recognise.

Her faith.

'Strengthen the weak hands and make firm the feeble knees,' she whispered. 'Be strong, do not fear, because here is your God.'

As she spoke the words of Isaiah, Chapter 35, the storm deepened and in the strengthening wind, it opened its apocalyptic curtains. She closed her eyes and allowed the images of 2035 to replay in her mind: the destruction of the churches, the desecration of places of worship and the ridicule of her father and anyone else who continued to walk in the path of religious scripture.

With each thought, the storm grew in strength and Ellie-Mae opened her eyes to see the lightning flash, its electric bolts cutting jagged shapes through the blackened sky. A rumble of thunder roared its anger and as the ground trembled, Ellie-Mae clasped the crucifixes around her neck and planted her feet.

The dark mass whirled around her, above her and in every direction as though searching for a weakness. But as the wind and the rain increased in intensity, the concentration of manmade chemicals dissipated in the overpowering elements of nature.

The synthetics opened their mouths for a second time, the dark mass gathering into demonic shapes that lifted and sharpened their outline into three-headed monsters. As the winged assassins swooped towards Ellie-Mae, a funnel of wind deflected their path and softened their screaming voices into whispers.

'You cannot harm me,' she said, as the dark mass evaporated once again. 'I am immune to everything you own and everything you think you own.'

'Take her,' shouted Lucius, his H.U.D. removed. 'Bring her to me. Now!'

A synthetic hand grabbed her arm, its metal fingers digging into her skin. She tried to escape, but the synthetic was too strong and for the first time since she'd climbed the barricade, the power of her faith wavered.

'Please, Ethan. Help me,' she cried. 'Samarah, stop them, I beg you!'

The synthetic warrior dragged Ellie-Mae towards the rest of its army, her knees scraping against the tarmac surface as she was hauled along the road. With every step of its mechanical feet and with every moment that passed, she could hear Lucius's voice shouting through the rain.

'Destroy the barricade, find the Objectors and kill every single person in this city.'

As the rage in his voice echoed across the bridge, she felt the grip on her arm loosen. This was it. Ellie-Mae knew she wouldn't get another chance and she clasped hold of its metal fingers and ripped them from her arm. She then kicked at its thighs with so much force, she fell back onto the ground.

The synthetic lunged towards Ellie-Mae and she scrambled across the rain-soaked tarmac in a desperate attempt to get out of its reach. When she looked again, she realised that something had changed. The warrior had stopped moving. Its shoulders were drooping forward and the previous glow in its eyes had extinguished.

Nothing happened at first. Nothing moved, but then its eyes offered a hint of light and its huge frame lifted to standing once again. Convinced the synthetic had come back to life, Ellie-Mae ran towards the barricade as quickly as she could. When she turned back, instead of chasing after her, the synthetic warrior had moved towards Lucius and was pointing its weapon at his chest.

'Do what I say,' Lucius screamed. 'Why are you not

listening to me?'

The synthetic ignored his desperate plea and retained its position with the tip of its silver weapon jabbing into Lucius and pushing him back. As the once self-proclaimed master of everything fell onto the wet tarmac, a different pair of figures came into view. Ethan and Samarah. Both had removed their visors and held them to their sides like astronauts who'd returned from a mission into space.

'Go on then,' said Samarah. 'Finish it.'

The other two remained behind Ellie-Mae as she strode towards Lucius, her shoulders back and her head lifted in triumph. 'For the second time,' she said. 'We accept your surrender.'

Chapter 39—Samarah

In the days that followed, the people of Exeter emerged from their different corners of the city to visit the bridge and the location of victory against the regime. Many of them spoke of exaggerated stories about those who took part.

'The angel, who rose from the dead and summoned the storm.'

'The blue-eyed boy with the powers to tame the synthetic army.'

Then of course, came the anecdotes about the *'great commander, the appointed leader of the uprising who'd seen into the future.'* Samarah had too much going on to even think about it. The newly named storm *'Ellie-Mae'* had littered the city with debris and Samarah placed herself in charge of tidying the streets.

'What about the barricade?' Ethan asked her.

'I think we should leave it,' she said. 'As a reminder of what we did.'

'Maybe we should make a gap in the middle,' Henry suggested. 'Just enough space to allow passage across the bridge.'

Samarah nodded, reluctantly. To the others, it might just seem like a pile of rubble but to her, its symbol of defiance was far more important than any words or stories. Even so, Henry was right. As well as the barricade, the army of synthetic warriors remained in the place they'd stood in the midst of the storm.

For three days, all of them stood in their rows of formation. Each of them held their silver weapons in statuesque poses, as though frozen in time and ready for a battle that was interrupted by the Objectors. All of them, that is, except one. It was standing in the second row and even though its arms and shoulders drooped, its eyes continued to glow a faint green.

'Is it safe?' Samarah asked, as she headed across the

bridge.

'As long as we keep Lucius locked up,' Ethan replied. 'I found a proper way into their network and when Ellie-Mae made him angry, I was able to use their voice recognition software to shut the program down. Except for the unique template in his voice, nothing else can fix it.'

There wasn't the opportunity for Samarah to ask any more questions. Ethan was the only person who knew anything about their technology and anyway, the time had come for Samarah and the others to head for the station.

Since the events on the bridge, vaccines for the sickness had been administered to everyone living in Exeter. In the following days, others arrived from different parts of the country and as their numbers increased, an isolation centre was set up to the north of the city.

The first group to have passed their period of quarantine was due to arrive at the station at any moment. Although she dreaded the thought, Samarah knew she had to be there when they arrived, especially as there'd been rumours of a select group on board who'd been chosen because of who they were.

She stood on the platform and tried to ignore the irony of how she'd been standing in a similar place only days before when the synthetics arrived.

'What do you think. Samarah?' Ethan asked. 'Can you tell us who is coming?'

She closed her eyes and concentrated on the rhythm of the wheels and sway of the carriages. She was even able to move within its steel walls and visualise the shapes of those inside.

'All I can tell you,' she replied. 'Is that they're human spirits, not synthetic.'

'That's good,' Ethan said. 'That's really good.'

227

She could tell he hadn't really listened to her reply and instead, Samarah could feel that his heart was filled with immeasurable hope. She looked at the others too. Ellie-Mae, Alex and Clara. In the last few hours, she'd heard their hushed conversations. Hopeful, nervous discussions about who the selected people might be.

They'd agreed it would be their loved ones as reward for what they'd done. Although she was happy for them, she also knew that other than Ethan and Ellie-Mae, she had no family and that no one would be coming for her. The steam machine stopped. The carriage doors opened and figures stepped down onto the platform.

A boy of about ten leapt in Ethan's direction and grabbed at his waist. 'You're my hero,' he said, then ran into the waiting crowd.

'You have a fan,' Samarah said, smiling.

Except for the boy, the rest of them were older with dispassionate expressions and as she looked at her friends on the platform, she realised that none of the passengers were who they were hoping to see.

'Who's in charge here?' a dark-haired woman demanded.

'Hi Sophia,' Ethan replied. 'How are the people in Birmingham?'

'Scared,' she replied. 'We need to act quickly. If we don't, the regime will regroup, populate the armoured trucks with human soldiers and fight their way into our cities.'

Behind Ethan, a different group were locked in conversation with Henry. 'The synthetic warriors are disabled, and the elite are retreating,' one of them said. 'This is our chance to destroy The Entitlement Party and everything they stand for.'

A woman with grey hair that Samarah recognised as someone she'd spoken to in Worcester was talking to

Ellie-Mae. 'We need to restore the monarchy,' Maggie said. 'The faithful city of Worcester demands it.'

'Let's get away from the station,' Henry said, 'we can discuss this in The Imperial Hotel.'

Samarah bowed her head and started the climb through the narrow alley back towards the road. 'Who are these people?' she asked. 'The way they're talking, they sound like Lucius and the elite.'

'City leaders, politicians and others who think they're important enough to have a say,' Henry replied.

'What about the people who matter? The families of Ethan, Ellie-Mae and the rest? What about them?'

'Another time,' Henry said, as he reached the road at the top of the hill, 'for now, we need to get them all inside the hotel and off the streets.'

The passengers from the train spilled out of the alley like ants and Samarah beckoned them to follow her trail across the road. Alex and Clara stood at the entrance to The Imperial Hotel and encouraged the crowd to head through the door.

'This isn't why we did this,' Ethan said. 'Why don't they understand?'

His words were lost as a man in a blue jacket bumped his shoulder into Samarah as he scurried past. She stepped out of his way. There was more than enough arguing and jostling for position already. The man in the blue jacket climbed onto a chair at the side of the room.

'We must form a new government today,' he said. 'We need people who can take control of the situation before it's too late.'

'I can't stand it. I'm getting out of here,' said Ethan. 'It was us who stood on the bridge. Us. Not a load of old people like them.'

'Where are the others?' Samarah asked, but as she looked around her, she realised that Ellie-Mae and everyone who meant anything to her were gone. Instead, the room was filled with raised voices repeating rhetorical phrases and cries of revenge.

Then, in a single moment, the shouting and hustling for position stopped.

The basement door opened with a crash of metal and stone. His eyes wide, his mouth wide open, the man in the blue jacket pointed towards a three-metre-high angular figure that appeared beneath the archway. Green uniform, piercing eyes, the synthetic warrior strode towards the centre of the room.

'Get down!' Samarah shouted.

The walls in the foyer shuddered at the force of the explosion, a reverberating pulse that shattered glass and hurled bodies. The sound of screams pierced into her soul and with gusts of heat burning her face, Samarah crawled past the man whose blue jacket was covered with blood. There were others too, charred, bloodied bodies lying on top of one another.

One of them moved, a woman with trembling hands whose eyes were filled with horror as she gazed towards the centre of the room. Samarah turned to look at the vision that had created such quivering fear. A macabre image of a headless synthetic. Its body was covered in flames and a swirl of grey smoke poured from its open neck.

'Samarah,' a voice said. 'Come with me.'

She wiped the ash from her face and allowed herself to be guided through the blood-soaked floor of the foyer. Once outside, Samarah followed a limping Henry and towards the steps that led to the basement at the back of the hotel.

'We've been betrayed,' he said, holding a set of broken chains. 'Lucius has gone.'

Chapter 40—Ethan

He'd crossed the bridge and was climbing the slope on his way back to the Cathedral when it happened. The all too familiar tremor beneath his feet, the brightness in the sky and the moment that time appeared to stop, retreat, then fast forward into chaos.

A cloud of black smoke spiralled above The Imperial Hotel to signal the location of the explosion. Ethan ran through the gap in the barricade, then stopped. He looked at the smoke, then back at the break in formation of synthetics that stood, immobilized on the bridge and noticed that one of them was missing.

It didn't take him long to realise which one. It was the synthetic that previously stood in the second row, with its drooping arms and eyes that glowed a faint green. It was the one he'd told the others not to worry about.

When he reached the hotel, his worst fears were confirmed. He'd witnessed enough explosions to know that this was a big one and when he saw the number of bodies being lifted through the main entrance, his thoughts turned to Samarah.

'Where is she?' he asked, as a feeling of dread intensified. 'Is she all right?'

'Alive,' Alex said, walking towards him, 'but not very happy.'

He soon found out the reason why. 'Do you recognise this?' Samarah asked, handing him a black leather case. 'Lucius left it behind for you.'

Ethan tapped his hand against the back of his jeans, but of course it was gone. 'The pickpocket,' he said, remembering the moment when the boy embraced him at the station. 'He must have stolen my phone.'

'No,' she said, sarcastically. 'You think?'

'What happened to the synthetic on the bridge?' Ethan

replied. 'The one that seemed alive.'

'It came here,' Alex said. 'The synthetic warrior was the bomb.'

Ethan looked at the smoking ruins of The Imperial Hotel and then towards the opened door that led to the basement. 'Where's Lucius? He must have activated the synthetic. No-one else could have done it.'

'Someone helped him escape,' Samarah said. 'Now we need to find out where he's gone.'

Desperate to redeem himself, Ethan opened the leather case that Samarah had given him. The phone was inside and he pressed the power button. Within seconds, the screen burst into life and a symbol appeared to announce the receipt of a message. Ethan clicked the symbol and a row of figures scrolled across the screen.

05:59:59, 05:59:58, 05:59:57…

'What is it?' Samarah asked.

The message faded, its symbol replaced with the same triumphant music Ethan had heard on many occasions. The ringtone of *The Ride of the Valkyries*.

'Perfect timing, Ethan, I knew I could rely on you,' Lucius said. 'The countdown has begun.'

'To what? What does it mean?'

'Ah, I have your attention, do I?' Lucius replied. 'Our headless friend in the hotel is the only one I could get to move, but it matters not. There are a few more like him placed at various locations around the country. Each one is pre-set with an emergency circuit that has now been activated and due to detonate at zero. Unlike the exploding little fellow we used in Exeter, some of the synthetics are filled with a nuclear device that will destroy everything within five kilometres.'

Ethan thought about the images he'd seen in the previous transmissions and the pictures of synthetics on the outskirts of Worcester, Birmingham and Chepstow.

There must have been hundreds, maybe thousands. Then of course, there were the ones that stood in rows on the bridge in Exeter.

'If anyone attempts to flee the cities, our soldiers will hunt them down in our armoured trucks,' Lucius said. 'Oh, and there's something else. If you try to interfere with the network or change the system in any way, the closing sequence will initiate immediately and the synthetics will detonate within minutes.'

'Why are you telling me this? Is there something you want me to do?'

'A bargain, eh?' Lucius said. 'Let's say you drive back to London, the three of you, the Objectors, and deliver the vaccine to the virus in person. That would be a start, wouldn't it? I might even think about stopping the mass detonations.'

The screen of the phone darkened and the countdown returned *05:58:02, 05:58:01…*

'He can't have gone far,' Samarah said. 'Maybe we can catch him up.'

'It's possible, but if you think about it, he wouldn't have programmed the synthetic bomb to explode until he was well on his way to London,' said Henry, lifting his keys from his pocket. 'Take my car, do whatever he tells you and buy us as much time as you can.'

Samarah snatched the keys to the Merlin 5. 'If Ethan is talking to captain viper, I'll drive and yes, I've spent enough time in the passenger seat to know how to drive this thing.'

'What will you do, Henry?' Ethan asked. 'You can't leave, otherwise the armoured trucks will come after you.'

'And don't forget the hogenas,' Samarah added. 'Lucius has set them free.'

'We'll send the word and tell the others to stay inside the city walls,' he replied. 'Then we'll do what we've always done in situations like this and dig for our lives.'

A cloud of smoke continued to drift from the entrance to the hotel. The survivors were being attended to by whoever was closest.

'I should stay here,' Ellie-Mae said. 'I should help to look after them.'

'I'm sorry, but you heard him,' Ethan replied. 'When he said he wanted delivery of the vaccine in person, I think he meant you.'

Henry hugged Ethan and then each of them in turn. 'Be careful,' he said. 'You three are more important than ever, especially now.'

'How do you mean?' Ethan asked.

Henry turned and looked towards the smoke that billowed into the sky. 'The hotel was full of people the uprising would have followed,' he said. 'Most of them are either dead or dying and if you defeat Lucius in his own domain, you will become the nation's true leaders in everyone's eyes.'

'Maybe they'll shower us with flowers and give us the keys to the kingdom,' Samarah said, sarcastically. 'I'll believe it when I see it.'

'If that's what it takes,' Henry said. 'I'll do it myself.'

The doors to the Merlin 5 had barely closed when the sound of triumphant music returned. Ethan lifted the phone from his pocket and placed it in the holder on the dashboard.

'The countdown goes on,' Lucius said. 'Hurry, hurry, hurry.'

'*05:53:38, 05:53:37…*'

Once they'd left the city of Exeter, a snarl of tangled cars forced Samarah to veer off the road towards a sloped embankment on one side. As she swerved the Merlin 5 back onto the tarmac, the phone was thrown to the floor, and the battery fell from within. Ethan started to put the pieces of the phone back together, only for Samarah to place her hand on his.

'Leave it,' she said. 'That's enough of Lucius for now, don't you think?'

The journey continued. Every now and then, Ethan would glance in Samarah's direction and they'd exchange a smile but nothing more.

'If the explosions happen,' Ellie-Mae said from the back seat. 'How many will survive?'

'Apart from Exeter, most of the synthetics are outside the walls,' Samarah answered. 'If the people in the cities dig deep enough, then wait for the nuclear clouds to disperse, they might be all right.'

Ethan was tempted to do something more and stop the detonations. Even though Lucius had warned him of the consequences of breaking the sequence, he was sure he could find the right code and spoof the system. He looked at the phone on the floor. All he'd need was a few minutes.

'Don't even think about it,' Samarah said. 'There will be one more chance for us, I can feel it.'

It had been a while since she'd appeared to read his mind. Now that he knew that Samarah was in there, he pushed any thoughts of interfering with networks to one side and repeated a single word instead.

Sorry.

It's OK, Ethan, and when this is over, we can talk about other things too.'

He smiled and looked out of the window. After what happened in Exeter, and the way he'd allowed the young boy to steal his phone, the mention of '*other things too'* was more than he could have hoped for.

She was beautiful in a way he'd never experienced, both inside and out and after what she'd implied, he started to believe that maybe there was a chance for them after all. For the second time since the journey began, Samarah

235

placed her hand on top of his.

A battered sign at the side of the road confirmed they were approaching the city of London. Not that they needed a map. The tumbled buildings and shattered windows of the underling suburbs were replaced with coils of barbed wire fixed to the top of marble walls and signs of '*HOME OF THE ELITE. KEEP OUT*'.

As they drove through Hyde Park and passed the grandeur of the '*Entitlement Palace*', Ethan clipped the battery into the phone and checked the screen.

'*02:22:23, 02:22:22…*'

Samarah slowed the speed of the Merlin 5 as they approached Vauxhall Bridge. In front of them, clouds of mist rose from beyond the wall that enclosed the protected zone of Clapham, Vauxhall, Brixton, Balham and Wandsworth.

'Does this feel like a trap to you?' Ethan asked, as the Merlin 5 stopped at the side of the road.

'I think this whole thing is a trap,' Samarah replied. 'Have you got any messages from Lucius?'

'Just the countdown,' he said.

'*02:12:09, 02:12:.08…*'

The portcullis at the end of Vauxhall Bridge was raised and Ethan walked through the gatehouse. The last time he was within the inner sanctum of the elite, the streets were filled with streamers and flags that honoured the Commandant and The Entitlement Party. Instead of the opulent, bustling city he was expecting, the streets were deserted.

Windows were covered with sheets of metal nailed to the walls. Items of clothing were strewn across the roads and car doors left open as though the inhabitants had moved on in a frantic hurry. It was almost as though London had lost its former splendour and descended into one of the oppressed towns in the north.

As the Objectors continued their approach to The Elimination Centre, a glimpse of the setting sun created ominous shadows that crept across the road. Ethan tensed his body, certain that a group of soldiers would appear at any moment.

Nothing came and instead, they soon reached the wall that encircled the bunkers at Clapham Common. The sliding gate was pushed to one side and the three of them headed onto the path. Still nothing. Nothing except for the lingering mist and the mounds of earth to signify the position of the bunkers. The sound of triumphant music broke the silence and Ethan's phone flashed with the image of Lucius.

'Head for the main hall inside The Elimination Centre,' he said. 'We've been waiting for you.'

Ethan pushed through the ironclad door at the top of the steps and descended into the bunker. The red haze of emergency lighting offered him a glimpse of the main hall and the steel columns that rose from floor to ceiling in each of the corners. Beside him, Samarah gasped and Ethan looked at the floor to see a wave of little black creatures scampering towards her, accompanied by the crackle of footsteps and the hiss of their voices.

'Get off me,' Samarah shouted, as they climbed onto her legs, her chest and her face.

She turned and ran through the exit of The Elimination Centre. When Ethan reached her, she was desperately brushing the creatures from her clothes.

'Those things,' he said. 'What are they?'

'Blood sucking insects, ' Samarah replied. 'My worst nightmare.'

'But they only came after you,' Ellie-Mae added.

Ethan looked at the creatures, then back at Ellie-Mae as he realised the awful truth. 'Genetically modified, then programmed in a lab,' he said. 'To attack Samarah.'

'Didn't you have them in your cell too? Is that what you're trying to tell me?' Samarah asked.

'No,' Ethan replied. 'It wouldn't have bothered me like it bothered you. Instead, they dragged me onto the common at different times of the day and night. Having to work in the freezing cold and digging into frozen ground was a reminder of my childhood. I used to do it on the farm and I hated it with a passion.'

'What about you, Ellie-Mae?' Samarah asked. 'Which nightmare did Lucius inflict on you?'

'Television screens and cameras in my cell. It meant I never had a moment's peace,' she replied, 'It was so bad, I wished I would die.'

The ringtone sounded to interrupt their conversation, *The Ride of the Valkyries* blasting from the phone.

'Go to bunker number five,' Lucius said. 'Ethan knows where it is.'

238

He was about to set off when a leaflet drifted towards him on the wind.

On one side, was an image of resistance he'd not seen before.

Ethan picked it up and turned it over to find a phrase in jagged handwriting. *'Never stop objecting. The people of England are behind you.'*

Ellie-Mae took the leaflet from him and looked towards a figure who was standing on the far side of the common. Even from a distance of fifty metres, Ethan recognised her face from his time at The Elimination Centre.

'It's Scarlett, the girl who said yes to Lucius,' Ellie-Mae said, separating from the others and heading across the common. 'She wants to speak to us.'

Chapter 41—Ellie-Mae

When Ellie-Mae reached her, Scarlett was standing beneath a clump of trees. Tattered clothes fell from her shoulders and her previously perfect auburn hair was scraped back behind her ears.

'I saw your message on the leaflet,' Ellie-Mae said. 'What can I do?'

'The southern uprising has started. The army is on their way and I thought it might help you to know what's happening,' Scarlett replied, her swollen face covered in cuts and bruises. 'Lucius is terrified of what they might do.'

'Shut up, Scarlett,' a voice said, from behind them both. 'You're in enough trouble already.'

Ellie-Mae turned to see a ginger-haired boy walking towards her. He was aiming a revolver at Scarlett. In response, she unzipped her fleece and pointed at the small mound on her belly.

'If you shoot me, Josh,' she said, 'Lucius's baby dies too.'

'You always have an answer for everything, Scarlett, but not for much longer,' he said, then adjusted his aim and pointed the gun at Ellie-Mae. 'You can come with me. Lucius wants to talk to you.'

She followed Josh towards the centre of Clapham Common. Samarah and Ethan were already there, surrounded by a group of soldiers. Behind them, a shallow wall overlooked a deep, circular cavern that was surrounded by a border of concrete.

'Bunker number five,' Josh said. 'The final reckoning for everyone you know.'

'Everyone?' Ellie-Mae asked. 'How can you be so sure?'

'Didn't you know, Ellie-Mae? Didn't you know, Ethan? Your families are in Chepstow with the rest of the lambs about to be slaughtered.'

Ellie-Mae took a sharp intake of breath and lifted her hands to her mouth.

'Thought that might shut you up,' Josh said.

From the depths of the cavern, a metal structure jolted, creaked then started to rise. At the top of the structure was a platform on which Lucius stood, his arms folded and his stare aimed at Ellie-Mae. Behind the platform were the peaks of four gargantuan missiles and each of them inscribed in tall, black lettering.

Birmingham
Chepstow
Worcester
Exeter

A metal gangway lifted, then unfolded and Lucius walked from the platform onto the common.

'Here we are, how nice,' he said. 'Together again, like one big happy family.'

Ellie-Mae tried to step out of his way, only for the tip of Josh's gun to nudge her in the back. Lucius cupped his hand, placed it against his ear and lifted his head to the sky.

'What's that, Ellie-Mae,' he said, mockingly. 'Could it be another storm? I don't think so, do you? Not this time.' He then fixed his attention on Ethan. 'What about you? Still think you can play with my networks?'

'The countdown is almost over,' Samarah said. 'You told us we should come here and we have. What now?'

'Ah yes, Samarah as well,' he said. 'Perfect. Move them into position.'

Ellie-Mae stumbled as a hand shoved her in the back. Ethan and Samarah were manoeuvred beside her as the three of them stood in front of the cavernous bunker.

'Say cheese,' Lucius said, as he grabbed a phone from his pocket and pointed the lens at the three Objectors.

He then turned the phone and showed them the photograph. 'History is about facts and the stories are always created by the victors,' he said. 'In the future, people will see this image of the so-called Objectors standing in front of our killer warheads, moments before they were sent on their way to the cities that once supported the uprising. Anyone who survives the massacre, will realise the truth of how the Traitor, the Judas and the Immigrant turned their backs on the underlings and joined the elite.'

Ellie-Mae looked at Samarah, then Ethan, their expressions betraying the same feelings of devastation as she herself was experiencing. Lucius had tricked them all. The synthetic bombs surrounded the cities. The armoured trucks and hogenas roamed the open ground and the rest of the underlings gathered in the places the warheads were programmed to strike.

She turned towards Lucius, hoping to make him understand the horror of what he was about to do. 'I am no Judas,' she said, 'and in the eyes of God, you will be accountable for your actions.'

'Still spouting your religious garbage are you, Ellie-Mae?' Lucius said, and turned towards Josh. 'Bring her with us into the bunkers. As well as providing a vaccine to the sickness, I could do with a plaything.'

'What about the other two?' Josh asked.

'Shoot them,' Lucius said. 'I have no use for either of them now.'

His expression hardening, Josh lifted his revolver and pointed its nozzle at Samarah, then Ethan, then back towards Samarah. 'Ladies first,' he said. 'It's how I roll.'

Ellie-Mae leapt in front of the gun. 'You mean nothing to any of them, can't you see?' she said. 'Do the right thing,

Josh, and you will be forgiven.'

He placed the revolver into its holster and lifted a black box from inside his coat. 'I don't need forgiveness, and if I mean nothing to them, why have I been given control of the detonator?' he said. 'Check your phone, Ethan, and tell me what it says.'

'42:48.'

Josh twisted a dial on the front of the box. 'And now?'

'39:21,' Ethan replied.

'And again.'

'31:15. Just over thirty minutes.'

'You see, Ellie-Mae,' Josh said. 'I'm more important than you think.'

One of the soldiers gasped. The others who were standing beside Samarah and Ethan stepped away, lowered their weapons and started to retreat from the circular cavern.

'Why are underlings so stupid?' Lucius said, his eyes narrowing as he stared at Josh.

He then turned and ran, his pace increasing in tandem with the soldiers who were sprinting towards The Elimination Centre.

'You've broken the sequence too early,' Ethan said, as a crash echoed from inside the cavern of missiles, followed by a cloud of smoke. 'This place is gonna' blow.'

'Keep back,' Josh said, lifting the gun from its holster. 'Or I'll shoot, I will, don't think I won't.'

He stepped towards the cavern, but as the ground shook, he lost his balance and dropped the revolver. As it fell to the ground, Ellie-Mae kicked the gun in Samarah's direction.

'Come with us, Josh,' Ethan said. 'You still have time.'

'No,' he said, as he stumbled across the metal gangway. 'I can fix this, and then I'll become one of the elite.'

The ground shook once again as black, acrid smoke

243

rose from within the cavern and swirled around the tips of the missiles.

'We need to get out of here,' Ethan said. 'Right now.'

Ellie-Mae looked towards a girl who was standing and looking in her direction. 'Scarlett,' she said. 'She mentioned something about a southern uprising. I think she can help us.'

'We need to get to the bridge,' Samarah said. 'Before they lock us in.'

'I'll be quick,' Ellie-Mae replied.

Even though her head was spinning and her thoughts were telling her it was the most dangerous thing she'd ever done, Ellie-Mae ran in the opposite direction to Ethan and Samarah.

'Let me die on my own,' Scarlett said, as Ellie-Mae reached the clump of trees at the edge of Clapham Common. 'It's what I deserve.'

'It isn't your fault,' Ellie-Mae replied. 'None of it is, and if you come with me, I will help you prove it.'

Scarlett's eyes reddened and blood-filled tears fell across the bruises on her face. 'Please go,' she said. 'His baby can die with me.'

Ellie-Mae took hold of her hand. 'Don't let Lucius win, he's not worth it,' she said, 'and without him, your baby needs to live, to love, and be part of a new beginning for all of us.'

It seemed to work. Scarlett wiped away the tears and together they ran through the smoke and past the sight of Josh clinging to the platform. A burst of flames lifted from inside the circular cavern and Ellie-Mae stumbled as a gust of heat knocked her to the ground.

She picked herself up, brushed the burning ash from her clothes and looked towards the gate at the edge of Clapham Common. She looked again, to make sure and then froze at the shock of a sudden realisation.

Ethan and Samarah had gone.

'I know a short-cut,' Scarlett said. 'We might even get there before they do.'

Chapter 42—Samarah

Samarah turned at the edge of the common. Black smoke billowed into the sky and flames rose from the cavern of bunker number five.

'Come on, Ellie-Mae. Where are you?'

Beside her, Ethan checked his phone. 'Eight minutes,' he said. 'If we get the car, we can come back and pick her up. She knows we're heading for the bridge.'

The last thing Samarah wanted to do was leave Ellie-Mae on her own, but Ethan was right. Time was running out and to have any chance of reaching safety, they needed to utilise every available second. With Ethan beside her, she ran through the streets of Larkhill and past the station for Little Portugal. Every few steps, she turned in the hope that Ellie-Mae was following behind, but each time she looked, the ibex was nowhere to be seen.

Even worse, as they reached the gatehouse at the bridge, the portcullis was closed as she feared, its metal frame blocking their exit and trapping them inside the protected zone. Her mouth dry, her pulse racing, Samarah aimed the revolver at the lock and fired, the shell of the bullet ricocheting onto the ground. She was about to fire again, when she noticed a shimmer of movement at the side of the gatehouse.

'Stop shooting. We're on your side.'

One of the square stones in the wall moved to one side and a girl with scraped back hair and a swollen face appeared from behind the stone as it slid along the ground. 'This way,' Scarlett said.

Samarah smiled. Only minutes before, she'd wanted to curse Ellie-Mae for her eternal faith in others and yet, in her willingness to believe in Scarlett, she'd found someone who knew this place better than any of them.

Samarah squeezed through the gap, climbed the steps

on the other side and raced across the bridge. At least the Merlin 5 was still in the place she'd parked and as the others jumped into their seats, Samarah pressed the ignition button.

'Go straight on, then right,' Scarlett said. 'We need to get away from the buildings.'

Samarah kicked her foot onto the accelerator. The response of the Merlin 5 was instant and she swerved into the right-hand turn.

'Now left,' Scarlett said.

The sky flashed and the car was thrown forward. Even so, Samarah did as Scarlett instructed, turned left and raced in the direction of a raised area of ground that rose above the rooftops of the buildings. In front of her, a narrow bridge swayed, tilted, then collapsed and she grabbed at the steering wheel.

The bridge crashed to the road and Samarah was winded in the locking bite of her seatbelt as the Merlin 5 thudded to a halt. Steam poured from its titanium bonnet and she grabbed the door handle. Fire engulfed the dashboard, the heat of the flames scorching the side of her face and with a stab of agony striking her shoulder, she leaned into the door that sprang open. Her hands snatched at the fastening on the seatbelt, her fingers wrenching it open and she tumbled onto the road.

'Samarah. Over here.'

She rolled across the tarmac to where Ethan was lying. 'Where are the others?'

'I'm here,' Ellie-Mae replied, 'and Scarlett, too.'

The ground trembled for a second time and the sky flashed an incandescent orange. Houses collapsed and the tiles from rooftops smashed onto the road as the explosion ripped its way through crumbling walls and shattered buildings.

'There,' Scarlett said, pointing at the sign for '*Hampstead*

247

Heath.'

As she climbed the hill, past the rocks and trees, Samarah was forced to stop at the shock of pain in her shoulder.

'Are you all right?' Ethan asked. 'Do you need some help?'

'Keep climbing,' she replied. 'I'll catch you up.'

She'd almost made it to the top of the hill when the blast of the third explosion caused her to turn. The streets of London, and the accepted home of the elite, was ablaze and the protected zone covered in a veil of black smoke that rose above the flames. A fourth explosion confirmed that the sequence of detonations was over, the payload of the final missile having blasted its volatile energy into the sky. As it did so, the fiery contents of bright light and smoke gathered into a single mushroom of venomous cloud.

'It can't be,' Ethan said.

Scarlett stepped forward. 'It isn't,' she said. 'Lucius boasted about nuclear weapons, but he never managed to get hold of any. He tried to buy them from Europe and beyond, but they all said no. They know what he's like.'

As the shape of the mushroom cloud dispersed, Samarah looked at the others beside her. Ellie-Mae, the girl with the timid exterior with the sureness of foot to traverse the most dangerous of terrains. Beside her was Ethan, the cub who'd grown into a lion.

Scarlett was there too. The girl carrying the viper's child. Samarah wondered what her life would be like and how she would survive the inevitable accusations and revulsion. As she glanced beyond the bruises on Scarlett's face, she could sense the persona of an Ox and a spirit that was bursting with strength and resilience. Samarah smiled at the realisation that no matter what happened, Scarlett would be fine.

She then closed her eyes, her mind reaching upward, outward. She wondered if she could locate a glimpse of the future and something to prove that everything would be all right. Nothing came, as if to suggest that fate was offering a blank canvas and that it was up to the survivors to choose its pattern.

'What about all those people in the bunkers?' said Ellie-Mae, breaking the silence. 'The soldiers, the families and members of the elite.'

Scarlett shrugged. 'In the last few weeks, Lucius has become even more paranoid,' she said. 'Then came the news about the southern uprising. The regime spent so much time concentrating on the battle of the north and the west, they forgot about the battle's closer to home.'

'Those leaflets we saw on the common,' Ethan said. 'The ones with the gas mask, the poppy and the slogan to *Rise Up Now*. Are you saying they're real?'

'Very real,' Scarlett said. 'Inspired by you three, the Objectors, the uprising was about to launch an attack on the protected zone. It's why Lucius was desperate to bring you here, discredit your name and fire his missiles into the other cities. It's also why he ordered members of the elite to hide in the bunkers.'

'How deep are they?' Samarah asked. 'The bunkers, I mean.'

'The ones I saw?' Scarlett replied. 'Not deep enough.'

The hush returned at the realisation of what they'd witnessed. The elite, and everything they stood for, had perished in front of them.

'What now?' Ellie-Mae asked. 'Will everything go back to the way it was?'

'Not if I have anything to do with it,' Samarah replied, 'and anyway, do you remember what Henry said? He told us if we defeat Lucius in his own domain, we'll become the nation's true leaders in everyone's eyes.'

'Whoever this guy Henry is, I think he's right,' Scarlett said.

The sun was setting, the last of its golden rays turning to red, matching the colours of the blazing city. As the sky darkened, she looked again at the others. Their faces were lifted to the flame-coloured sky as though, like her, they were using the power of its crimson haze to rid themselves of the lies, the hate and the violence of the past.

'*You are the masters of the new age. It's up to you to put things right,*' Ethan said. 'It's something my uncle once told me. I didn't understand him at the time, but I think I do now.'

'If the three of us are going to change the world, we might need some help.' Ellie-Mae said, turning to Scarlett. 'By the way. Does anyone know where we are?'

'The perfect place to start a government filled with young, visionary voices and create something amazing for everyone,' Samarah said, pointing towards a sign that was partly hidden beneath one of the trees.

Parliament Hill, it said.

None of them moved and as Samarah stood there, she could feel the sudden weight of responsibility that had been thrust on their shoulders. She wished she could feel the same, absolute confidence as they did, but the longer they stood there, an increasing feeling of doubt crept into her mind to outweigh any sense of hope for the future.

She couldn't help but think that maybe, in a week, or even a month, everything they'd done would be forgotten. She'd already seen what happened in Exeter after the battle of the bridge. She'd witnessed the so-called city leaders and different factions of the uprising fight amongst each other and jostle for power.

Although the Objectors had risked more than anyone to win this war, in the cold light of a new day, she couldn't help wondering that in the minds of many, Ethan, Ellie-Mae and herself were just three, ordinary people to be thrown aside.

Her moment of reverie was broken by the rumbling sound of an engine. She looked up and at first, it looked like a bird, parting clouds and smoke as it flew towards them.

As the helicopter came closer, she noticed a set of guns at its side, readied for attack. Samarah looked into the windows and tried to gain a sense of who the pilot might be. As she reached out to the spirit of the animal within, the same word repeated in her mind.

Reptile.

'Get down,' she shouted, convinced the viper had returned.

The others did as she said, the four of them diving onto the damp grass of Parliament Hill. The rattle of metal confirmed that the machine guns had opened fire, but instead of bullets, the air, the ground, and the backs of the Objectors were covered in white poppies.

Samarah was the first to grasp what had happened. She remembered the conversation with Henry, the sarcastic comment she'd made of being showered with flowers and being given the keys to the kingdom.

'If that's what it takes,' Henry had said. *'I'll do it myself.'*

She looked again and recognised the pilot as the chameleon himself. *'I have a helicopter, too, not that I use it,'* he'd once told her, and she smiled at the memory of how she didn't believe him at the time. Even though she thought she knew him, there were moments when Samarah realised that she barely knew him at all.

She smiled at the thought, thrilled that the chameleon had been able to surprise her in such an incredible way. She then giggled and threw a handful of poppies at Ethan. Ellie-Mae joined in, laughing and crying tears of joy, as the Objectors hurled the gentle symbols of peace at one another like confetti. It was as though, for a few seconds at least, they were children again.

Then, with one more swoop of the helicopter towards Parliament Hill, the rotation of its blades lifted the cloud of white poppies high into the London sky.

Cast of Characters

The Objectors:

Ethan—an Objector, from a family of Quakers who conscientiously objected in WWI and WWII.

Ellie-Mae—an Objector and Christian with strong religious beliefs.

Samarah—an Objector, of Afro-Caribbean origin from a spiritual upbringing

Leading figures of the regime:

The Commandant—the former head of the regime, who died in 2038.

Lucius—the face of the regime, also known as the viper.

Mark I and Mark II synthetics—used by the regime as a form of control and destruction

Those with a speaking part, in the order they appear in the story:

William Eastern—the leader of the uprising.

Neil / Mr Roberts—the gunslinger in the Wild West simulation in The Elimination Centre

Josh—a ginger-haired cadet and platoon leader from The Elimination Centre.

Billy—a cadet from The Elimination Centre, originally from Birmingham.

Scarlett and Clara—cadets from The Elimination Centre

Daniel Quartz—a cadet who completed his contract of elimination.

Fabian—a lieutenant in the regime's army and based in Sheffield.

Aaron and Francesca—cadets who, alongside Samarah, are sent for 'special training.'

Hannah Williams—an underling selected for elimination

Harrison—a platoon leader in Wakefield.

Amelia—a cadet in Wakefield.

Alex—a cadet from Worcester, who'd previously worked in the wastelands.

Maggie—city leader of Worcester.

Henry Slater—owner of the Merlin 5 supercar. Also known as the chameleon.

Arthur—a knight, who lives in Worcester.

Joseph—a refugee, displaced from the northern towns.

Sophia—city leader of Birmingham.

Paul Worthington—Scarlett's father.

Dr Patterson—a surgeon from Worcester.

Thanks

This story began in 2018, as part of a dissertation at the University of Worcester. The plot is based on a society of 'haves' and 'have nots' and the belief that even in midst of selfish actions and violence, there can be hope and togetherness. Seen through the eyes of three main characters, its purpose was always to demonstrate the power of objection and the right to stand up for what we believe.

I am grateful to those who have assisted in the development of this story. To Mark Billen, who always reads my stories at their most raw. To Family Falcon who read this so diligently and offered me feedback on a multi-generational level. To Roz Levens and Holly Yuille, who offered such insightful comments and suggestions for improvement. I'd also like to thank Worcester Writers' Circle for their encouragement and my wife, Jill, for helping me with the linguistics and for her continued support in my writing. I am also grateful to the young readers who offered me such incredible assistance in making sure that the book was aimed at a Young Adult readership. Their details are noted at the beginning of the book.

Finally, I'd like to say a big thank you to Black Pear Press for their assistance and continued support in elevating this story to the place it is today.